'You can't do this. I will not allow it, Anna.'

He stared at her in disbelief and caught the gleam of her eyes and the faint shine of her moist lips in the moonlight.

'You cannot stop me! I am no longer your responsibility.'

'I saved your life,' he said, losing his temper and pulling her into his arms. 'Whilst I am alive, I will always feel I bear some responsibility for you.'

'Now who is talking nonsense?' She struggled to free herself, but it was as if she was a butterfly imprisoned in an iron fist. Suddenly she wondered why she was trying to escape when she was where she wanted to be. She drooped against him and rested her head against his chest.

Her submission was so unexpected that Jack was at a loss as to what to do next. Really he should release her and walk away, but instead he wanted to go on holding her. Hatred and grief had held him captive far too long.

June Francis's interest in old wives' tales and folk customs led her into a writing career. History has always fascinated her, and her first five novels were set in Medieval times. She has also written fourteen sagas based in Liverpool and Chester. Married with three grown-up sons, she lives on Merseyside. On a clear day she can see the sea and the distant Welsh hills from her house. She enjoys swimming, fell-walking, music, lunching with friends and smoochie dancing with her husband. More information about June can be found at her website: www.junefrancis.co.uk

Previous novels by this author:

TAMED BY THE BARBARIAN
ROWAN'S REVENGE

REBEL LADY, CONVENIENT WIFE

June Francis

MILLS & BOON®

Pure reading pleasure™

First published in Great Britain 2008
Large Print edition 2008
Harlequin Mills & Boon Limited,
Eton House, 18-24 Paradise Road, Richmond, Surrey TW9 1SR

© June Francis 2008

ISBN: 978 0 263 20174 1

Set in Times Roman 16 on 18¼ pt.
42-1108-79452

Printed and bound in Great Britain
by CPI Antony Rowe, Chippenham, Wiltshire

REBEL LADY,
CONVENIENT WIFE

My thanks and appreciation to my agent, Caroline Montgomery, and senior editor, Linda Fildew, for giving me a second chance to enjoy writing Historicals for Harlequin Mills & Boon again, as well as to my editor, Suzanne Clarke, for being so enthusiastic and encouraging about my writing.

Prologue

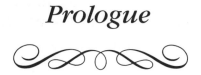

France, 1469

Jack Milburn groaned, twisting and turning in the bunk. Perspiration dampened his dark hair as, in his dreams, he relived the nightmarish times again.

'Go quickly! *Allez vite!*' he ordered, ears alert to the sound of splintering wood.

'*Mais, M'sieur Milburn, où—?*' cried Hortense.

'*Ne pas demander aux questions,*' he interrupted, pushing the maid who was carrying his son in her arms from the chamber. He hurried her along the passage that led to the alley at the back of the house and opened the door.

'*Papa!*' screamed Philippe, stretching out a hand to his father.

With tears in his eyes, Jack took the small hand and kissed it before turning to Hortense. '*Courez!*

Courez vite!' His expression was bleak as he closed the door quietly behind them. Taking a deep breath, he drew his sword and headed for the entrance hall to face the man who had killed his lover, Monique.

The Comte de Briand stood in the doorway, a dark looming presence. Jack did not need him to step forward into the candlelight to recognise Monique's bestial husband. The Comte's lank hair was yellowish white and fell to his huge shoulders. His nose was a squashed blob of dough in the centre of his swarthy face and the black-and-white streaked moustache and beard almost concealed the plump lips that snarled, *'Chien anglais!'* as he lunged forward with his sword. Jack parried the blow, aware that two other men had entered the chamber behind his enemy.

Jack ground his teeth, experiencing a familiar fury as the scene played in his head. Odds of three to one meant that the chance of his surviving the conflict was unlikely. Still, he was determined to fight for all he was worth, so as to give Hortense plenty of time to get away with Philippe. It was too late to save Monique, but he was prepared to sacrifice his life to enable his son's survival. His sword arm felt as heavy as lead each time he lunged and parried, and he felt as if he were wading through honey. Then came an agonising pain in his right cheek and, after that, a blow to the head that finished the fight.

'Monique! Philippe!'

He was vaguely aware that someone was bending over him and could hear the slap of waves against the hull of a ship. For a moment he was convinced that he was in his own cabin on the *Hercules* and it was the Comte de Briand bending over him. He could picture his smirking face, mouthing *'Your son is dead.'* Jack felt the scream welling up inside him and he prayed for death. But his instant death was the last thing on his enemy's mind.

'Signor Milburn, wake up! The physician is here to see you.'

Someone was shaking his shoulder and Jack struggled to escape the shackles that imprisoned him as he trudged on through the desert wasteland. It was sheer stubbornness that was keeping him moving, gripped as he was by an impotent rage. One day he would return to France and avenge the deaths of Monique and his son. He would seek out the Comte de Briand and kill him if it was the last thing he did.

Chapter One

England, summer 1475

The air felt hot and humid. As she left the village, Lady Anna Fenwick could hear the rumble of thunder in the distance. If she was to reach home before the rain came, then she was going to have to hurry.

Something sharp hit her on the cheek and she heard a man's whispering voice say, 'Take that, witch! May God strike you down dead.'

Shock brought her to a halt as blood trickled from a cut on her face. Only recently had she become aware of the servants looking at her askance and whispering in corners. Her heart was heavy as she recalled a couple of village women holding out horn-shaped amulets, believed to be effective against the evil eye, as she passed by.

'Murderess! Adulteress!' hissed the voice.

Anna wanted to shut her ears to the accusations. But what good would that do? She found it difficult to believe that anyone who knew her could speak of her in such a way. It was a year since her four-year-old son, Joshua, had died of the whooping cough. Her grief had been almost unbearable, worse than when her husband, Sir Giles, had died a year earlier. During the last few months she had felt ill at ease in her own home with just the servants and Giles's nephew, the son of his dead sister, and his wife, Marjorie, for company. Whilst Giles had been alive, Will's manner towards her had always been circumspect but she knew he resented her. He had lived with Giles since being orphaned as a youth and had been his heir until, at the age of forty, Giles had fallen in love with Anna and married her. On his death bed her husband had told her about the marital agreement that he and her eldest half-brother, Owain ap Rowan, had drawn up on the eve of Anna and Giles's wedding.

'You'll burn in hell,' said the voice, forgetting to whisper this time.

She recognised the voice and a shudder passed through her. Will! What a fool she had been to trust him this past year, but her sorrow had blinded her temporarily to his devious ways. He had believed he would inherit Fenwick Manor on Joshua's death, but he had been mistaken. A codicil in Giles's will had left all to Anna should aught happen to their son.

After Joshua had been laid to rest with his father, she had been emotionally exhausted and hoped that the goodly sum of money that Giles had left Will would suffice to keep him happy. She'd had reason to believe that was so, for the following day he had been so caring that she had willingly accepted his suggestion that he and Marjorie continue to live with her to keep her company. Feeling numb after this second terrible blow, she had been glad of his help in running her manor. But slowly she had come alive again and shown a determination to manage her own affairs. It was then that Will had begun to reveal a much darker side to his nature and Marjorie had become less than friendly. Yet if Anna had not overheard the gossip whispered behind her back, it would never have occurred to her that they might wish her dead.

'Murderess,' whispered the voice, again.

Her heart beat rapidly. 'Come out of there and face me if you dare!' she cried.

There was a rustling in the hedge that bordered the field of ripening corn. 'You'll get your deserts. Like mother, like daughter, you'll meet the same fate as she did,' called the voice.

The words puzzled her and she turned full circle in an attempt to pinpoint Will's location. 'My mother died in childbirth. Explain yourself!'

'They lied to you.'

'If you're referring to Owain and Kate, I don't believe you, Will,' said Anna firmly, peering through the thicket of hawthorn, but unable to see him. 'Anyway, I've had enough. I'm for home before the storm breaks. You and Marjorie can pack your bags and leave Fenwick.'

A flash of lightning and a crash of thunder almost drowned out her voice, warning her that the storm was nigh. Picking up her black skirts, she raced for home, wanting to be indoors before the rain came.

She took a shortcut through the herb garden where the fragrance of lavender, thyme and gilly-flowers filled her senses. The air was stifling and the earth was thirsty for moisture. She tore open the wicket gate and ran towards the back of the house. Once indoors she expected to find some of the servants in the kitchen but it was empty. She searched the ground floor, but there was no one there. Had they all decided to desert her whilst she was out of the house? What about Marjorie, who had still been abed when Anna had left to walk to the village an hour or so ago? Perhaps she and her maid were upstairs.

Anna took the stairs two at a time to the first floor but she saw no one as she made her way along the passage to her bedchamber. She felt hot and sticky and decided to change her garments as soon as she was in the safety of its confines. She pushed open the door and froze as a figure stepped out of the shadows. There was a crash of thunder and it seemed to echo the pounding of her heart as she gazed at the demonic red face with horns protruding from its head. A red cloak swirled about the black-clad apparition as it moved towards her. She backed away and would have turned to run if the door had not slammed behind her.

'Have your way with her quickly and then I'll see she burns,' said Will's voice behind her.

Terror overwhelmed her as she felt a shove in her back that catapulted her towards the gruesome figure. Black-gloved hands seized her, holding her in a vice-like grip. She was aware of heavy breathing and averted her face. On doing so, she realised that a couple of inches of flesh showed between glove and sleeve. This creature was no devil, but human. Anna sank her teeth into his wrist and drew blood. A curse issued from beneath the devilish mask and then he was tearing at her clothes. She struggled violently, aware of Will's laughter in the background.

'You'll regret this,' she panted, attempting to prise the man's hands from her breast.

As soon as she spoke those words a flash lit up the darkened sky outside her window and there was a violent crash of thunder that shook the whole house. Her captor jumped violently as there came a roar and a crackle from overhead. She looked up and saw smoke issuing from a break in the ceiling. He began to shake and released her abruptly.

She glanced at Will and saw the fear in his face. She put out a steadying hand to the bedpost and clutched her torn garments so that they covered her nakedness. 'How dare you lay hands on me! You will pay for this infamy,' cried Anna, pointing an accusing finger at him. 'Leave now or it will be you and your accomplice who will burn.'

Will's eyes darted from her to that devilish figure. Then he wrenched open the door and shot out of the chamber. Anna's assailant quickly followed hot on his heels. She collapsed on to the bed. Her shaking hands still clutching her ruined gown of black linsey-woolsey. She could hear the thudding of their feet on the stairs as they made their escape. For a moment, she did not move and then the smell of smoke caused her to gaze upwards. More thin streams of smoke were issuing through other cracks in the ceiling and she realised the thatch must be alight. She had to get out of there!

She sprang to her feet, thinking there were items that were precious to her in this room that she must save, in case the whole house caught fire. She changed out of her torn garments and into another gown. She hurried to pack a few clothes, legal papers, Giles's precious parchments, as well as items essential for her toilet. Then she fastened a pouch, containing as much coin as she could carry, about her waist. The sound of breaking glass, as the window shattered, caused her to jump out of her skin. She must make haste. From the chest at the foot of the bed, she took out her tapestry work and then lifted her lute from the wall. The instrument had been a Christmas gift from her half-brother Owain, made in Venice and delivered into her hands by merchant venturer Jack Milburn. He had vanished whilst in France six years ago.

Swiftly she wrapped the instrument in the folds of the tapestry and tucked it under her arm. She gave one last glance about the room. Here she had spent many contented moments, as well as heart-breaking ones. Giles had breathed his last and her son had died in her arms in this bed. With tears trickling down her cheeks, she hurried from the bedchamber. With a bundle held up to her nose and mouth against the smoke, she raced along the passage, only to pause when she reached the door of Will and Marjorie's bedchamber.

She could hear snoring and remembered that she had been going to look in on Marjorie. She banged on their door. 'Marjorie! Is that you in there? Wake up! The roof is on fire and you must get out of the house.'

There was no reply, but Anna thought she heard a break in the snoring. She lifted the latch, but the door did not yield so she banged again. 'Marjorie, you must get up!'

A sleepy voice called, 'Go away!'

'No! Rise and save yourself,' said Anna, attempting to open the door once more.

'I will not!' Marjorie yawned. 'Will said I must not listen to aught you say because you will cast a spell on me.'

An exasperated Anna said, 'It is not true! I don't know why Will should say such things, but I am no witch. Do get up or you could die in your bed.'

'I'm not listening,' said Marjorie in a sing-song voice. 'I have my hands over my ears.'

Anna groaned. 'Marjorie, don't be a fool! If you do not leave now, it could be the end of you.' When there was no answer, her heart sank. If she herself did not hurry, then she, too, could be trapped in the house by the fire. What was Will thinking of to leave his own wife possibly to die in her bed? And whose face was behind that devilish mask? She prayed to God to protect her from the pair if they were laying in wait for her somewhere downstairs, or in the grounds. She called to Marjorie again but she did not answer her.

With a terrible sense of foreboding, Anna hurried downstairs. She went through the hall, but it was deserted. Cautiously, she entered the kitchen, but that, too, was empty. She went outside, but there was no sign of anyone. She placed her belongings outside the stable and then gazed up at her house. The whole roof was aflame. Pausing only to remove the veiling that covered her wimple, she soaked it in a water butt before running back to the house. She had to try to persuade Marjorie to leave one more time.

Anna covered her nose and mouth with the wet veiling and hurried upstairs as fast as she could through the ever-increasing smoke. She found Marjorie lying prone outside her bedchamber door. She was still alive, but scarcely breathing. Anna wiped Marjorie's face with the damp cloth, but still she did not stir. Anna felt a rising panic and struggled to lift the other woman to her feet, but she could not do it, so instead she dragged her along the passage towards the stairs.

Anna's chest was wheezing and she was fighting for breath by the time she got Marjorie outside. Then she herself collapsed on to the ground beside her. It seemed an age before Anna felt able to make the effort to pull Marjorie farther away from the house on to the grass. There she sank to the ground again and this time it seemed longer still before she had the strength to get to her knees. To her dismay, Marjorie had ceased breathing despite all Anna's efforts.

She staggered to her feet and gazed at her house; she could only stand by helplessly as the flames consumed her home. Her heart felt like a stone inside her. She had loved this house, but with her husband and son gone from this earth, it had been a lasting reminder of the sadness of their deaths.

She wept afresh for them and the happy times spent inside its walls, as well as for Marjorie.

'Why has fate dealt me such agonising blows?' cried Anna to the skies. 'Are you punishing me, God?'

No heavenly voice answered her and, frustratingly, the storm clouds had passed, spilling hardly any rain. But where was Will and his accomplice? She could not place any faith in his caring about her safety, but what about his wife? She doubted he would accept that she had tried to save Marjorie. Instead, she was convinced he would use that timely flash of lightning and his wife's death to strengthen his accusation that Anna was a witch. A chill of fear ran through her. She had to leave here now, in case the two men returned, and ride for her old home at Rowan Manor. Owain and his wife, Kate, had reared her from babyhood and she could trust them to help her.

Fortunately the fire had not spread to the outbuildings and she went in search of her saddle and bridle. On finding them, she paused only long enough to drink some water and pack her belongings in a pair of saddlebags, before hurrying to where her horse was cropping the grass in a nearby field. Nervously, she kept looking over her shoulder. No doubt Will would realise she had survived the flames when he saw that her horse was missing. It was possible that he might even guess her destination and follow her. But hopefully, she would have enough of a head start to manage to escape his clutches. Rowan Manor lay several leagues away; although she felt weary with fear and grief, she prayed that God would have mercy and enable her to reach Owain and Kate before nightfall.

Anna darted a look behind her and thought she caught sight of a lone rider half a mile or so to her rear. Terror caused her heart to jerk within her breast. She could not see him clearly, but was convinced it was Will and wondered what had happened to his accomplice. She had ridden some five leagues along byways and tracks through the Palatine of Chester and her whole body ached after her ordeal. But she was now within a couple of miles of Rowan Manor and urged her palfrey from a canter to a gallop. She was relieved that the sky had cleared and the ground was neither too wet nor too dry, only yielding slightly beneath her horse's hooves. God willing, she would reach Rowan before Will caught up with her. She whispered encouragement in her horse's ear and dared to risk another glance behind her.

To her dismay, the rider was now close enough for her to recognise Will's cadaverous features and tall, bony figure. She told herself that she must not let fear disable her, causing her to lose control of her horse. Ahead lay the crossroads that signalled the turning into the lane that led to Rowan. Once she was within the bounds of Owain's lands, then most likely there would be men in the fields and she would be safe.

As her horse took the turning, Anna saw too late the sycamore split in half, so that part had fallen and blocked the path. Her horse reared and, despite all her effort to remain in the saddle, she was thrown to the ground. Luckily she landed on grass, but the breath was knocked out of her. The shock of the fall affected her vision so that colours appeared to be washed out of everything. Feeling half-blind, she gasped for breath, scared that her horse would lose its balance and crush her. She forced herself to make the attempt to claw her way out of the reach of its flailing hooves. Then, unexpectedly, she was seized by the back of her cloak and hoisted into the air. Deposited in a sprawling heap in front of a saddlebow, she was aware of the scent of sandalwood and male muskiness. She struggled frantically to gain control of her limbs and get a grip on the horse.

'Hold tight,' ordered an unfamiliar, steely voice.

Relieved that it was not Will who had arrived on the scene first, Anna did her best to comply with the man's order. Still suffering from the effects of her fall, obedience proved difficult; she could feel herself slipping from the beast. Simultaneously, she realised that her rescuer had managed to control her horse. Its front hooves were on the ground; despite a great deal of snorting and blowing from the animal, all this had been accomplished in a matter of moments. But before Anna could catch a proper look at the man, she completely lost her balance and toppled to the ground.

This time she managed to land on her feet. Finally upright, on solid ground, her first thought was for the horse that had been hers since it was a foal. She loved her mare dearly and hastened to comfort her, stroking her nose and whispering soothing words into its flickering ear. So it came as a complete surprise to find herself being seized again from behind. This time she felt as if she was being strangled as she was yanked off her feet and placed face down across a very different horse.

She was in no doubt about who dared to mishandle her in such a way.

A hand pressed down on her head and Will snarled, 'Keep your eyes away from me, witch's daughter, or it will be the worse for you.'

'By the Trinity, what do you think you're doing?' demanded Anna's rescuer in a harsh voice. 'Release her at once or you will taste steel!'

She tried to get to get a glimpse of him, but that proved impossible with Will's hand crushing her face into his horse's neck. 'Keep out of my affairs,' said Will. 'This one's a witch and a murderess, just like her mother, and will burn for her latest foul deed.'

'It's not true,' gasped Anna in a muffled voice.

'Shut your mouth, madam!' ordered Will, pressing down harder on her head.

'Did you not hear me?' thundered her rescuer. 'Release her at once, I say.'

'If you value your life, I suggest you keep out of this,' warned Will. 'I repeat, this woman is a witch and she is dangerous.'

'If that were true, then you should have more sense than to treat her so disgracefully,' said her rescuer, his tone deceptively soft. 'I will not ask you again to release her.'

'Who are you that I should obey such commands?' sneered Will, reaching for the amulet about his neck. 'This protects me. Now go before she bewitches you.'

As soon as Anna felt Will remove his hand, she lifted her head so as to see how her rescuer would respond. He had manoeuvred his horse alongside Will's mount and her first sight of him was of long muscular legs clad in black hose and leather boots, clamped against his horse's flanks. Raising her eyes, she saw that he sat tall in the saddle. His shoulders were broad beneath a black woollen doublet that was open at the neck to reveal a white shirt and sunburnt throat. A scar snaked down his right cheek, lending a certain harshness to his features. Suddenly she became aware of chilling blue-grey eyes beneath hooded dark brows returning her gaze. Her heart performed a peculiar somersault; there was something familiar about this man. Yet she could not remember where she had seen him before.

Even so she said, 'Of your courtesy, sir, I beg you not to listen to him. None of what he says is true.'

Her rescuer inclined his dark head. 'From my experience it is a great mistake to leave women to the mercy of cruel bullies.'

Will flushed with anger. 'You should not have gazed upon her. Already, she has bewitched you. I tell you that she has bad blood in her. Not only is she a witch, but murdered her husband because she had a lover!'

'You speak false,' cried Anna indignantly, digging her gloved fingers into Will's leg in an attempt to drag herself upright. Instantly he slapped her hand away.

Within seconds her rescuer had seized Will's wrist and had his knife at his throat. 'I did warn you,' he said in an icy tone.

Will's eyes glinted with fury. 'You'll rue this day, for daring to set your will against mine, stranger.'

'You would be wiser thinking before you open your mouth. First, you threaten a so-called witch and then the man holding a knife to your throat. You will beg the lady's pardon or I will slit you from ear to ear.'

Her rescuer's voice reminded Anna of iron encased in velvet and she shivered, despite herself.

'If you—you think you c-can get away with m-my murder then you're mistaken,' stuttered Will. 'There are those who know my errand and she will burn and so will you.'

'I don't know how you can live with your conscience, Will,' cried Anna angrily. 'And what about Marjorie? Where were you when my house was burning and she was in need of rescue? You lied to her, too, and so you are to blame for her death!'

An unexpected sob broke from Will. 'I did not intend for her to die. I thought she would have gone with the servants. Only they said...' His face turned ugly again. 'It is your fault, you witch!'

Without hesitation the stranger slashed the ties that fastened Will's cloak, causing him to squeal in terror. Hastily he stammered out an apology to Anna.

'Louder,' ordered his captor.

Will swore, but the prick of the blade drawing blood had him yelling out the words.

Anna did not feel sorry for him at all; she wanted to get down from his horse and be rid of him. She had done her best by him, but he had betrayed her. 'Thank you, sir,' she said to the stranger. 'But I deem that will do for now.'

'If that is your wish.' Her rescuer replaced the dagger at his belt and loosened his grip on Will's wrist. Immediately the villain attempted to push Anna to the ground, but the other man acted with speed, seizing her by the waist and dragging her on to his horse. Will cursed the pair of them and then digging his spurs into his stallion's flanks, he rode off in the opposite direction to Rowan Manor.

Weak with relief, Anna clung to the front of her rescuer's doublet, conscious of the strength in the arm that held her. 'I'm afraid that, by rescuing me, you've made an enemy, sir.'

'I would have done the same for any woman in distress,' he said coolly, disturbed by the response of a certain part of his anatomy to the close proximity of her soft curves and the scent of lavender that mingled with a strong smell of smoke. He told himself this would not do; he could not allow himself to be distracted from the task he had set himself. 'What is your destination?' he asked, slackening his grasp on her waist.

'I am on my way to Rowan Manor, the home of my half-brother Owain ap Rowan. But let me introduce myself—I am Lady Anna Fenwick.' She proffered him a hand gloved in dirty tan kid.

He stared at her intently before shaking that small, firm hand. 'I deem we are already acquainted, Lady Fenwick, although it is some time since we met. My name is Milburn. I will escort you to Rowan as that is also my destination.'

Anna's grimy brow knitted as she gazed into his weatherbeaten face. It had been some time since last she had visited Matt Milburn's manor in Yorkshire. 'My thanks to you. Your escort is much appreciated, as was your coming to my aid.' He gave a brief nod of acceptance for her words of gratitude. She marvelled at his strong features and wondered about the scar on his face. She was almost tempted to touch it, but reminded herself that he was a married man with children. Such an act would be unseemly and, after Will's accusation of her being an adulteress, her behaviour must be above reproach. Even so she could not resist saying, 'That scar—' She stopped abruptly for there was embarrassment and some deep sorrow in his face. 'I beg your pardon. I shouldn't have mentioned it. If you could set me down, Master Milburn, I will ride my own mount.'

Relieved to have temptation so swiftly removed, he helped her to the ground, watching Anna as she went over to her horse. She called over her shoulder, 'When did you leave Yorkshire? It must have taken you several days to get here.'

'I did not ride. I have a ship, the *Hercules*, anchored off West Kirby in the Dee estuary.'

His words surprised her into turning and staring at him. 'Now that I did not expect to hear. Have you had news of Jack after all this time or are you here to buy horses from Owain?'

He smiled faintly. 'You mistake me for my twin, Lady Fenwick. I *am* Jack Milburn.' His eyes fastened on her luscious lips as they parted in astonishment. He took the opportunity to have a proper look at her for a few seconds. Beneath her light summer cloak, she wore a loose black gown made of quality linsey-woolsey cloth that did little to conceal her curves. Wisps of red-gold hair escaped her wimple to curl on a bloodied and grimy cheek. Had that swine attacked her? She appeared lost for words—but was that surprising considering the years he had been missing?

He noticed the lute poking from a fold of material in a saddlebag and memories flooded back as he was reminded of the year his father had been murdered in Bruges. He remembered a mischievous-eyed girl, whose elfin features had beamed with delight when he had presented her with the Venetian crafted lute. She had seemed so alive, her red hair like a flame about her pretty little face. He had been fifteen at the time and, in any other circumstances, a future marriage might have been on his mind, only that year had proved to him that the life of a merchant venturer was extremely risky. Taking a wife would have to wait until he had made his fortune and the time was ripe to settle down in one place.

Anna found her voice. 'But—but you've been missing for years! We thought you were dead. We even had a requiem mass said for you.'

'So I was informed by your half-brother Davy.'

'Davy? What has your absence to do with him?'

'It has naught to do with him,' replied Jack, hastening to add, 'It is solely that he was on business in Europe when I returned and he performed a commission for me. I'm surprised that you have not heard that I'd...come back from the dead.'

She looked bemused. 'It is a while since I have visited Rowan, but I agree that it is strange that Kate did not send word of your safe return. Maybe it was due to my closeting myself in the house after my son died, although my late husband's nephew and his wife lived with me and they would have been there to take a message.' A shadow crossed her face. 'I wonder if Will destroyed it. Possibly it might have arrived when I sought spiritual consolation in a nearby convent.'

So the man he had just scared off was her husband's nephew, mused Jack, wondering why the man was so intent on convincing folk that

Anna was a witch. But he must not involve himself in her affairs as he had enough on his mind without concerning himself about her. 'I'd heard you lost your husband and son. I can understand how that must feel and extend my condolences,' said Jack with a stiffness in his manner that was almost cold.

'Thank you,' she said, debating whether he could really understand how painful was the loss of a dearly loved child and husband, for as far as she knew he had never wed. Unless…perhaps he thought that losing a parent was equal to the terrible wrenching grief that was the loss of one's child. She took a deep steadying breath. 'I am pleased to see you alive, Jack. What happened to you? That scar—' She stopped abruptly. 'There I go again. Obviously, the memory is painful. You have suffered, too.' She felt tears well up in her eyes and hastily brushed them away.

'Damn you,' muttered Jack, turning his back to her.

How he hated seeing a woman in tears. It put him too much in mind of his final parting from Monique and Philippe before he had left for England, knowing he would not see either of them for a month or more. He would have taken them both with him, but Monique had refused to cross the Channel. Some happening in her past had filled her with a fear of the sea and he could not shift her from her decision. If he had suspected that her husband was on their trail, then he would have insisted that she and Philippe accompany him.

'I should not have asked. I beg your pardon for prying in your affairs,' apologised Anna in a low voice that roused Jack from his thoughts.

'There's no need for you to do so,' he said tersely, keeping his back to her, determined not to allow the sight of her tear-stained face to weaken him. 'Naturally you're curious about what happened to me. Another time, perhaps, I will tell you.'

He considered how strange it was that he had been able to recall Anna's childish features so quickly. Yet, during his enslavement in Arabia, he'd had difficulty remembering Monique's face. It was not that he had forgotten the colour of her hair and eyes or the shape of her nose and the feel of her lips. What he'd been unable to do was compose an actual image of her whole face. Yet his son's face continued to haunt his dreams. Reason enough for him to not allow a sudden protective feeling and tug of attraction to the mature Anna to sway him from his chosen path.

'I look forward to hearing your story,' murmured Anna, gazing at his strong back before giving her attention to her horse once more. Suddenly she noticed that a girth strap hung loose. 'Jack, if you please, I would have you look at this strap.'

He walked over to her and took hold of the girth strap she proffered. He noticed the leather was not only partially torn, but also sawn through. 'You believe this was done deliberately?' he asked, raising his dark brows.

'I am the only one who uses this saddle.' Anna's eyes were angry as she tapped a finger against the leather. 'I am certain Will must have done this, to bring me down if I managed to ride for help. If I broke my neck, it would save his having to rile the villagers further into burning me. I deem that he believes by destroying me he will gain Fenwick Manor.'

'That would make sense of his insistence on your being a witch and wanting rid of you,' said Jack, reluctantly drawn into a discussion. 'Yet why should he gain it on your death…unless there was a clause in your husband's will?'

'There was no such clause. Neither is he my nearest kin that it would pass to him on my death.'

Jack's frown deepened. 'It does not make sense.'

Anna nodded. 'But envy is a terrible emotion, Jack.'

He agreed, fingering the cut girth strap, knowing she would not remain in the saddle with the strap in that state. Yet for her to share his horse would be untenable. As for her riding his stallion...

'Enough of such talk,' murmured Anna, noticing the sun dipping beyond the horizon. 'It is time we made a move. I'll lead my horse as the house is only a short distance away. I suggest, Jack, that you ride on and inform Owain and Kate to expect me.'

'I would offer you my hired horse but I doubt you'd be able to handle him.'

She looked up at the stallion's powerful shoulders and knew he spoke the truth. Taking hold of her horse's bridle, she nodded in the direction of the manor. 'You go ahead. I will follow.'

Jack hesitated. He knew he could not leave her to walk alone. That cur of a nephew might return. But he hated being ordered about; he'd had enough of that in captivity. He experienced one of those flashbacks that left him cold. He was being forced to his knees and could almost feel the lash of the whip flaying his back. He had not even known why he was being punished, understanding little of the language of his master. It was then he had determined to learn Arabic and to escape.

'Why do you linger, Jack? Mount your horse and ride on. I will be perfectly safe,' reassured Anna.

Jack scowled down at her, resenting the instruction. 'I say it is a fine evening and there will be light in the sky long enough for us both to walk and reach the house before it gets dark.'

Anna flashed him a smile. 'If that is your wish. No doubt both horses will be glad to be relieved of their burdens for a while. I have ridden mine hard and presumably you have, too.' She heaved a sigh. 'What a day it has been and it is not over yet.'

She was aware of a terrible sense of displacement, realising afresh that she was homeless. Although the loss she felt at the destruction of her home could not compare to the grief she still felt for her son, this was just another pain to bear. Tears pricked the back of her eyes and she blinked them away, knowing she must not give way to weakness.

She looked up and caught Jack Milburn watching her. There was a bleakness in his expression that caused her to wonder what had happened to him during the years he had been missing. For the rest of the journey, she kept her eyes fixed on the road ahead, thinking how he had changed almost out of all recognition from the youth she remembered.

Chapter Two

It was a relief to see the sandstone walls of Rowan Manor. Anna's heart lifted and she thanked the Trinity that soon she would be inside its walls to be welcomed by Kate and Owain and the rest of the family.

She handed her horse over to one of the grooms and removed her saddlebags and lute. Jack, who was unsaddling his own mount, said, 'Leave them. I'll carry them in for you when I'm ready.'

She thanked him. So many thoughts were running through her head that she felt quite dizzy. She did not wish to upset Kate and Owain too much and knew she was going to have to think hard about what she should tell them. Turning back to Jack, she said, 'Please, I beg you, do not mention your confrontation with Will to Kate. They will be deeply concerned about the evil that has befallen me without having to worry about my involving you in my affairs.'

He was about to say he thought she was making a mistake, then he remembered the secret he had kept hidden for years, even from his twin. Besides, hadn't he decided to not involve himself further with her?

Filled with trepidation, Anna hurried towards the walled garden at the back of the house, guessing that at that time of evening Kate and Owain would be in their parlour. She was not mistaken. Both were sitting in the candlelit room.

As soon as Anna entered the parlour, Kate, a curvaceous woman in her early forties, set aside her sewing and rose to her feet. 'Anna, what are you doing here? We did not expect to see you until the Michaelmas Fair. My goodness! You're filthy! What has happened? Is there something amiss at Fenwick?'

'Indeed there is,' replied Anna. 'The house was struck by lightning and all my servants had vanished, so there was no one to help me to douse the flames.'

Kate gasped and, going over to her, enveloped Anna in an embrace. 'My poor Anna, what a dreadful thing to happen! What of Will and his wife?'

'Marjorie was sleeping at the time. I managed to get her out of the house, but she died!' Anna's voice shook and she tore herself from Kate's embrace and began to pace the room. 'It was terrifying. Will had accused me of—' She stopped abruptly, realising what she had said.

'Accused you of what?' asked Kate, starting forward.

Anna shrugged and tried to smile. 'It does not matter.'

'Of course it matters,' said Owain, a handsome man in his mid-forties with dark hair silvering at the temples. 'You've been through so much these past two years and now this! If we are to help you, then you must be honest with us.'

Anna's face quivered. She had talked herself into a trap and knew she would have to tell them some of what Will had said. 'He—he accused me of—of being an adulteress—just like my mother!' She put a hand over her mouth. She had not meant to say the latter either. It showed the state of her mind. Kate and Owain exchanged startled glances. 'Aye, you might well look like that,' Anna muttered.

'What nonsense!' cried Kate, putting an arm about Anna's shoulder and noticing the cut on her face. 'Your cheek is all bloodied! Did that happen while you were trying to escape the fire?'

'No. Will threw a stone at me,' said Anna, taking a kerchief from a pocket and dabbing at the cut and then cleaning her face, realising she would have to tell them a little more. 'I deem he wanted me to believe it was someone from the village, but I recognised his voice. I fear that he wishes to discredit me with the servants and villagers and seize Fenwick.'

'He must be crazed,' said Kate, aghast. 'Owain, you must sort this matter out as soon as possible.'

'I certainly will,' said Owain firmly. 'Although, with the house burnt down and his wife dead, I suspect it is the village where I'll need to search for him. I'd best take some men with me.'

'If he is not there, you could try my man-of-business's house in Chester,' said Anna. 'No doubt Will shall try and persuade him that I'm not a fit person to own Fenwick.'

'You really believe so?' said Owain, looking deeply concerned. He rose from a table littered with papers. 'Sit down. You're obviously distraught and exhausted and need to rest. Kate, fetch some wine.'

Anna sighed. 'How can I relax? I have lost all

that I held dear and now I am at a loss how to go on with my life.'

Kate looked disturbed. 'Hush, love. All will be well.'

'That is so easy to say,' cried Anna, tears filling her eyes. 'I know a house can be rebuilt—but what would be the point? It would not be a home. I might as well go live in a nunnery.'

'Now that is nonsense,' said Kate. 'You're too young and comely. All you need is to stay with us for a while. I thought when Joshua died that it was a mistake for you to shut yourself away at Fenwick.'

Anna turned on her. 'You have not lost a son! How can you speak so when you have no experience of what I was suffering?'

'Talking about it might have helped,' said Kate quietly. 'But you wouldn't let us share your pain.'

'Enough, love,' said Owain, giving her a warning look.

She sighed and nodded. 'I'll fetch the wine.'

'Wait!' said Anna, ashamed of herself for losing control. Staying Kate with an outstretched hand, she swallowed hard before continuing. 'I beg your pardon for what I said, but now you've reminded me that I have forgotten to tell you that Jack

Milburn is here. He says that he has come to see Davy. I mistook him for his twin. Why did you not let me know that Jack had been found?'

'Jack is here!' Kate's blue eyes lit up. 'It is true we knew he was alive and have been expecting him. But believe me, Anna, I did send word to you at Fenwick with the good news.'

Anna frowned. 'Who did you send?'

'Hal.'

'Hal!' Anna darted a look at Owain. Hal was the youngest of the Rowan brothers and still unwed despite being almost forty years old. 'Perhaps he did not deliver the message…or, if he did, Will kept it from me. But why should he do so?'

'I have no idea,' said Owain. 'We could ask Hal when he comes in.'

Anna shrugged. 'What does it matter now Jack is here?'

Owain and Kate looked relieved.

'I'll leave you two then,' said Kate, smiling. 'I'll have one of the maids make ready your old bed-chamber, Anna, while I find my dear stepbrother. We will drink wine together and drink each other's health. Are you hungry?'

Anna nodded. 'I have not eaten since breakfast and no doubt Jack will be hungry, too.'

'Then I will see that food is brought here.' Kate left them alone at last.

'Do you know what happened to Jack during his absence, Owain?' asked Anna.

'He was sold into slavery,' he said, his expression grim.

Anna's mouth fell open. For a moment she could only stare at him and then she collected her wits. 'He sent word telling you of this?'

'Nay. His twin did,' replied Owain. 'Matt never gave up hope, even when we did. He kept in touch with Jack's agents in Europe and had them hire men to search for him. Eventually, when Matt began to doubt his instinct that Jack was in trouble but alive, a courier arrived with the news that he was in Venice.'

'No wonder Jack has changed! How was he captured and how did he escape?'

'I know only what Davy told me and that was little enough,' said Owain, pulling up a chair and sitting opposite her.

'Jack told me Davy was in Europe when he returned. I presume he was delivering horses.'

'Aye. But he also had other business there and was in Bruges when Jack's courier turned up at the agent's house. Apparently Jack was suffering from

a fever and that's why he was unable to leave
Venice. He feared he might die and wanted Matt
to know of his abduction and his years of slavery.'

'So Davy brought the message to Matt and then
came here?'

Owain shook his head. 'Davy arranged for a
courier to deliver the news to Matt whilst he travelled to Venice. He found Jack recovered and jour-
neyed with him to Bruges before going on further
business for him to France. Davy returned home
a week ago, just in time to see his daughter born.'

'Joan has had a daughter!' Despite her grief at the
loss of her only son, Anna was delighted for the
couple, who had five sons. 'I must buy the child a
birth gift when next I visit Chester,' she added.

'I'm sure Davy will tell you that you're welcome
to visit them,' said Owain, smiling. 'And I'll have
no talk of nunneries.' He shook his head. 'You
know you're welcome to stay here at Rowan as
long as you wish. It'll be good for you to be
amongst your family again.'

Anna was silent. She had been away from
Rowan too long to fit easily into her former
position in the family. Yet where else could she go
where she would be safe but here or behind the
walls of a convent?

Restlessly, she rose and went over to the window aperture and gazed out over the darkened garden. The happenings of the day played over in her head and she felt sick with the remembrance of the disgust and terror she had felt when confronted by Will and that figure in the devilish mask. She felt her head was going to burst as images overrode each other. She turned round to face Owain and blurted out, 'Tell me...did my mother have a lover? Did she cuckold our father?'

Owain's expression was enough to make her wish that she had not spoken. Then a sound at the door shattered the strained atmosphere. 'Did who cuckold our father?' asked Davy, entering the parlour.

Anna felt the blood rush to her head and could only gaze at this giant of a man. He was the middle of the Rowan brothers and she knew him the least best of the three. He had married before she was born and lived on the Wirral with his wife and children, having his own stud farm. Suddenly she realised that Kate and Jack Milburn had followed him into the room. Anna wished she could disappear in a puff of smoke. Instead, she turned her back on them.

The moon had risen and she could make out the shapes of bushes and plants. Then, unexpectedly, she saw a devilish face loom out of the darkness. Her masked attacker! She could see the horns on its head and the same gaping, evil grin. She froze with fear. Was it a projection of her overwrought mind?

She managed to tear her gaze away and face the room. 'There's someone out there!' she cried.

'You look like you've seen a ghost,' said Davy.

'A devil's face! It was grinning at me,' she gasped.

'It can't be,' said Kate, hurrying over to her.

'There *was* someone out there,' whispered Anna. 'It had a red face and horns!' She just stopped herself from saying that she had seen it before.

Davy and Owain exchanged glances. 'One of my sons playing a trick with that old mask?' suggested the latter.

'What mask?' asked Anna, shooting him a glance. 'Are you telling me that you have such a mask in this house?'

Owain nodded. 'I'm sorry it gave you such a fright. I'll tan the hide off whichever of my sons did this to you,' he said angrily.

'But why should your boys play such a jape on me?' asked Anna, unconvinced that either Gareth or his younger brother were responsible.

Kate said apologetically, 'Boys will be boys. I'm so sorry, Anna.'

Jack frowned. He knew only to well the kind of ploys that boys could get up to, but this was not amusing. The sight of Anna's strained pale face made him feel he had to find the boys and prove to her that it was simply a foolish prank. He left the parlour and followed the passage to the door that led outside.

He was instantly aware of the scent of honeysuckle, roses and gillyflowers combined with a strong smell of smoke, but there was no one in the garden. He thought he heard a faint sound coming from the stable yard and made his way there. But it, too, was deserted. He went into the stables and asked one of the men there had he seen either of the Rowan lads. He shook his head.

Frowning, Jack returned to the garden, wondering if Anna's imagination had run away with her. It was not so surprising, considering all she had endured that day. Even so, he thought to check the soil beneath the window and saw large footprints. There was the proof that someone had stood here. He went inside the house and walked into the parlour.

'Well?' asked Owain, glancing in Jack's direction. 'Did you see anyone?'

Jack shook his head. 'But there are footprints in

the soil outside.' He kept silent about the prints being the size of a man's.

Anna thanked him. 'At least you've proven to me that I'm not losing my wits.' She told herself that there was probably more than one such devil's mask in the Palatine of Chester. They were made for mummers' plays or the mystery ones acted out at certain holy festivals.

'It is to be expected that you might be a little light-headed and confused after all you've been through,' said Kate sympathetically. 'I'll give you a sleeping draught, so you can have a good night's sleep. From now on we'll take care of you.'

Instead of easing Anna's mind, Kate's words made her feel uncomfortable. She did not relish being treated like a child again. Fortunately, at that moment several servants entered the parlour, carrying trays of food and wine.

'Refreshments at last,' said Kate, sounding relieved.

With an effort Anna set aside her anxieties. Now she knew a little more about what Jack had suffered, she wondered whether she might be able to draw him out on the subject. But she lost the opportunity because Owain had taken him aside and she heard him say, 'It's wonderful to see you again, Jack. From the little I've heard of your adventures, you're fortunate to be alive.'

Jack shrugged broad shoulders. 'I'm glad to have been given a second chance.'

Owain looked vaguely puzzled. 'You mean that this time you're in England you plan to find yourself a wife and raise a family. I have a daughter who might suit you.'

His words surprised Anna into joining in their conversation. 'I thought you'd found a husband for Beth, Owain.'

'No. She refused him,' he said with a grimace. 'Her head is filled with romantic tales of handsome knights in armour, prepared to commit acts of derring-do for a lady. Alas, a wealthy goldsmith with a fine house in Chester is not good enough for my daughter.'

Anna said wryly, 'I remember dreaming of handsome knights once upon a time.'

'You did marry a knight,' reminded Owain.

'That is true. Giles fought in King Henry's French wars when he was young.' She turned to Jack. 'You never met my husband, did you?'

'Alas, no. I was in France on business when you were betrothed,' he said smoothly.

'Of course. How could I forget.' Anna removed

her soiled gloves and folded them inside her girdle. She accepted a goblet of wine from a serving-man. 'Sir Giles was a kind and generous husband and I grew to love him. You chose well, Owain, when you accepted his offer for my hand.'

'Thank you, Anna,' said Owain, looking gratified. 'Will you repeat those words to my daughter when you see her? At the moment she is staying at Joan and Davy's house, helping with the children.' He turned to Jack. 'So what do you say to my suggestion? Beth will come to you with a generous dowry if you were to take her for wife.'

'I doubt I'd fit Beth's notion of a handsome husband with this scarred ugly face of mine,' replied Jack in a stilted voice.

Anna made a murmur of protest. 'Not ugly, Jack.'

He raised disbelieving eyebrows. 'There's no need to pretend, Anna. Besides, I'm not looking for a bride. As it is, I can only stay for one night as I still have business in France that occupies my mind.'

Owain's smile faded. 'You would leave us so soon?'

'I have no choice in the matter. The news of events in France, which Davy has brought me, means I mustn't delay. We both plan to leave at first light and will travel part of the road together.'

'I will not ask you what this business is, but you will take care?' said Owain. 'We do not want to lose you again.'

'You must not worry about me, Owain,' said Jack, his expression uncompromising.

Anna wondered if his business in France had aught to do with what had happened to him six years ago, but received the impression that questions would be unwelcome.

'Then let us drink a toast to Jack,' said Owain.

'Indeed, we will,' said Kate, smiling at her stepbrother. 'To your good health, Jack.' She raised her goblet.

Anna echoed her words as she gazed at the man who had rescued her. He had been handsome before, but he was mistaken in believing she considered him ugly. There was that about his face now which went deeper than pure good looks. Suddenly she wanted to know the man behind that scarred visage. 'This is a fine wine,' she said, sipping the rioja.

'Is it one we supplied to you, Owain?' asked Jack.

'Aye. You can trust your agents. They carried on your business as if you were still there giving them their orders,' he replied.

Jack agreed inwardly that they had proved their

worth, but reckoned that was due to his older twin's belief and determination that he still lived. Perhaps if he had not been so secretive about his relationship with Monique, then Matt might have been able to trace him to Arabia. But what was the use of thinking such thoughts? It was too late for regrets. He had still not told him the true reason for his abduction or about what took him to France, knowing that if he had done so, then his twin would have been furious with him and done all in his power to prevent him.

Jack moved over to the table, which had been cleared of papers and now displayed several dishes of food. The slices of beef, cheese and bread, cakes and tartlets made his mouth water. Anna followed him and, as they helped themselves, she murmured, 'Owain says that you were sold into slavery, Jack. I find it difficult to believe that such a thing could happen.'

He frowned as he fixed her with a stare. 'You believe I speak falsely?'

She flushed. 'No, but it seems so incredible that it could happen in a so-called civilised country.'

'There are thousands taken into slavery in this world, Anna,' he rasped. 'Not only in France but Spain, Africa and Arabia. You find it unbelievable because those worlds are beyond your experience. Yet look at what your husband's nephew planned for you. He would see you burn. Now that I find incredible and there are questions I would like to ask.' He paused, before adding, 'But it really is none of my business and you should tell Owain everything. Now, if you will excuse me.'

She felt the colour deepen in her cheeks and came to the conclusion that the sooner Jack left the better. He had played the role of knight errant, yet now he was doubting whether she was as innocent as she had appeared. Perhaps he now believed she was a witch. She thought back to the moment when he had come to her rescue. If he had not done so, then she might not have lived to see this night through and she would always be grateful to him. But she no longer felt hungry and, draining her goblet of wine, slipped out of the parlour.

Jack caught the glimpse of a whisk of black skirts as Anna left the room. Obviously she'd had enough of the small gathering. However caring a family, when one had lived a different life away from them, it was never easy for either party to adjust to the changes. He knew he had offended her and regretted it. He wondered what she would think of him if she knew he had murder in his heart. No doubt she would be shocked and attempt to dissuade him from such a course.

He had sworn Davy to secrecy about his intentions—not that he had told him the absolute truth—but hopefully he could be trusted with what he did know. Jack had no desire to cause his kinfolk further worry, but it was his life and he must do what he believed was just. He knew Matt sensed his distress, but the pain of being treated as of less worth than a beast of burden had gone too deep to talk of it easily, even to his twin. His experience would always set him apart and that made him feel very alone. Perhaps that was why he sympathised so much with Anna—being accused of being a witch made her an outcast, too.

He must stop thinking about her! Sympathy could weaken a man and result in death. During his captivity, he had immersed himself in bitterness and hatred and used any method necessary to ensure his survival. He was not proud that there had been a time when he'd had to act in ways that now made him feel ashamed. Anna would certainly not approve of his behaviour.

Anna had no sooner left the parlour than she encountered one of the servants in the passage outside. She was a pleasant-faced woman with greying brown hair and soft hazel eyes.

'I was coming to tell you that your bedchamber is ready, Lady Anna,' she said. 'There's hot water if you wish to cleanse yourself from the dust of travel. Your baggage has been taken up. It is a pleasure to see you back here at Rowan.'

'Thank you, Megan,' said Anna absently. The maid had worked on her half-brother's manor as long as she could remember.

'I'm so sorry your house burned down. Yet perhaps it's fate that has brought you here.'

Anna was too weary and full of aches and pains to bother asking her what she meant by those last words. 'Goodnight, Megan. I'll manage to undress without help.'

'But there is something I must—' began Megan.

'Not now.' Anna left her behind and made her way upstairs to the bedchamber that had been hers all her growing years.

A branch of candles had been lit and stood on a small table. It was a well-appointed room and its window looked out over the vegetable garden and the paddocks where Owain's fine brood mares and stud horses grazed. She wondered whether to bother unpacking the few clothes she had managed to save from the fire. Perhaps just her night rail and toiletries for now, she decided. She gazed at the bed and wanted to collapse on it and sleep for hours and hours, but first she must wash. At least her gloves had protected her hands and they were reasonably clean still.

There was a tablet of Kate's special lavender oil soap on the stand and a thickly woven drying cloth. No doubt it had come from Bruges and had been delivered to this household by a carrier who had worked for Jack.

She undressed, throwing her smoke-impregnated gown into a corner of the room. She stood naked a moment, inspecting her bruised arms and scratched breast. A shadow darkened her eyes and a tear fell on her cheek as she remembered those terrifying moments in her bedchamber. Whose face had been behind that devil's mask?

Should she do as Jack had said and tell Owain everything that had happened that day? Forewarned was forearmed; if her half-brother was to represent her and challenge Will at the local court, then perhaps he should know that, besides accusing her of adultery, Will had said that she was a murderess and witch, as well. Due to the difference in their ages, Owain had been more of a father to her than a brother. Both he and Kate deserved her honesty, but the accusation against her mother continued to nag at her.

Anna sighed, taking her night rail from a saddle-bag. She sniffed the garment and discovered that it, too, stank of smoke. Should she dress again and go and ask Kate might she borrow a nightgown? Perhaps not. Anna was in no mood for a heart to heart with the woman who had been as a mother to her. She felt guilty for feeling the way she did, so instead she thought of Jack.

His refusal to talk about his time spent in captivity spoke to her of great suffering. How would she have coped with being a slave? Of course, wives were to some degree considered chattels by their husbands, but this could not compare with slavery such as Jack had experienced. Giles, who had been almost twice her age, had adored and spoilt her. She missed him still, but time had lessened her grief. He had left her well provided for, and even if she were to remarry she would not lose by it. She was only twenty-three, so still young enough to bear children. The thought caused her a mixture of anguish and hope. Although something had died inside her when she had lost Joshua, she knew that she still had more love to give. But not now—not yet.

She put on her night rail and then unpinned her red-gold hair so that it rippled down her back. As she combed it, her mind drifted over all that had happened that day. Would she ever be rid of the images of Will's hissing voice accusing her of adultery and witchcraft, of that devil's mask, her house aflame, poor Marjorie dead and Jack plucking her from danger? She wondered what thoughts lay behind those fine steely blue-grey eyes of his. She wished she might help him. After all, he had come to her aid when she was in dire peril.

Anna finished combing her hair and then knelt by her bedside and prayed for mercy, forgiveness, guidance and protection from evil. She was just about to climb into bed when there came a knock. For a moment she thought of pretending she was asleep, but curiosity sent her over to the door.

She pressed her ear against the wood. 'Who is it?'

There was no answer.

The knock came again.

'Who is it?' she repeated.

Again no answer, but she could hear heavy breathing. Her heart began to thud. What should she do? Perhaps it was the children playing games with her? She flung open the door, only to be confronted by an adult male holding the devilish mask up to his face. The light from a nearby wall lantern shone on his flaxen hair. She caught her breath as he lowered the mask and the face behind it looked even more terrifying in the flickering light.

'Well, so-called sister of mine, have you never wondered why your hair is the colour it is?' Hal sneered. 'Your mother, Gwendolyn, had a lover!'

Anna started backwards, feeling sick inside. She could not believe that a person she had known all her life could treat her like this, even though they had never been the best of friends. 'I don't believe you,' she croaked.

'Believe what you want, but it's true. Owain and Kate lied to you. You've bad blood in you, Anna.'

'Why do you torment me so?' she whispered.

His mouth twisted in an ugly smile. 'Because you were born in sin. Your father was a Frenchman, the Comte d'Azay, and you're his daughter.'

Anna felt as if ice suddenly encased her heart. 'It—it can't be true,' she stammered, although there had been a time when she had asked Owain whether they had kin with red-gold hair. He had hinted that her great-grandmother had hair the same colour as hers and she had believed him.

'That's silenced you, hasn't it?' sneered Hal, his

eyes alighting on the curtain of hair that rippled down over her breasts.

'Leave me alone,' she gasped. 'I would have naught to do with you.'

'By the devil, you're lovely.' He spoke in a hoarse voice and reached out a hand towards her.

She noticed the teethmarks on his wrist and that was proof enough for her that Hal and the man who had attacked her in her bedchamber really were one and the same person. 'How dare you! Haven't you hurt and insulted me enough?' she raged, knocking his hand aside.

'Insult you? I'm the only one in this family who's told you the truth.' Hal sounded quite indignant. 'The rest have been living a lie for years. You're no kin to the ap Rowans. Your mother bewitched and killed my father with an enchantment. You've inherited her power and cast a spell on me. If you won't break it, then you must accept the consequences.' He lunged at her.

Anna backed into her bedchamber and tried to slam the door shut. He was too quick for her and, brushing her hair aside, seized the neck of her night rail with rough hands and tore it. She screamed.

'Shush, shush,' he muttered, placing a hand over her mouth. 'We don't want anyone coming, do we?'

'God's blood! What do you think you're doing?' bellowed a familiar voice.

Hal was dragged away from her. Anna sagged against the doorjamb and watched him struggle in Jack's hold, cursing him and blaming her for being a witch and a Jezebel for the way he had acted. She watched as Jack closed his mouth with a punch to the jaw and sent him crashing into the opposite wall before he slumped to the floor.

Jack licked his bloodied knuckles and glanced at Anna. She fumbled for the torn silk to cover her bare breasts. He could not look away. Such perfect breasts. It seemed an eternity since he had found comfort and pleasure in a woman. Guilt twisted his gut and now he felt angry with Anna for making him desire her. Then he looked into her terrified face.

'My thanks, Jack,' she said hoarsely, concealing herself behind the door, the full horror of what might have been suddenly registering with her. 'I have not spoken of it, but I deem it was Hal who attacked me in my own house before the lightning struck,' she added.

A groan from the man on the floor drew Jack's attention and he knelt beside him. A curse escaped Hal. 'How could you torment Anna in such a way, you cur?' demanded Jack.

'She has bad blood in her. Murderer's—adulterer's—witch's blood,' snarled Hal.

'You lie!' cried Anna, wrapping the bed coverlet about her and coming out into the passage.

'Enough of this,' growled Jack. 'Get back inside your bedchamber, Anna. I'll deal with him.'

She gripped his arm. 'Get him out of my sight. I don't want to ever see him again.' She returned to her bedchamber and closed and bolted the door behind her.

Jack yanked Hal to his feet. 'Take a word of advice from me, you cur, and stay away from Anna,' he growled.

Hal cursed him. 'Who are you to give me advice? You know naught of Anna or what went on here years ago.'

'Whatever happened, it is no excuse for your behaviour towards a lady, so just do what I say,' warned Jack, 'or I will kill you.'

'You just want her for yourself,' accused Hal.

Jack didn't demean himself by denying Hal's words, but his eyes were cold chips of ice. 'Take my advice and leave. Owain is not going to be pleased with you when he hears of this.'

Hal glared at him. 'You'll regret your interference in my affairs.'

Jack laughed. 'You are a fool if you would threaten me.' He drew his sword and dug its point in Hal's large stomach. 'Now move!' He spun him round and now the point was in his back.

Still cursing him, Hal did as he was told, stumbling along the passage. Jack brought up the rear, determined to see him off Rowan Manor, relieved to be leaving in the morning. Twice he had embroiled himself in Anna's affairs. There must not be a third time.

Chapter Three

Anna stepped away from the other side of the door and sank on to the bed. She felt deeply embarrassed that for a second time Jack had rescued her from the attentions of a man who had levelled such terrible accusations at her. Some men might have believed there was an element of truth in them, especially when one of her accusers had known her since her birth. She felt sick with the fear that her mother truly had committed adultery with a French lover and that she, herself, was a bastard child. Had Jack overheard that earlier part of Hal's accusation? She thought not—surely he would have interfered earlier if he had done so.

Anna closed her eyes tightly, trying to recall the name of the Frenchman. He was a Comte and his name begun with a D…d'Azay! That's what Hal had called him and she could not deny there had been a ring of truth in his voice. Besides, she did not believe that Hal could have conjured up a French aristocrat for her mother's lover? If he had wanted to simply blacken her name, surely it would have been more believable to name an English or Welsh man? Anna did not want to believe in this French aristocrat lover, but she did. Which meant Owain and Kate and others had lied to her. It pained her that they had kept the truth from her all these years, but it did not hurt as much as the realisation that they were not kin to her. Their blood did not run in her veins. She was no real member of their family. She was alone. Truly an outcast.

She shivered and climbed into bed and snuggled beneath the covers. Tears trickled down her cheeks. How could she stay here, knowing that she did not belong? She certainly had no intention of returning to Fenwick and was uncertain if she would ever go back there again. Obviously Hal and Will were in cahoots with each other and determined to destroy her. She felt deeply hurt that two men she had trusted could behave so wickedly towards her. Did they really believe the accusations levelled at her? Or had they spoken in such a way purely to undermine her confidence and strength of will to help them get what they wanted from her?

What was she to do? She felt desperately unhappy, worried and confused. How could she make a sensible decision whilst in such a state of mind? Oh, God, why did you have to take Giles and my son from me? Was it because my sins are manifold due to my having been conceived in an adulterous relationship? What is your purpose in punishing me? How can I absolve myself from this sin? Or is it my parents' sin that needs absolving and only I can do it? She desperately wanted to know and was reminded of the psalmist in Holy Scripture who cried to God from the depths of his being to be rescued from the pit of despair.

There came a knock on the door, causing her to start up. Who could it be this time? Jack? Her emotions immediately ran riot. Was there some truth in Hal's accusation that Jack wanted her for himself? He had not denied it. Perhaps he believed what Hal had said and deemed she would welcome him into her bed?

Her head began to throb.

'Lady Anna, it's Megan. I have your sleeping draught here.'

Anna's relief was overwhelming and her suspicions that Jack might be devious faded. She tumbled out of bed and hurried over to the door and opened it. 'Do come in.'

The maid viewed her with concern. 'You looked flushed. I hope you aren't about to come down with a fever.'

'No, no,' said Anna, taking the steaming cup from her and breathing in its fruity, herby fragrance. 'My mind is in a whirl, that is all. So much has happened today that many thoughts are playing round and round in my head.'

'You've been through a bad time, my lady, but now you're home, matters will sort themselves out.'

Anna had known Megan all her life. Was it possible she would know if her mother really had had a French lover? She could not blurt out such a question to a servant, but maybe there was a way of finding out without asking a direct question. 'Master Hal has said such dreadful things to me about my mother since my return that I am at a loss what to do about it.' Anna climbed back into bed and told the maid to sit down. 'I fear that certain truths have been kept from me. Sir Hywel, perhaps he was not my—'

'Ha!' exclaimed Megan, sitting down on the chest at the foot of the bed. 'Master Hal couldn't keep his mouth shut—begging your pardon, my lady, for speaking disrespectful of him.'

'So it's true,' said Anna, her heart sinking.

'Aye, my lady. Lady Gwendolyn was crazy with love for the French Comte.'

'She was!' Anna's spirits lightened in an amazing way.

'Aye. Not that he was her first love, but he was her last.'

'She never loved my—my father, Sir Hywel?'

'No-oo. He married her when he shouldn't have. He was almost old enough to be her grandfather.' Megan lowered her hand and smoothed the coverlet with a steady hand. 'But then Lady Gwendolyn was a beauty and thought she deserved position and power.' She lifted her head and smiled at Anna. 'Now, you drink that potion down. There's naught like a good night's sleep to help you see things clearly. Master Owain and Mistress Kate love you dearly.'

'I deem you're right, Megan,' said Anna, her smile false. 'I am certain that in the morning I will see everything in a different light. Thank you.'

'God grant you rest and peace of mind, Lady Anna,' said Megan, getting up.

Anna watched her leave and, placing the cup on

the chair by her bedside, went and bolted the door. Then she returned to her bed and drank the sleeping potion. Was her father alive or dead? If alive, was he living in France? Did he have a family? Had they known about her mother? Was he aware that he had a daughter? If so, was it possible he might love her for her mother's sake? Her eyelids drooped. Placing the empty cup on the chair, she snuggled beneath the covers. Exhausted, she drifted into sleep.

Anna had no idea of how long she had slept before she dreamed that she was in Chester with Giles and Joshua, watching one of the mystery plays. It was the story of Jesus's temptation in the Wilderness when he confronted Satan. Suddenly the actor playing the role was no longer someone acting out a part, but he was a devil threatening to take her to his fiery kingdom. She broke out in perspiration and started awake with the image of that evil laughing face burning in her mind.

Trembling, Anna rose from her bed and went and splashed cold water on her face. She had to get away from this Palatine of Chester, otherwise she would go mad. There were too many questions that she dared not ask, and she did not want to upset Kate and Owain. She would not be deserting Joshua and Giles because the memory of them lived in her head and her heart. She would carry them with her wherever she went.

Dawn was not far off and she dressed in clothes that still bore traces of the smell of smoke. She allowed herself time to repair her torn night rail before placing it in a saddlebag. Remembering to pick up her lute, she checked the strings had not been damaged from the journey.

She left the bedchamber and tiptoed downstairs, following the fragrant smell of freshly baked bread to the kitchen. There she found Cook and enquired as to whether Master Davy was up and about. He informed her that he and Master Milburn had partaken of breakfast and left a few moments ago. Instantly, she begged of him some fresh bread rolls and spread them with honey. She also filled her leather flask with small ale. Having packed them in one of her saddlebags, she asked Cook to give Owain a message.

'Tell him not to worry about me, I need some time alone. Most likely I shall go to the convent where I found some peace once before.' She had decided on this ruse so that Owain and Kate would not worry about her. Somehow she must find a way to get to France.

'Certainly, my lady,' he said, scarcely able to conceal his curiosity.

She bid him good day and left.

The sky was streaked with pearly pink-and-cream streamers of cloud. Anna was glad that the day was so fine after yesterday's thunderstorm and hurried to the stables, hoping Jack and Davy had not yet left. She found them in the stable yard, where Jack was digging out a stone from his horse's hoof.

'What are you doing up so early?' asked Davy, gazing at her in surprise.

'I have a couple of questions to ask you,' she said.

'You'll have to be quick. We'll be leaving soon.'

Both men eyed her saddlebags. 'Where are you going?' asked Jack.

'On retreat to a convent where I have stayed before,' she said, with assumed cheerfulness.

'Does Owain know you're leaving?' enquired Jack.

She thought she detected a note of censure in his voice and stiffened. He looked as if he had not slept well. There were circles beneath his eyes and the scar on his cheek stood out vividly in the cool morning air.

'I am a widow and past twenty-three summers, Jack Milburn,' she said firmly. 'I have had the ordering of my own life since my husband died. I do not have to answer for my actions to any man but the king.'

Jack rubbed his unshaven jaw. 'That's as may be, *Lady* Fenwick, but a woman travelling alone, whatever her standing in the world, is a fool not to consult those who have her well-being at heart.'

She flushed. 'You would judge me, Jack? I appreciate what you did for me yesterday, but now I must do what is needful for my peace of mind. If you must know, I've left a message with Cook for Owain, informing him of my destination.'

He hesitated. 'What about an escort? Who knows what villains might be lurking ahead?'

'I doubt the villains would be abroad at this early hour.' She gave him a haughty look. 'If you'll excuse me, I need to saddle up my horse.' She added in a low voice to Davy, 'If you can spare me a few moments?' With a flurry of black skirts, she vanished inside the nearest stable.

Davy rolled his eyes at Jack and followed her.

Jack's expression was grim. He was annoyed because last night Anna had invaded his dreams.

Not only had he been plagued by the recurring nightmare of his son being torn from him, but now a terrified Anna being dragged away by a devilish creature had joined that image. He had sensed the devil's aim was to toss her on to a burning fire and knew he had to prevent it. Yet as he tried to rescue her, something kept dragging him back.

On waking, he had felt drained of all strength, similar in fashion to the aftermath of the fever he had caught in Arabia. He had reasoned with himself that the nightmare was the result of yesterday's events, but he could not deny the dream had greatly disturbed him, rousing that protective instinct within him again. He wondered what she wanted with her half-brother and waited impatiently for the two to reappear.

Inside the stable, Anna was pleased to find that her broken girth strap had been replaced and she saddled up her horse.

'So what is it you want from me?' asked Davy, impatiently.

She gazed at him. 'I do not want you to mention what I am going to say to Owain or Kate. The Comte d'Azay! What do you know of him?'

'Who told you about him?' asked a startled Davy.

'Hal said that he was my father. Did you ever

meet him? What kind of man was he? What did he look like? Where did he come from in France?'

Davy's expression was dour. 'You'd be wiser putting the past behind you, Anna.'

Her eyes flashed with anger. 'That's a bit difficult when I've only *just* discovered this part of the past that relates to me. I cannot possibly forget that my father is not the man I believed him to be. I need to know more about this Comte. I cannot ask Owain or Kate. I cannot bear to distress them further.'

Davy hesitated. 'The Comte was a handsome man with foxy red hair. It was the colour of his hair that convinced me that Gwendolyn had played Father false. Also, it was obvious that she was besotted with him.'

'Did you believe she was also a witch?'

'No. Hal did. He was for ever saying that Gwendolyn had bewitched Father into marrying her. Your mother was a lovely creature with hair as black as a raven's wing. She was reared in our household and treated like the daughter of the house. Father was wrong to marry her and deserved what happened to him. But there was naught supernatural about it.'

Anna felt a lot better. 'Do you know how she met the Comte?'

'Through her uncle, but he's dead. Owain knew

both men better than any of us. He met them at Domfront in Normandy, where our eldest brother, Martin, is buried. Does that satisfy your thirst for knowledge?'

She nodded. 'My thanks to you.'

Davy's face softened. 'You were brought up an ap Rowan and that's what you are at heart, Anna.' He left her standing by her horse.

Anna's emotions were in turmoil. What Megan and Davy had told her about her parents was enlightening and it was also a relief. They had given her an impression of them that was altogether different to that of Hal's. She now believed that the Comte and Gwendolyn had fallen in love and herself conceived in a moment of passion. She definitely had to find out if her father was still alive. He might have left for France before her birth. Something to do with the unrest between their countries, perhaps. But how was she to get to France? Her first step was out of this stable. She attached her belongings to her horse and led the beast outside.

Davy and Jack were still in the yard. At the sound of the clatter of her horse's hooves, both men lifted their heads and stared at her. Then Jack came striding across the yard towards her. 'I'll help you mount,' he said tersely.

She glanced at the mounting block. 'It really isn't necessary. I can manage on my own.'

'I'm sure you can. But allow me to help you this one last time.'

His words startled her. 'Will we not meet again, Jack? No doubt you will be glad to see the back of me. I cannot deny that our encounters must have proved troublesome to you.'

'Have I complained? Who knows, Anna, what lies in the future? Travel is a risky business.'

'Yet you survived.'

'Aye. But it was not easy.' He bent and formed a cradle with his hands. For a moment she did not move, but gazed down at his bare head. She was aware of an urge to stretch out her hand and smooth his untidy dark hair. Her thoughts even travelled as far as imagining being held close to him. She sensed that if he made love to her, then her fear and loneliness might vanish. How ridiculous a thought was that in the light of what they knew of each other? He glanced up at her and their eyes met. She felt a dart of sensation in her breast and a rippling in her stomach.

'What are you waiting for? I'm in a hurry,' he rasped.

'You offered your assistance, I did not ask for

it,' snapped Anna, placing a hand on his shoulder. She was instantly aware of the strength in the muscles there and placed her foot in his laced hands. She felt his fingers brush her ankle above the short boot and experienced a frisson of pleasure. Then her breath caught in her throat as he raised her into the air as if she weighed no more than a dandelion clock. The moment was spoilt when he threw her into the saddle as if he could not wait to be rid of her.

She scrabbled for the reins with one hand, whilst attempting to arrange her skirts decorously with the other. She was about to thank him for his assistance, but he had turned away and was crossing the yard to his own horse. She watched him haul himself into the saddle and gather up the reins. She turned her head away for a thought had suddenly occurred to her—one so shocking that she questioned her sanity.

Jack caught Davy's gaze on him. 'What?' he demanded.

The older man smiled faintly. 'Did I speak, lad? So, what are we going to do about her? We can hardly allow her to ride off alone.'

Jack's face was grim. 'You heard her. She has the ordering of her own life and answers to no man but the king. I deem she would not even take orders from Edward, the mood she is in. Although he is in France, so we cannot put that to the test. She's your sister. You deal with her.'

Davy half-opened his mouth and then clamped it shut. He watched Anna ride out of the yard and thought that, on horseback, she truly was an ap Rowan.

Jack's eyes smouldered as he gazed after her. He wondered what had been on her mind when he had caught her watching him a moment ago. If he were superstitious like Hal, he might have believed she was attempting to enslave him with the power of her lovely eyes. He shook his head as if to rid himself of the thought, telling himself that he must not blame Anna for the lust she roused in him. She had an excellent seat. Remembering her fall from her horse yesterday, he was filled with admiration. Surely she must be suffering some after-effects after all that had happened to her. Yet she made no complaint. If only life were different. But he must put her out of his mind.

Anna was seized by doubt. She must be mad to be considering travelling to France. It was true what Jack had said. Travel was a risky business. She wondered who had been responsible for selling Jack into slavery. Could it have been a business rival? Giles had told her that there was a lot of money to be made from trade. The best woollen cloth, parchments, tapestries, gold and silver and other luxury goods could fetch a goodly price. Yet how could an English man such as Jack outdo the merchants on the Continent, whose transport costs would slice his profits? It didn't make sense for a foreign rival to get rid of him. Unless it had been a fellow countryman?

She nibbled on her lip. What was the point of puzzling over the matter? She would be eternally grateful to Jack for coming to her assistance, but she could expect no more help from him. Soon, their ways would part. Once they reached the highway, she would go in the direction of Chester on the pretence that she intended seeking sanctuary at the convent and he and Davy would turn in the other direction towards the Wirral and Birkenhead Priory, where one could take a ferry across the Mersey to Liverpool. Even at this early hour, the road would be busy with monks and clerics bound for St Werburgh's Abbey, as well as peasants, merchants and others going to market, so there was no need for them to worry about her.

If it had not been for their earlier exchange in the yard, Anna might have been tempted to ask Jack outright to give her passage on his ship to France, but she doubted he would agree. If only she could smuggle herself aboard and not be discovered until they were out at sea. But that plan was out of the question if his ship was anchored in the Dee estuary.

She came to the end of the lane and there she waited for the two men to draw alongside her. 'So, Anna, you're still of a mind to go to the convent?' asked Davy. 'You could come and stay with Joan and me for a few days and see the new baby.'

She was warmed by his thoughtfulness. 'It's kind of you to ask me, Davy. Perhaps another time. At the moment I would not make cheerful company and that might upset the children. Besides, you have Beth with you.'

'Give it a sennight then and we'll look to see you.' He leaned forward and kissed her cheek.

'Give Joan and the children my warmest regards,' she said softly.

He nodded and drew his horse away from hers.

Anna was aware of Jack's frowning eyes upon her. 'Why so glum, Jack?'

'Are you sure you'll be safe travelling without a companion to this convent? I hope you have no plans to take the veil?' His tone was brusque.

She stiffened. 'Now there is a thought.'

His frown deepened. 'You wouldn't, Anna?'

'Why not, if it is God's will for me?'

'To shut yourself away from the world and never see all those you hold dear? You can have no idea what that is like,' he rasped.

'And you do, Jack?'

His smile was grim. 'Don't do it, Anna! Return to Rowan. Owain will protect you.' His horse was growing skittish and chaffing at the bit and he knew he would have to go.

She smiled. 'I hope you have a safe journey, Jack. By the way, what is the name of your ship?'

'*Hercules.*'

'It's a fine name for a ship.' She held out a hand to him. 'Fare thee well.'

He clasped her hand briefly and then relinquished it and rode after Davy.

Anna remained where she was for several minutes, deliberating which path to take to West Kirby that would not bring her into contact with Jack before it was absolutely necessary. The back lanes would be best as they were less frequented.

With luck she might reach there before him, although the success of her plan to get aboard his ship was dependant on the tide. When the tide was out at West Kirby, a great expanse of sand was exposed, so that no ships could sail right up to the water front. At such times one could walk out to the three islands in the estuary. The furthest was two miles away, so one needed plenty of time to reach it. Otherwise, there was the possibility of drowning on the incoming tide or being forced to spend several hours on Hilbre, the largest of the islands, waiting for the tide to retreat again.

She wondered how Jack's master mariner knew when to come inshore to pick up Jack if the ship was anchored out in the bay. Perhaps they had worked out a signal or maybe Jack intended hiring a boatman to row him out to the vessel from the island. If the tide was out, then she was presented with a severe problem. But, after the events of yesterday, and the dreams she had had, she was curiously reckless. Most likely the feeling would not last and she would descend into that pit of despair again, but for the moment her mind was fixed on going to France. So she rode towards a lane that would eventually bring her to West Kirby and the sea.

* * *

Jack gazed out over the expanse of sand between the mainland and the small islands in the Dee estuary where the *Hercules* was anchored. According to a couple of fishermen mending their nets, it was going to be a few hours before the tide turned. They had given him directions concerning the safest path to walk to the largest island two miles away—a path he had traversed with others on his arrival, but he had appreciated being given fresh directions for the return journey. He had handed over his hired horse to the stables and quaffed a tankard of ale and eaten some bread and cheese at the inn and was now about to set out. His eyes narrowed against the sun glistening on the sand. He guessed it would take him about an hour to reach Hilbre Island where he would signal to his ship. He could see the silhouettes of people making a similar voyage, so he knew he was not alone. Putting his best foot forward, he headed across the sands.

Anna arrived in West Kirby half an hour or so later. Whilst leaving her horse in the charge of a stable boy, she recognised the stallion that Jack had ridden. 'How long since this horse's rider left?' she asked.

'An hour or more,' he replied.

She thanked him and made her way to the waterfront. Her heart sank when she saw that the tide was out. After making a quick search of the small fishing village without seeing any sign of Jack, she gazed across the sands where she could make out figures crossing to and from the largest island. Was Jack amongst them? Her brow creased in thought and she decided to have a word with one of the fishermen mending his nets.

He confirmed her supposition that Jack had set out to walk to Hilbre Island. Filled with dismay, she was now having second thoughts about the risk involved in following him. Yet if she delayed, she could be caught out by the tide. Coming to a decision, she hurried to the stable and discussed with the stable boy the care of her horse. Money changed hands and then she removed her belongings and set out after Jack.

Anna knew from a previous occasion that she must not walk directly to the largest island but go via the two smaller ones, Little Eye and Middle Eye. She was over halfway across the sands when she started to question whether she had been a fool to set out so late, burdened as she was with her possessions. Shielding her eyes from the sun, she thought she could catch a glimpse of its rays sparkling on water towards one end of the island. If that was so, then the tide had turned and was coming in. It was too late to go back, so she must walk faster.

She managed to cover the next quarter of a mile with great speed and now Hilbre Island loomed closer. But already the sea was starting to trickle through grooves in the sand at her feet. Her saddlebags and lute were weighing her down and damp sand clung to the hem of her gown, which was flapping against her legs and hampering her progress. Determinedly, she forced her painful limbs on, keeping her eyes fixed on the hump of the island, where she could now see grass. Water swirled about her ankles, soaking her boots and the bottom inches of her gown. She trudged on, aware the sea was creeping higher. She told herself that she must not panic, for she was almost there.

With aching arms, she scarcely managed to fling her saddlebags on to a rock and was reluctant to throw her lute after them. As she hesitated, a harsh voice said, 'God's blood, Anna! What are you doing here?'

Her heart leapt in her breast at the sound of

Jack's voice. He seemed to have appeared out of nowhere and now loomed over her. His expression was thunderous as he snatched the lute from her and placed it beside her saddlebags. Before he could drag her up beside him, she placed her hands on the pinkish-brown rock and clawed herself up out of the water as it sucked about her thighs.

'Your wits, my lady, have gone begging,' he snapped, seizing her arm and hoisting her into a standing position.

'I would not deny it,' gasped Anna, staggering against him. 'I will understand if you wish to toss me back into the sea.'

'Don't tempt me!' His eyes narrowed. 'Why are you here? You're supposed to be on your way to the convent.'

'I changed my mind. I wish you to take me to France,' she said breathlessly. 'I will pay for my passage. I have coin on me.'

He stared at her in horror. 'You must be mad! I have no intention of taking you anywhere.'

'I thought you might not and that's my reason for not asking you earlier.' Anna managed to avoid his gaze by reaching down and taking a handful of sodden skirt. She attempted to wring it out, but her efforts achieved little. There was no doubt in her mind that another of her gowns was ruined and would never be the same again.

He swore and ran a hand through his wind-ruffled hair. 'If you knew that, then why did you make such a risky journey across the sands?' She gave him a look of entreaty. 'I thought that by making such an effort, you might take pity on me. I have to get away, Jack. Somewhere completely different, where no one knows me. Please, do not reject me out of hand?'

Jack determined not to weaken, but knew he would have a struggle with his conscience. 'I don't believe in insulting people by showing them pity. Why do you want to go to France? Don't you know that King Edward's army has invaded the country to do battle with King Louis?'

'I knew of it, but it escaped my mind,' she said in a trembling voice. 'Anyway, I don't see why either army should be bothered with me.'

The sudden heat in his gaze seemed to scorch her. 'Those are the most idiotic words I've ever heard a woman say,' he roared, startling her so much that she lost her footing and would have fallen into the sea if he hadn't shot out an arm and dragged her back.

'See what you did?' she cried, trembling as she clutched his sleeve. 'There really is no need to shout.' Jack took a deep breath. 'There's naught a soldier loves more than a stray wench sauntering around the countryside.'

She fought down a blush and said in a dignified voice, 'I am no wench and I have no intention of sauntering. I have my reasons for going to France and they are not for dallying with soldiers.'

'I know. You want to get away somewhere different where no one knows you. But why France? Why not another place in England? There must be another reason for your wanting to go there.'

'Of course.' Anna was convinced that if she told him the truth then he would definitely refuse to take her. 'Do you think we might move from this rock?' she asked, needing time to think of an answer that should be acceptable to him.

Jack stepped on to another rock and then grass, avoiding a clump of sea thrift. She lifted her skirts and leapt towards him. He glowered at her as he picked up her saddlebags and began to walk. 'Your other reason had better be good, or I will leave you on this island to wait until the tide ebbs and you'll have no choice but to trek back to the mainland.'

Chapter Four

Anna stared after him in dismay and, picking up her lute, hurried after him. 'But it will be dark by then and I might wander into soft sand and never be seen again.'

'You should have thought of that before leaving the safety of the mainland,' he said tersely. 'What about Owain sorting out your affairs? What about Kate worrying herself to flinders about you?' he raged, striding along at a heart-racing pace, so that she had trouble keeping up with him.

'They'll believe I'm staying at the convent.' Her sodden skirts caked with wet sand clung to her legs most unpleasantly, but she dared not suggest that he slowed down. 'I left a message with the stable boy in West Kirby to take care of my horse. If I have not returned by the time the money I gave him runs out, then he is to return my horse to Rowan Manor. Only then is he to tell Owain that I have gone to France with you.'

Jack stopped in his tracks and stared at her. 'You have completely lost your wits. I did notice there was a full moon last night.'

'I am not a lunatic,' she said indignantly. 'Although it would not be surprising if I were half-crazed. Surely it is obvious to you that Will and Hal between them are determined to be rid of me?'

'I think Hal had something else in mind for you altogether,' he growled. 'You should have told all to Owain. Running away to France is no way to deal with this matter.'

'I have my reasons for not doing so,' she said firmly. 'And it did not occur to me that I was running away. Rather I have something completely different in mind. But at least I should be safe from Hal and Will in France.'

'But there are other dangers that lurk for the unwary traveller abroad and sea travel is not without its risks,' he said, exasperated. 'I really should leave you here.'

'Please, Jack, don't do that.' She prayed fervently for words that would convince him to take her with him. Then an idea struck her that she believed was truly inspired. 'I asked for God's guidance and I feel he has told me the path I must take,' she said piously.

He glanced at her with suspicion in his eyes. 'And what path is that?'

'A pilgrimage.'

He smiled grimly. 'You're not serious.'

She was taken aback. 'Why not?'

Jack began to walk again and his pace was just as brisk as before. 'Have you given this pilgrimage much thought?'

Thinking quickly, Anna said smoothly, 'I have it in mind to follow Kate's journey through France, taking in the various shrines on the way to Spain.'

'Your words only serve to convince me that you have scarcely thought about what such a pilgrimage entails,' said Jack, shaking his head. 'St James's feast day was in July, so you're much too late to get to Santiago de Compostela in time for the celebrations.'

Anna groaned. 'You're so right, Jack. I haven't given it enough thought. I can only say that during my last retreat, one of the lay sisters suggested that a pilgrimage would be good for me. I thought little of it until this recent débâcle with Will and Hal.'

Jack's dour expression relaxed a little. 'Now

that sounds more probable, but a pilgrimage in our own land would serve your purpose just as well.'

Anna tried to conceal her dismay at this suggestion. 'But I have to go to France.' At the look on his face, she added hastily, 'Although, I suppose, had I thought of it sooner, I could have travelled the pilgrims' way through England and then crossed to France with other pilgrims.'

'There's no reason why you still can't travel one of the pilgrim ways in England,' he said reasonably. 'Of course it goes without saying that it would be wise to take a companion. A lady travelling alone, even with a group of like-minded folk, can still meet with trouble.'

Anna tried to look pleased with the idea and nodded meekly. 'You're right, of course, Jack. But I really don't want to have to go back to the mainland and start again. Perhaps you might suggest where I could start my pilgrimage now I am on this island, seeing that you are so knowledgeable about such ventures?'

He looked at her with an expression that said he didn't quite trust her when she tried to flatter him. 'I need to think about that. I cannot stress enough, Anna, that travel is about discomfort and danger. I am not saying that it doesn't have its excitements and amusing sides, but a journey demands careful planning. You must always be on your guard. It's not like a stroll to the nearest village.'

Her eyes flashed with annoyance. 'Why do you speak to me as if I am a fool? You were a witness to the way Will and Hal behaved towards me. You can have no notion of what it is like to be accused of being an adulteress, a murderess and a witch and thre-threatened with b-burning!' Her bottom lip quivered and she turned her face away from him, blinking back tears.

Immediately, Jack saw himself as an unfeeling monster. He didn't know who he blamed the most, himself or Anna. 'If you had not told me to keep silent, I would have spoken out about what I had witnessed and all would be well.'

Anna kept her back to him. 'You're mistaken. All would not be well. I know most likely it would be safe for me to stay at Rowan, but I am not a child any more. I have been a wife, a mother and now I am a widow and need to stand alone. I've made a decision to cut all ties with home and family.' For the moment, she added inwardly.

He was shocked. 'You've no idea, Anna, what it feels like to be completely alone,' he snapped, out of all patience with her.

She turned and stared at him. 'Of course I do. I presume you deem you know better than I because you felt so alone when you were cut off from your family when you were a slave.'

'Aye. But it's not only that. Women aren't meant to stand alone,' he rasped.

'Sometimes we have no choice, Jack,' she retorted. 'And there are different kinds of solitude.'

'This debate is getting us nowhere,' he said, walking away.

Even as he did so, he was remembering how he had hated not having the ordering of his own life when he was a slave. But Anna was a woman and it was different for women. He believed that God had ordained men to be the dominant gender so as to protect and cherish women. Although not all women were vulnerable and weak. He had known many strong women in his time. His sister, Cissie, had a very strong will and had shown amazing strength of character after the murder of their father. Fortunately, she had met a man of under-standing and a similar strength of character. Mackillin had loved Cissie and needed a strong woman to stand at his side in the Border country. Monique had been a different kind of woman al-together, beautiful, vulnerable and so easily frightened into doing what she was told without question. She had believed she had no choice but to obey her husband's perverted orders. She had roused Jack's finer feelings and he had determined to rescue her from what he had regarded as the slavery of her marriage. Anna was different again. He had never met any woman quite like her. There was a contrariness about her that filled Jack with a whole barrel-load of conflicting emotions. He should have known how to handle her, but didn't.

'So are you going to give me passage to France on your ship, or not, Jack?' asked Anna, interrupting his thoughts. He did not answer because he had not made up his mind. 'Am I going to get the silent treatment? Giles would do that sometimes when he was vexed with me, but did not want to argue.'

'I don't want to argue with you either, Anna,' said Jack. 'But I have to make the decision of what is best for you.'

She sighed. 'What else can I say that might persuade you to help me? Maybe if I told you that I believe by giving up my comfort and risking my life on pilgrimage that God will grant places for my loved ones in Heaven in appreciation of my sacrifice. I would like to think that my child and a good man like Giles would be welcomed straight into Heaven, but according to the Church I have to doubt it.'

Jack could so easily have been drawn into voicing his feelings about such teachings, having read some of the scriptures translated from the Latin, but again that control over his speech and temper that he'd had to exert during his years of exile meant he was able to keep silent.

'You talk of risks,' said Anna. 'Yet we both know that Kate travelled abroad on pilgrimage and lived to tell the tale. I deem that it is your experience of being abducted and sold into slavery that makes you so immune to my plea to give me passage to France.'

Jack felt his control slipping. 'Of course what happened to me affects the advice I give you,' he snapped. 'Knowing that, you should be prepared to see the sense in what I say. If you were abducted, my fine lady, and were to end up in a sultan's harem, you'd soon regret you'd ever been born.'

She flinched at being on the receiving end of such anger, but put a brave face on it. 'I don't know what a harem is, but I beg your pardon for annoying you. I do not mean to harass or make you angry. It's just that I desperately want to go to France. I am convinced my fate lies there.'

Jack's anger abated. He could understand only

too well what it felt like to labour under a conviction so strong that one would risk all to achieve one's goal. He realised she had got under his guard again and knew that he should harden his heart and refuse to take her. Yet if he left her here on the island to make her own way back to the mainland there was no guarantee that his conscience would be clear. Rather he would not be able to get her out of his mind, wondering if she had made it safely back to the mainland and then to Rowan.

He looked away from her and out over the estuary and was able to pick out the *Hercules* from other ships anchored in the estuary. He took a polished circle of steel from a pouch about his waist and flashed a signal to his ship. He was pretty certain that his master mariner would be watching out for his signal. There were several small rowing boats with oarsmen pulled up on the shore. He did not immediately make a move to approach one. Despite what he had said to Anna earlier about pity, he did feel compassion for her. The struggle he had was with himself, knowing that by having her aboard his ship, day in, day out, the physical attraction she held for him could endanger his mission. Having decided that, he doubted she would welcome any advances he might have made, not with his scarred face that filled him with shame.

He glanced at Anna and saw that her eyes were closed and her lips moving in what must be silent prayer; she also had her fingers crossed. His doubts evaporated and the corner of his mouth twitched. Who was he to argue with God? He would just have to pray for strength to resist as he'd done in the past.

'Come on, Anna. Let's go.'

She opened her eyes and gave him a sparkling glance. 'You are taking me to France with you?'

'I'm not yet sure about France, my fine lady,' he answered with a grim smile. 'I have to consider your safety. Maybe I will land you at a port on the south coast of England. There you will be able to find lodgings at the nearest religious house. You will be able to ask whoever is in charge for their advice concerning pilgrimages. I have no doubt they will provide you with a pilgrim's habit and staff if your calling is true. If you decide to travel to Canterbury, you are bound to meet numerous other pilgrims intent on crossing the channel to Europe.'

Anna was disappointed and almost tempted to tell him that she would stay on the island overnight and walk back across the sands in daylight. Yet if she were to accept his offer, then at least she would be that much closer to France. 'You are all kindness, Jack,' she said lightly. 'I will bear in mind what you say.'

Within the hour Jack was helping Anna up the rope ladder dropped over the side of his ship. He was conscious of her warm softness beneath his hands, but was determined to ignore the physical effect she was having on him. 'Do not look for luxury or comfort aboard my ship,' he said shortly.

Anna called down over her shoulder. 'I assure you I am not so ignorant that I would expect luxury on any ship. I will regard this voyage as part of my pilgrimage and the discomfort the penance I must pay for my sins.'

Suddenly she became aware of the astonished face of a bewhiskered mariner waiting to help her aboard. She thanked him prettily as she held out a hand to him and he assisted her over the side and on to the deck.

As Jack handed up her saddlebags and lute, aware of the effect she was having on at least one of his sailors, he could only hope none of them would fall in love with her. The last thing he wanted on his ship was lovesick sailors. His expression was formidable as he stepped aboard himself. Immediately, he saw that Anna was introducing herself to his master mariner, Peter Dunn. Hastily Jack took over from her.

'This is Lady Anna Fenwick, who is kin to my stepsister, Mistress ap Rowan. We will land her on the south coast before sailing for Calais. You can weigh anchor now,' he ordered.

'It's a pleasure to meet you, Lady Fenwick,' said Master Dunn, obviously trying to conceal his surprise at her presence.

Anna thanked him for his welcome. She could feel the deck shifting beneath her feet and it gave her an odd feeling. She noticed chickens in coops on the deck and thought they seemed completely unbothered by their surroundings. It was not the first time she had sailed on a ship and she prayed that she would be as good a sailor this time as when she and Giles had visited the town of Caernarfon on the Welsh coast. Of course they had been fortunate with the weather and she could only hope the sea would remain calm as it was at that moment.

She was suddenly aware of Jack at her shoulder. 'I'll show you to my quarters, Anna. I'll remove my possessions and you can make yourself at home.'

She glanced up into his strong scarred features. 'I did not intend ousting you from your sleeping quarters.'

He said brusquely, 'Where did you expect to sleep, Anna? Under the awning with the men?'

She was taken aback by his comment, thinking that it was uncalled for. She might have said so, if he had not picked up her saddlebags and turned away. She tucked her lute under her arm and trailed after him, across the deck in the opposite direction from the fo'csle to a deckhouse. She was aware of the men's eyes upon her and hoped it was untrue that many mariners were superstitious about having a woman aboard. If so, she was fortunate indeed that none knew of the accusation levelled against her of being a witch. She felt a sinking of the heart, thinking of Will's deviousness, and Marjorie, who had lost her life because of his lies.

As soon as Anna stepped inside Jack's quarters, she knew what he had said about there being a lack of comfort and luxury was true. The cabin was cramped and contained only a bunk bed above a couple of drawers with brass handles. She presumed the hinged drop piece of wood would serve as a table and there was a chair screwed to the floor.

'I do not envy the life of a mariner,' she murmured.

'There are worse conditions for a man to live in,' said Jack, his expression austere.

Due to the smallness of the cabin, their bodies were almost touching and she felt a sudden breathlessness, aware of that mixture of male muskiness and sandalwood in a way that she had not been on their walk across the island. She inched backwards and the wooden rim of the bunk caught the back of her knees so that she toppled on to the bed.

'Are you all right?' asked Jack, bending over her.

'I just lost my balance,' she replied.

'Hopefully, you'll soon get your sea legs.' He offered her his hand to help her up.

She took hold of it and was yanked to her feet. Her breasts brushed against his chest and a thrill raced through her. Although the cabin was dimly lit, she could see an expression in his eyes that took her completely unawares. Neither moved. She could feel the thud of his heart echoing the beat of her own. Her lips felt dry and she licked them nervously. He lowered his head. For a moment she was convinced he was about to kiss her and was shocked to realise that she would welcome his kiss. Then he released her hand and left the cabin. This time when Anna fell back on to the bed, she remained there, hoping he had not considered her behaviour unseemly. Yet she sensed he had wanted to kiss her and that made her feel less guilty.

Jack drove his fist against the main mast, then moved away when he became aware of a couple of sailors' eyes upon him. How could he have almost succumbed to Anna's charms so swiftly? Thank God he had not kissed her. What was it about her that made him feel like this? In all the years of his captivity he had resisted his baser instincts and refused to take a woman. It had not been easy when his body had cried out for release but he had sworn to be faithful to Monique's memory, at least until he had fulfilled his oath to kill her murderer. If he managed to do so and survived the encounter then he planned to marry a woman of sense, who would not expect a love match.

He glanced up at the billowing sail before going over to the side of the ship. He stared at Hilbre Island receding into the distance and wished he had left Anna ashore when he had had the chance. There was no question of going back now. He would have to live with the decision he had made and was going to have to make sure not to be alone in her company again. With God's good grace and a fair wind they should reach the south coast within a sennight. He would land her at Plymouth harbour and see her safely to one of the religious houses. Then he could concentrate all his will on avenging the deaths of Monique and his son.

He allowed his thoughts to drift to his conversation with Davy when they had met in the hall at Rowan Manor. He had told Jack that the Comte de Briand was alive, but absent from his chateau in Maine. King Edward's invasion had ensured his joining the acolytes surrounding Louis of France in Amiens. The news had not pleased Jack because it was in Amiens that he had rented a house for Monique after she had discovered herself with child and fled from her husband. Now, it seemed, Edward's army was camped outside its city gates which, surprisingly, were left open. Apparently, there was much coming and going to and from the city. Tournaments were taking place outside its walls to keep the English knights occupied and competitions at the butts were organised for the archers to practise their skill as well.

'It is a strange war that both kings are waging,' Jack remembered saying, puzzled by the situation.

'Aye,' retorted Davy. 'But it does mean that you will be able to enter the city without any trouble.'

Jack had agreed, wondering what Davy would have thought if he had told him the whole truth, instead of only that the Comte de Briand had been the man responsible for selling him into slavery and that he intended avenging that dastardly deed.

Davy's parting words had been, 'Don't make me regret helping you to settle old scores with the cur, Jack. If you were to lose your life now after coming back from the dead, I'd be in dire trouble with the family.'

Jack wished he'd not had to involve Davy in his plans, but that recurring bout of fever had left him too weak to confront the Comte in those early months after his return to Europe. Originally he had not planned to return to England before facing the Comte; now he was glad he had been reunited with his twin. Jack had seen for himself Matt's wife and his children, as well as his sister, Cissie. She and her husband, Rory Mackillin, and their two sons, had sailed from Scotland to Yorkshire in order to check that all was well with him. He had put on a good act and they had gone away content.

Jack rested his chin on his folded arms and

stared moodily out over the shimmering sea. He had wished that he and Monique could have wed. Instead they'd had no choice but to live in mortal sin. Yet he considered that the church's sin was greater by countenancing marriages between children and old men. Jack ground his teeth, remembering when they had first made love. Monique had spilled many a tear after revealing the terrible truth about what her castrated, former philandering husband had forced her to do. She had begged Jack to forgive her, but he had assured her that there was naught to forgive. How could he hold her accountable for that cur's bullying ways? After that, they met clandestinely until Monique became pregnant.

He felt weary and the noise of the swishing waves against the ship's hull began to lull him into a somnolent state. He imagined he could hear music and dreamed he was inside Amiens cathedral in company with Monique and hundreds of others, listening to the songs of the great eleventh-century visionary, poetess and composer, the Abbess Hildegard of Bingen.

'She makes a lovely noise does the lady,' said a voice close to his ear.

Jack forced open his eyelids and yawned. He

could still hear music! Where was it coming from? Then he remembered Anna had her lute with her in his cabin. Why had he not thought that she might actually be skilled on the instrument? As for her singing...

He began to listen in earnest. She had a pure sweet voice that unlocked something in his soul and he knew this would not do. Moving away from the side of the ship, he went over to the deck-house and called, 'Cease that caterwauling!'

Instantly he heard the sailors murmuring and staring at him as if he had lost his wits. Maybe they were right and his memories were driving him mad. But the singing had not stopped and the musical notes reminded him of dancing water. Had she not heard him or was she pretending not to have done so? Tears filled his eyes as a vision of his three-year-old son splashing in the pool with the spray from a fountain falling on his naked shoulders came to mind. He knew he had to stop her or the music would completely unman him.

He opened the cabin door and popped his dark head inside. 'Anna! I asked you to stop!' he growled.

Her fingers stilled on the strings of the lute and her voice trailed off in mid-note. 'Do you not know this melody? I consider it most tranquil. I first heard it in Chester after a performance of one of the mystery plays.'

'I know it,' he said tersely.

She smiled. 'I thought it likely that you would because Kate told me how much you enjoy music. I remember that you play an instrument yourself, don't you? Is it the drum?'

For a moment he did not know how to answer her questions. Her words were reminding him of another time that was lost to him. Happy family times in Yorkshire. If he were to start believing it was possible to find such joy in music and family again, then it would prove even more difficult for him to hold to his course.

'That was a long time ago,' he said testily. 'I would rather not be reminded of it. If you could resist playing your lute while aboard this ship I would appreciate it.'

'If that is your wish,' said Anna, her voice subdued. She set her lute aside. 'Is there aught else you would rather have me do? Although we had a cook at home, Kate made certain I learnt to make a few simple dishes.'

Jack experienced a mixture of guilt and disbelief. 'You're a lady now. It would be unseemly for you to perform such menial tasks. Besides, we have a ship's cook.'

'Then I am glad that I brought my tapestry work with me.' She paused. 'Tell me, Jack, what do you do to pass the time when aboard ship? If you have Master Dunn to deal with the everyday running of the vessel, it must leave you with time on your hands.'

He looked startled. 'Not at all. He consults me on disciplining the men and I share other responsibilities with him. I know how to navigate and can read the stars. My brother-in-law, Lord Mackillin, made certain I knew all that was involved in sailing a vessel, just in case I ever found myself in a situation where I was minus a master mariner or a couple of crewmen.' He bowed his head politely in her direction. 'Now if you will excuse me. I'll go and see what Cook is preparing for our meal this evening.'

'I hope it's appetizing, whatever it is,' she murmured. 'It seems a long time since I ate the bread and honey on the way to West Kirby.'

He, too, was hungry and relaxed his stern mood enough to assure her that as it was only a few days since they had taken on fresh provisions and no doubt some of the men had been fishing, supper should be adequate.

As he wrenched the door open, he called over his shoulder, 'We'll dine out on deck whilst the weather is fine.'

She nodded, wondering what it was about her music that had disturbed him and why he no longer played himself. In the early days of her bereavement she had not had the heart to touch her lute. Would the time ever come when she could ask him why he no longer received pleasure from music? She sighed. What should she do next? Her tapestry work? No. First she must change out of her damp gown. She should have done so earlier, but the need for the calming influence of music had won out over common sense. She had but two gowns in her baggage, one black, one grey. Both would be creased but there was naught she could do about it. Placing her lute against the door, she proceeded to change out of her ruined gown.

Supper did prove satisfying, hunger lending an edge to their appetites. Both Jack and Anna ate their fill of fried herring with peas and onion served with oaten bread, followed by a sweet cheese flan. They sat on kegs either side of a table that consisted of a plank atop a couple of barrels. The food was washed down by ale for Jack and elderflower wine for Anna. They ate in silence, both unwilling to say aught that would annoy the other.

The sun had set by the time they had finished eating but, as the sky still showed streaks of gold, silver and apricot in the west, neither was in a hurry to retire to their sleeping quarters. By then the wine had mellowed their moods. 'This wine is quite delicious,' said Anna, after several cups of the brew. 'Where did you purchase it?'

'It was a gift from my brother,' Jack replied. 'Apparently his wife puts the servants and children to gather the blossoms in June. This is last year's brew and quite potent.' He reached out a hand for her cup. 'I deem you've probably had enough by now, my lady.'

She frowned and held her cup against her. 'That is for me to decide. Why do you now call me my lady instead of Anna? Of course it is more acceptable than being called a witch or a wanton, but it is formal for two people who've known each other for a long time.'

He told himself that perhaps he was instinctively trying to put some distance between them, but he could not say so to her. 'You were a girl when last we met and we have seen little of each other since. I realise now that perhaps I should have called you *my lady* from the moment you told me who you were.'

She frowned. 'There is no need for such formality, Jack, so you must call me Anna. Owain and Kate often spoke of you. Also, when your sister and her husband visited or your brother came, they talked of you and kept your memory alive. You were to me a great adventurer and I was sad when the news came that you had disappeared.' She could scarcely see his expression, but the way his shoulders stiffened was enough to convince her that he was still reluctant to talk about those times.

'It is time you went to bed,' he said, despite his emotions being stirred by her revelation.

She nodded, then said sleepily, 'But perhaps, Jack, during my time on this ship…' Her voice trailed off and her eyelids drooped.

He stared at her, wondering if she had fallen asleep. If so, then he would have to carry her to bed. The thought of her soft yielding body in his arms was enough to arouse him and proved sufficient to help bring him to his senses. He leaned forward and shook her. 'Anna, wake up! You were saying that perhaps during your time on this ship…'

She half-opened her eyes and gazed at him from

beneath sweeping eyelashes. What had she been going to say? Ahhh, she remembered. 'Perhaps we can get to know each other better, Jack.'

'Maybe,' he replied in a clipped voice, although he had no intention of doing so for that way temptation beckoned; rather he said that word to placate her and to bring the evening to an end.

Chapter Five

Anna huddled inside her cloak and gazed into the mist. It was several days since they had set sail and during that time she and Jack had hardly spoken to each other. The mood of contentment she had felt that first evening aboard the *Hercules* had evaporated. It was obvious to her that Jack intended keeping her at a distance.

She went hot and cold with embarrassment, re-membering his refusal to enter the cabin with her later that evening. This despite her telling him that her invitation was purely so he could collect his belongs from the drawers beneath the bunk. She might as well have saved her breath. He had said that the drink had gone to her head. Surely she must realise that with the eyes of the sailors upon them, he must do all that was proper to protect her reputation. She had only partly believed him. From the fiery expression in his eyes it seemed to her that he believed she had seduction in mind.

Snatches of conversation went round and round in her head. Maybe Will saying to Jack that she had murdered her husband and had a lover had stuck in Jack's mind despite all he had said to the contrary. She was certainly still having difficulty trying to forget such an accusation. Yet she was at least assured that, for the moment, she was safe from Hal and Will and in the care of a man, who, despite his stern manner, had appointed himself her protector. Yet he had admitted to not wanting her on his ship. It was obvious he was not going to waste time talking to her and could not wait to be rid of her.

Her ears caught the mournful tolling of the ship's bell and it felt as if it echoed her mood. If only the mist would lift and they could get on with their journey, but at the moment they were becalmed off the coast of Pembrokeshire. She prayed for a breeze and that the sun would break through the mist. She feared that, despite the bell warning of their presence they could be in danger of colliding with another vessel.

She heaved a sigh. She should never have risked that walk across the sands. Her wits must have gone begging because otherwise how had she, normally a woman of good sense, convinced herself that the father who most likely didn't know of her existence would be glad to see her? It was possible that she might end up in more trouble than when she had set out from Fenwick. For a start, she had lied to Jack about her reason for wanting to go to France and no doubt God would punish her for her sin. But perhaps causing Jack to carry out his plan to set her ashore on the south coast of England would compensate for her wrongdoing?

What if she told him the truth? No! She still had hopes that she could get to France; if he knew of her plan, he might not be so keen to leave her to her own devices in England. She also knew that, if she told him, she would be admitting to being a bastard child, and she just couldn't do it. This despite her belief that her parents had loved each other.

She wondered if Jack had ever been in love. He had told Owain that he was not in the market for a bride. Did that mean he had no intention of ever marrying, or not just yet? If he did marry, would he make a marriage of convenience or had he delayed taking a wife because he was looking for love? She found herself remembering that frisson of pleasure and excitement when he had held her in his arms. Just thinking about it caused a tingle inside her.

How had her thoughts strayed into such realms? She told herself that she needed something to do. The devil found work for idle hands. A shiver ran through her as she remembered her nightmare the last night she had slept in a proper bed. Suddenly she was aware of the slightest movement of the ship and the faintest creaking of ropes. It was like being rocked gently in a giant cradle.

She stared out into the fog. Ireland would be to starboard and beyond that country lay the great ocean, where sea monsters were rumoured to swim in the deep cold waters. She tried to imagine what they looked like and what she would do if one should suddenly loom out of the grey curtain of the mist. Shout for Jack? She felt he was a man like St George, capable of fighting dragons for a woman. The voices of the crew sounded loud in the still air. Were they prepared for such an event? If only a breeze would spring up and the sun come out, then she could sit on the deck with her tapestry and think some more about how to persuade Jack to take her to France.

'You'll catch a chill if you remain here much

longer,' said Jack, appearing suddenly out of the mist and startling her. He placed his hands on the side of the ship, next to her elbow. He was muffled in a cloak and tiny droplets of mist clung to the dark fringe of hair curling on his forehead. She felt that tug of physical attraction. Had he deliberately come in search of her? Or had he just come upon her, without realising she was here?

'Have you any idea when the mist will lift?' she asked, more as a means of making conversation than expecting him to know the answer.

He surprised her by giving her a definite answer. 'Within an hour or so. There's a change in the air on the starboard side.'

She crinkled her brow. 'I can't feel any hint of a breeze.'

'You soon will. In the meantime, perhaps you should sit in your cabin until the sun breaks through.' He straightened up as if to move away.

'I'd rather remain on deck,' she said firmly. 'I'll enjoy watching the mist evaporate in the sun.'

Jack said, 'I saw a painting in Venice once. It was a picture of the sun piercing the mist over part of the city, the lagoon and its islands. Its rays gilded the domes of buildings so they seemed to float above the clouds as if by magic. If I could have afforded the artist's price I would have bought it, but at the time…' He shrugged broad shoulders beneath the brown cloak.

'I've heard that the Venetians are talented in many ways, painting, sculpture, glassmaking…and, of course, I can vouch for their skill at making musical instruments,' she added with a smile.

'I never realised you could play the lute so well,' said Jack.

She looked him straight in the eye. 'If you deem I play well, then why are you so against my playing? It seems foolish to deprive not only yourself of pleasure, but also the crew.'

'I have my reasons,' he said shortly.

'Name them?' she challenged.

He looked away and over the side of the ship. 'I don't have to explain myself,' he rasped. 'This is my ship and what I say goes.'

'When it involves the safety and the navigation of this vessel I agree,' said Anna. 'But how can a little music endanger this voyage?'

He lifted his head and sighed. 'You ask too many questions. We either change the subject or…'

'You will distance yourself from me again,' she said lightly.

'I have to guard your reputation.'

'To the extent that you scarcely do more than exchange greetings with me,' she said coolly. 'Or is your real reason because you believe me a witch and a wanton after all and that I seek to ensnare you in my coils?' She realised immediately that her words had struck home. His hand tightened on the wood and for a moment she thought he would express his disapproval of her honesty by walking away.

Instead, he said gruffly, 'Of course not! I can only ask for your understanding. For a long time I was cut off from the company of decent women and I am out of the habit of making polite conversation. I find it especially difficult in the company of a lady such as yourself. Perhaps you don't realise how comely you are.'

She felt the heat rise in her cheeks. 'I confess it is a long time since a man has paid me a compliment.'

'If you had stayed at Rowan, then no doubt you'd have met the kind of men who would seek you out and pay court to you.'

'That thought had not occurred to me. Just like you, I am not in the market for a spouse.'

'Why not? Owain found you one good husband. No doubt he could do the same again. He has your well-being at heart and is a good judge of character.'

'You almost persuade me, Jack, that I should have done what you said and stayed at Rowan,' she said in a mocking voice. 'But it is too late now. Besides, the past has a habit of coming back to haunt us and who is to say that Hal and Will might not already be spreading rumours about me, saying that I was responsible for Marjorie's death.'

'You should not have run away.'

Her eyes sparkled. 'I didn't.'

'If you'd stayed and taken them to court, you could have demanded they produce proof of their slander.'

'They would have accused me of witchcraft and so many people are superstitious and act irrationally in such circumstances. You must know that, Jack,' she said earnestly. 'Not all folk are as enlightened as you are.'

Jack made no answer. For he was remembering part of a conversation he had overheard between his father and stepmother. It had involved Owain. Apparently he had been acquitted after being brought to trial for the manslaughter of a nobleman suspected of murdering a knight. The murder had taken place at the ap Rowans' other manor in Lancashire. He had only been a boy at the time and he could have misheard some of the conversation but he seemed to remember witch-craft had been suspected at first but in the end it was proved otherwise.

'I think you misjudge the common sense of most folk, Anna.'

'You think so?' She sighed. 'I wish the past was not always with us.'

He nodded. 'Sometimes I manage to put the past behind me but then suddenly it comes back to haunt me in dreams and I am back in Bruges or Amiens or Arabia. Whenever the fever recurs my nightmares are particularly vivid.'

Anna placed her hand on his arm. 'This fever—have you any notion what causes it? How often does it recur?'

Jack recognised a genuine interest in her lovely eyes. Unexpectedly she reminded him of someone, but he could not immediately put a name to the person.

'If you do not wish to speak of your suffering, I understand,' said Anna gently, watching the differing expression flutter across his scarred face.

'This I do not mind talking about,' said Jack with a faint smile. 'The ague came upon me after I was bitten by a mosquito. So many perish of the fever after such a bite, but I was fortunate. My mistress consulted her physician as soon as I fell ill. For a long time I hovered between life and death, but, as you can see, I survived.'

'Your owner was a woman?'

'She was one of several owners, but the others were men.'

'She must have valued you greatly to consult her own physician for healing.'

He jerked a nod. 'She paid good money for me. I was grateful and I worked hard for her. She dragged me out of the pit and I vowed I would never fall so low again.'

'She sounds a good woman,' said Anna.

'She was a widow…a dealer in cloth and dyes…and treated me like a son,' he murmured.

Anna was pleased that he had been more forthcoming about the years of his enslavement. 'You say she dragged you out of a pit…'

'I was not speaking literally,' he said shortly. 'Now, no more questions.'

She knew that she must be patient if one day she was to hear more of the years he had spent as a slave. 'Forgive me, Jack. I will not pry.'

He did not reply and she realised that she no longer had his attention. He had lifted his head and was gazing in the direction of the mainsail. Anna's eyes followed his and she saw that the canvas was stirring. 'Your breeze is coming,' she said.

'Aye!' His face was animated. He excused himself and hurried away to consult with Master Dunn.

With the weather in their favour once more, they made good progress during the next couple of days. But any hope Anna had that Jack would tell her more of his past was frustrated, for he resorted once again to keeping himself aloof from her. She felt slighted, but she adopted an attitude of not caring and worked at her tapestry, picking out a cornflower in woollen thread dyed with woad here and a poppy in red there. She sang softly as she worked to help keep her spirits up. She was vexed with Jack. What was wrong with the man that he could not at least be sociable? He had his freedom, so should be making the most of it. Life was too short to be wasted dwelling on what one could not change. Often she thought of Giles and her son, trying to find some comfort these days in recalling the happy times they had spent together.

But sometimes her thoughts dwelt on what Jack had said about the widow who had treated him like a son. Had he regretted leaving her behind when he escaped? How had he escaped? She wanted to learn more about this man, but knew she would have to be patient.

Fortunately, at mealtimes they were joined by Peter Dunn. Jack's master mariner was a man of medium height, whose weatherbeaten face was half-concealed by a great gingery moustache and beard. He had many a story to tell about sea monsters, as well as sirens who would lure a sailor to his death, if he didn't have the God-given sense to close his ears to them. Anna was amused by his tales but, more often than not, she spent hours on her own with much too much time to think. There were times when she thought of her natural father and whether he had a wife and children. If he was a family man and she was to find him, how she could make herself known to him without hurting them? It was a question that demanded an answer.

They were somewhere off the Cornish coast when Anna decided as a change from working on her tapestry that she would inspect Giles's collection of parchments. So being of a mind to try to read some of the script, she unrolled the vellum and placed it on its cloth wrapping on the plank that served as a table. She could feel the sun on her back and the breeze caressed her cheek as she leaned over the manuscript and began to translate the Latin.

'What have you there, Lady Fenwick?'

She glanced up at Master Dunn and smiled. 'It's a parchment from the twelfth century, written by a monk.'

'You can read the writing?' he asked in amazement.

'Some of it; the rest I guess.' She hesitated before adding, 'When I showed interest in learning the songs and hymns of the Abbess Hildegard, my half-brother paid for one of the nuns at a local convent to teach me Latin. Owain, himself, taught me some French as several of her songs were translated into that tongue.'

'Master Jack will be interested,' he said eagerly. 'As well as other costly goods, he used to trade in old parchments. Of course, this was before he was abducted.'

Anna secreted away this new information. She also decided to take the opportunity to ask Master Dunn whether he knew who had abducted Jack.

'A rival in business, so he told us,' replied the mariner, stroking his beard. 'And it's true there is rivalry between the different merchant houses, my lady. He was a Frenchman.'

'I suppose Jack often visited France?'

'Aye, regularly. We would set him ashore somewhere off the northern coast. Sometimes we would sail to Calais and tie up at one of the quays there, but more often than not he preferred a quiet stretch of shore.'

Anna was puzzled. 'Why was that?'

'Didn't want any enemies knowing his every move.'

'I see,' she said thoughtfully. 'If Jack has enemies in France, what business takes him there now?'

'Unfinished business, I should think. Master Jack is no fool and he does have many acquaintances and friends in France—so, no need for you to worry about him,' said the master mariner.

'What's this, Peter, taking your ease?' asked Jack, coming up behind him.

'Nay, Master Jack,' he replied hastily. 'I was just admiring Lady Fenwick's ability to understand this here ancient manuscript. She says it's three hundred years old.'

'Then she should not have it out in the sun,' said Jack, his dark brows knitting as he gazed down at the parchment. 'The light will cause the ink to fade.'

Anna realised she should have considered that possibility and gave a wry smile. 'You're right,

Jack. But I did not want to closet myself in the cabin on such a fine day.'

'Then perhaps you should go beneath the awning,' said Jack, bringing his head on level with hers, so he could inspect the parchment more closely. 'Can you really read this script, Anna?'

'I deem you suspect me of deceiving your master mariner, Jack,' she said in a mocking voice. 'Do you believe I am only admiring this beautifully illuminated work with its paintings of animals and fruit, demons, men and angels?'

Jack smiled. 'You have to admit, Anna, it is unusual to find a lady able to read a parchment such as this.'

'She can read French as well as Latin, Master Jack—says her half-brother taught her so as to help her sing her songs,' was Peter's parting shot as he left them alone.

Jack lifted his gaze and looked at Anna. Her cheeks were flushed by the sun, her eyes were bright and her lips were curved in a smile. He imagined how it would feel to plant a kiss on those soft lips and instantly had to clamp down on the thought. 'You must get out of the sun.'

'I will,' she murmured.

'Is your knowledge of written French one of the

reasons why you believe yourself able to cope if you do go on pilgrimage through France?' he asked.

'I can speak some French and certainly I would hope that would be of some use to me,' said Anna, shading the manuscript from the sun with her upper body. 'I am certainly still of a mind to visit that country.'

His expression was not encouraging. 'You will find it nigh impossible to understand the different dialects of the provinces that make up France, Anna. As for its people understanding your attempts at speaking their language, no doubt they will find your accent just as baffling.'

She drew in her breath with a hiss. 'Jack Milburn, I would have you know that I have not only sung in French but Owain conversed with me in that language, as did my husband, Sir Giles. I think I told you that he fought in King Henry's wars in his youth?'

'You did. But what you say makes no difference to my decision to set you down in Plymouth,' said Jack, his jaw set firm. 'If it weren't for the danger of rocks on the Cornish coast, I would drop you off now. I've heard there are several interesting places of pilgrimage in Cornwall to do with the Celtic saints.'

'Parting company with you cannot come quickly enough for me,' responded Anna hotly. 'Now, if you would leave me be, I will continue with my perusal of this parchment.'

'Why did you bring such a costly item with you?' he said irritably. 'It was foolish. Footpads haunt the lonely tracks across the moors and it could be stolen. Unless you originally had in mind to find a buyer for it in Chester?'

'I had no choice but to bring it with me, for I rescued it with others from my burning house,' replied Anna.

He was astounded. 'You have more than one?'

'Aye. Giles was a collector.'

He swore beneath his breath. 'You would have been wiser leaving them in Owain's safe keeping, Anna.'

'Well, I didn't,' she snapped, annoyed with his oh-so-sensible remark. 'If you are so worried a robber might snatch them away, I will donate the whole lot to a religious house once you set me ashore. Then neither of us will need to worry about them.'

'That would indeed be a generous act, but use your sense. You will need the money they could fetch in the market place to rebuild your house. I don't know how comfortably your husband left you when he died, but unless you remarry, it's possible you'll have to support yourself for some twenty years or more.'

'Unless I go into a nunnery,' she flung at him. He looked aghast. 'You can't still be contemplating doing so. I cannot understand your desire to live the secluded life when you should have no difficulty finding another husband.'

'I thank you for the compliment, *Master Milburn,* but I have no intention of remarrying unless my heart is involved,' she said rashly. 'I understand you are concerned about my wellbeing, but I will make my own decision about what is right for me. At the moment I have made no decisions about my future when I return home—if I return home. Still, I agree with you that a widow woman out in the world can never have too much money. So perhaps I should hand the parchments over to you to sell when you reach France.'

He opened his mouth and then snapped it shut. He was astounded by the generosity of her offer after his rudeness to her. 'You would trust me to do that for you?'

'Aye. Just because you make me angry does not mean I don't trust you. You are a merchant venturer and I am sure you would be able to get the best price for them. So, what do you say to my proposal? If your estimation of their value is true, then your commission will be a goodly sum.'

Jack did not know what to say. She had put him in a quandary. In different circumstances he would have accepted her proposal, but if he was to stay true to his vow, then he must refuse. After all, there was no guarantee he would survive the confrontation with the Comte de Briand. But how could he refuse her offer without hurting her feelings? Then he had an idea.

'I suggest, Anna, that you hold on to the parchments for a while. It is likely that, due to the development of the printing press, they will increase in value as more leaflets, documents and books are printed by machinery. They will become even more of a rarity, so I suggest we find somewhere safe to put them. That is unless you are desperately in need of coin right now?'

'Not desperately, but I have no French coin, so perhaps we could sell one or two?'

Jack sighed and ran a hand through his hair. 'I confess, Anna, that there are other merchant venturers more knowledgeable of the present market than I am after an absence of six years.'

She nodded. 'I understand that, but I would

rather you gained when the parchments are sold—just to show you how much I appreciate your help.'

'That really is unnecessary,' said Jack, a muscle in his cheek twitching.

'Nevertheless, let us seal our agreement by shaking hands,' she said, holding out her hand.

He had no choice but to take that small but capable hand in his and was compelled to lift it to his lips and kiss it. Her fingers trembled in his grasp and swiftly he dropped her hand as if it were a hot chestnut. He cleared his throat. 'To business.' Carefully he picked up the parchment. 'May I see the others too? I will sit beneath the awning and you can join me there.'

Anna nodded, feeling her cheeks grow slightly pink. The fingers that he had kissed still tingled and she found herself humming as she crossed the deck. Then suddenly she saw a sight that completely made her forget the business in hand. 'Jack, what is that great fish?' she cried, pointing out to sea. 'Look! It is leaping out of the water.'

His head was not the only one to turn, but it was Jack who stood up and came over to her. 'It's a porpoise. Sometimes one sees a whole school of them, leaping and diving after the smaller fish.'

'Now that would be a sight worth seeing,' she murmured, her eyes fixed on the graceful animal.

'What wonders you must have seen on your journeying, Jack! I wish I could have been with you.'

Jack felt a warmth at his heart. He was glad that she was happy at the sight of the frolicking porpoise and felt a momentary sadness that he had become accustomed to such sights and no longer marvelled. He imagined what a pleasant companion Anna would have been in Venice, Bruges, Spain, as well as the frozen islands to the north. He stayed at her side, watching as several more porpoises joined the first one. He felt strangely at peace sharing her pleasure. Monique had had no taste for travel, otherwise he would have taken her with him. A sigh escaped him and he told himself that he must bring the moment to an end. He asked Anna to fetch the other parchments.

She did so, and for the next couple of hours the pair of them admired the talents of the men responsible for creating such beautiful drawings and skilful writing. She was pleased that she and Jack were on good terms again and hoped that this boded well for the remaining time she would be spending in his company.

The previous evening Anna had gone to bed and slept deeply, completely unaware that during the night the wind rose mightily. When she woke she realised by the bucking of the ship that the weather had changed. It filled her with dismay as she came out on deck to see that the sails were reefed and there was no land in sight. As for the deck, it was going up and down in an extremely alarming manner. It was also much colder than yesterday and there was no scent of wood smoke from the cook's fire. Seeing Jack on the fo'csle, she staggered across the deck towards him.

'Where are we?' she shouted.

'We've been blown off course. There'll be no landing you on the south coast now,' he said loudly, gazing down at her with frowning eyes.

A chill of fear raced down her spine. 'Are we on the great ocean?'

'Aye.' The muscles of his face were taut and his scar gleamed silvery white against his tanned skin. 'Start praying that the wind will change and blow us eastwards to Europe.'

'And if it does—where will we make landfall?' Her knuckles gleamed white as she clung to the banister of the stairway that led up to the fo'csle. She had forgotten to put on her cloak and the wind felt as if it were blowing right through her.

'Hopefully France, unless we are blown further

south,' he shouted. 'You'd best get back to your cabin. Unfortunately, there'll be no hot food or fresh bread until this wind dies down.' At that moment Peter spoke to him and he turned away.

Anna faced the way she had come with some trepidation. At least inside her cabin she would be out of the wind. She prayed it would change direction, abate somewhat and blow them all the way to France. She lowered her head and decided to make a run across the deck, tacking this way and that. Halfway across, she felt the ship veer round and heard a warning shout. The next moment she was drenched by a wave and lost her footing and was swept across the desk. Gasping with fright and the shock of the cold water, she tried to claw her way up the slanting planks but the undertow of the retreating wave began to drag her with it. She screamed.

Then Jack was there, seizing her by the arms and pulling her to safety. Anna slumped against his chest, weeping and spluttering out water. She was aware that he was shouting out an order and men were making haste to obey him. 'Hush, hush, you're safe. I'll soon have you off this deck and in your cabin,' he said against her ear. She felt herself being lifted and it was as much as she could do to prevent her teeth from chattering. Her hands were that cold she could not even cling on to Jack.

'Please, Anna, don't cry,' he muttered, managing somehow to carry her with one arm, while hanging on to a rope that had been rapidly slung from the mast and tied to the handle of her cabin door.

One of the mariners had gone ahead of Jack and now held the door open for them. Then Anna and Jack were inside out of the wind and he set her down on her feet. She immediately staggered against him. 'Here, Anna, hold on to the wooden strut of the bunk, whilst I get some dry clothes for you,' he said.

'I—I—I can't. I—I've no f-feeling in my hands,' she stuttered.

'Then just lean against the door!' he shouted.

For a moment back there he had thought she was going to be swept overboard. He should never have brought her with him, he thought savagely, moving her aside and easing himself round her. He balanced himself on his haunches and pulled out the drawer beneath the bed and rooted through the items there before dragging out what he considered essential female apparel.

'Here, put these on,' he said brusquely, tossing them on to the bed.

Anna was incapable of doing what he said and could not understand why he was so angry with her. 'W-why are y-you shouting at me?'

'You could have died, you foolish woman! We could all still die! Why did you have to follow me? Haven't I seen enough of death? A fine protector, I am!' he ranted, hitting the wooden strut at the side of the bunk with his head. He swore.

'D-don't talk so—so stupid!' she managed through chattering teeth. 'Y-you saved my life. Instead of complaining, help me!'

He stared at her from angry eyes. 'Haven't I done enough for you?'

She returned his stare and whispered, 'Do—do this one last act of kindness?'

The space was so cramped that she was able to remain where she was and stretch out a hand and touch him. At that moment the ship tilted and they were thrown together. Jack had no choice but to put his arms round her. He could feel her shuddering and then she began to hiccup. He could not bear the sound, reminded of the noise Philippe used to make when trying to stifle a sob after falling and grazing his hands. Jack was suddenly at the end of his tether.

'Stop moaning, Anna! Get on to the bunk and take off your clothes,' he ordered

Anna was so taken aback by his words that she stopped hiccupping 'That is an improper suggestion to make, Jack.'

'Don't be foolish! You could catch a chill and die! The last thought in my mind is of ravishing you.'

'Well, I'm relieved to hear it. But—but I can't do what you say because my—my hands are too cold.'

She had scarcely got the words out when the ship tilted again and they were thrown apart. She ended up on top of the bunk whether she liked it or not. Jack dragged himself off the floor and climbed on to the foot of it. He reached for her hands and began to chafe them. There was no way he could trust himself to help her undress.

'Ouch! That hurts. I th-think I must have a splinter down my nail from clawing at the deck.'

He dropped her hands. 'I'll have to leave you.'

'Of course. But you'll have to undo my fastenings first.' She could not wait to be rid of the horrible feel of the cold, wet material against her skin. And the bed was getting damp.

Jack removed his sodden gloves and crouched over her. He had difficulty with the first fastening because the fabric was so wet, but at last it was undone. His fingers moved on to the second and he managed better this time. Then he came to the third one, but when the back of his hand brushed the upper curve of her breast, he knew that if he continued then he was in serious danger of losing control. He could only hope that she was unaware of what was stirring below. Only a few more buttons and then he was out of there.

Chapter Six

Anna was no green girl and her sluggish pulse began to increase as her cold body warmed in response to Jack's arousal. She was aware that his breathing had deepened and his fingers had stilled. Perhaps he was waiting for the ship to roll the other way. In the meantime she had to think of something to take her thoughts away from the intimacy of their position.

'T-tell me, Jack, do you know of a t-town called Domfront in N-Normandy? I thought that p-perhaps on your travels...'

He was so relieved to hear her voice sound normal that he did not ponder why she should ask such a question. 'It stands on a hill on the main road from Brittany to Paris.' He spoke rapidly. 'Eleanor of Aquitaine, the wife of the second Henry Plantagenet, was born there.' He managed to undo the last fastening and sprang away from her like a scalded cat.

'Wait!' said Anna, stretching out a hand to him. 'You have been to Domfront?'

He was impatient to be gone, but was curious as to why she persisted with her questioning. 'Aye. Why do you ask? Did Kate mention the town to you? As far as I know there are no relics there; although St Thomas Becket once stayed in the castle and celebrated mass in the church.'

'Nay, not Kate. Just one more question, Jack, and then you can go. Did you ever meet the Comte d'Azay when you were there?'

Jack stared at her in astonishment. 'How do you know that name? What has Raoul to do with you?'

'You know the Comte?' Her voice rose almost to a squeak.

'Aye. But now is not the time. Get out of those clothes and into dry ones. Stay here until the wind abates.' He managed to get out of the cabin before she could ask him aught else.

Anna hastened to do what he said and removed her sodden clothes. She was shivering again and trying to keep her balance as she reached for her drying cloth. She winced as one of her fingernails caught on the material and immediately inspected the nail. There was the tiny point of the splinter showing. Perhaps she could remove it without Jack's help. Any more enforced closeness might embarrass them both and she did not want him to retreat into his shell again. She rubbed herself vigorously until her skin tingled, trying not to think about his arousal and her reaction. Schooling her wayward thoughts, she wondered how he knew her father. Had she misheard or had he really called the Comte by his Christian name? Ra-Raoul! He had also pronounced d'Azay slightly differently. How much did she dare ask Jack about her father without having to reveal her reason for asking?

She donned her sole remaining clean undergarments and gown. If she told him the truth now, then she would have to admit to having lied to him about her reason for wanting to go to France. What would he think of her then? That she could not be trusted and possibly there might be some truth in Will and Hal's accusations? She shivered. If they reached France, then she was going to need Jack's help. Should she continue with the pretence of a pilgrimage?

A rumbling in her tummy reminded her that she had not yet eaten. But she was going to have to remain hungry until the wind died down. She would pray the storm would abate and that they would safely reach land. In the meantime, she must remove the damp blanket, wrap herself in her cloak and try not to think about the ship capsizing.

By evening the sea had calmed down enough for her to come out on deck. To her relief, she was assured by Peter Dunn that the grey smudge on the horizon, which she had thought was a cloud, was the coast of France.

'By my reckoning it should be Brittany,' he said.

'Shall we go ashore there? Will it be safe?' she asked with a mixture of excitement and trepidation.

'Never had much trouble with the Bretons in the past, although those roundabouts St Malo have been known to indulge in piracy—so much depends on where we make landfall. What with King Edward declaring war on King Louis, it could be that Master Jack will wait until we reach Normandy before going ashore.' Peter gazed in the direction of the fo'csle. 'Here he is now, so you could ask him yourself, Lady Fenwick.'

Anna glanced over her shoulder and saw Jack approaching. His expression was stern and she wondered if he was annoyed with her about what had happened that morning. Whatever his mood, she decided not to wait for him to speak. 'Good even, Jack. Peter tells me that is Brittany in the distance. Will we be going ashore there?'

He narrowed his eyes as if calculating the distance to the coast from the ship. 'Maybe on the morrow, we'll get in closer and drop anchor in a secluded bay and take on fresh water.' He glanced at Peter Dunn and indicated with a movement of his head that he wanted to speak privately to Anna. The mariner excused himself and walked away.

Anna looked at Jack. 'Where do you plan to set me ashore?'

'If it is to Domfront you wish to travel, then you might as well remain on the ship until we reach the Normandy coast. Although if it was Raoul d'Azay you wish to meet, then I doubt you'll find him there. I'm curious to know how you know Raoul's name and your interest in him. I wondered if perhaps your husband had heard of him in connection with his being a collector of parchments. When last I saw Raoul, more than six years ago, he was doing a fair trade in them.'

Now here was something that Anna had not even considered—that her father should have similar interests to Jack and her husband. Also Jack had given her a perfect opening to find out more about her father. 'I never heard Giles speak of the Comte by his Christian name. You knew him well?'

'Aye. We were friends.'

That news did surprise Anna. Surely there must be a gap of fifteen years or more between their ages. 'I was under the impression that he lived at Domfront, but you said I wouldn't find him there.'

Jack shook his head. 'His father might have had kin there once, but that was years ago. He wasted Raoul's inheritance, from what I have been told, and his lands were taken from him.'

'How terrible! So where does the Comte live and how does he support himself?'

'I first met him at a fair in Bruges. Likely now he belongs to the newly formed French Company of Merchant Venturers in Vitré.'

Anna sat down on one of the kegs and gathered her cloak about her for the air was cool after the storm. 'I must say, I never thought of your meeting him in such a way.'

'I'm surprised he never mentioned me to your husband, or vice versa—after all, Raoul knew of my interest in parchments and that I had kin in the Palatine of Chester.'

Anna avoided his eyes. 'Perhaps the Comte had his reasons. Can you tell me more about him?'

'Why?' Jack seated himself opposite her and his eyes narrowed as he scrutinised her delicate but strong features. 'Now you have brought up the subject of Raoul, I am thinking is it possible that he is the main reason you wished to go to France and your excuse of a pilgrimage was thought up on the spur of the moment.'

Anna coloured faintly. 'It—it is true that I want to meet him, but...'

'But what? You have lied to me, Anna!' He had never felt so angry for a long time. 'Is it that you met him when he visited Wales and the north of England the year I was abducted and you fell in love with him?'

Anna did not heard the last few words. Her spirits had soared. 'He came to England!' she cried.

'Perhaps now you're a widow, you feel there is a future for the two of you, together,' said Jack, glaring at her.

'He came to England,' she repeated happily. Had her father come in search of her, but Owain had sent him away, denying all knowledge of her?

'Aye, he went to England,' growled Jack. 'We've established that! But do you plan to marry him? Was it to him you intended to give the parchments?'

This time Anna heeded what Jack had said and

stared at him in astonishment. 'Marry him? Of course not. Alas, Jack, I have to confess that I had not heard of the Comte d'Azay until Hal spoke of him to me when you rescued me from his assault. I knew soon after that I had to come to France and find him, however dangerous it might be.'

For a moment Jack could not grasp what she was saying and struggled to control his irritation. He was completely baffled. 'You say Hal told you about him? I don't understand. What did he say to you about him?'

Her heart was beating heavily for she knew the time had come to tell Jack the truth, if she was to have his continuing help. She dropped her voice and said, 'That the Comte is my father.'

There was a stunned silence.

'That's impossible!' exclaimed Jack.

Anna's face fell. 'What do you mean it—it's impossible?'

'Raoul's far too young to be your father.'

Anna's spirits were plummeting rapidly. 'I don't understand. He is the Comte d'Azay?' She pronounced the name the way Jack had.

'Aye. But Raoul and I are of a similar age, so unless…' There was a sudden arrested expression on Jack's face.

'Unless what?' cried Anna, unable to bear the thought that she had after all come on a wild goose chase.

Jack laughed. 'Surely you can reason it out yourself, Anna? If Raoul, a man of my age, is now the Comte d'Azay, then...?' He cocked a dark eyebrow.

She closed her eyes tightly and then opened them again. 'You're saying my father is dead,' she whispered.

'If he was your father,' said Jack, feeling sorry for her. 'How can you believe aught Hal says when you already know him for a slanderer?'

'Davy said it, too,' murmured Anna in a strained voice.

Jack frowned. 'That sheds an altogether different light on the matter.' He stared at her and then cleared his throat. 'It perhaps also explains why I keep thinking you reminded me of someone—and it was not an ap Rowan.'

He saw her wince. 'That thought pains you.'

'Of course it pains me,' she murmured, toying with her sore finger. She was now vaguely aware of the sailors on the deck and wondered if they had overheard any of the conversation. 'Wouldn't it hurt you if you discovered you were not a Milburn after all? That your family had deceived you about who you were—and then to be told by the man you called "brother" that you had bad blood. I am extremely fond of Owain and Davy, their wives and their children. Then suddenly I learned that they are not kin to me. I no longer belonged.' Her voice broke and she put her hands up to her face and her shoulders shook.

Jack struggled with the urge to reach out and touch her. 'You know that's nonsense,' he said harshly. 'Please, don't cry! I understand now why you were prepared to take so many risks to reach France. Obviously you had an overly sentimental notion that your real father would welcome you with open arms.'

She lowered her hands to reveal a tear-stained face. 'No, that is not true! Although I confess I did hope that my mother and the Comte cared for each other deeply and that I was born of love.'

His face softened. 'That could possibly be true. There are marriages of convenience where either the wife or husband are deeply unhappy and they look elsewhere for love.' He was thinking of Monique and the man she had been forced to marry.

Anna scrubbed at her face and felt a little less

sad. 'Raoul,' she murmured. 'You deem there is a likeness between us?'

'I think the similarity I see is to his cousin Francesca.'

'I have a cousin, too?' A faint smile lightened her face.

'Aye, but…' Jack hesitated, not wanting to see that tentative smile vanish. His eyes lighted on the tiny scar on her cheek. Anna had been through much grief and disappointment and he was regretting already that he had to make her face up to certain possibilities. He leaned towards her and took her hand. 'Anna, you must realise that it is more than six years since I have seen them and a lot can change during that time. You also have to consider that, if they are safe and well, they might not wish to meet you.'

He hated himself as he watched the smile die in her face and a shadow darken her eyes. 'You might as well say it,' she said in a tight small voice. 'I am the bastard child of the other woman.'

Jack felt a stab of pain in the region of his heart as he was reminded of his alliance with Monique and the child they had conceived outside marriage. 'The sin is not yours, but that of the church,' he said harshly, dropping her hand.

Anna was taken aback by his vehemence. 'You blame the church?'

'Aye.' For a moment he was very close to telling her the truth about his dead lover and the son whom he regarded as an innocent in the whole affair. She looked at him oddly. 'My thoughts are all in a muddle. I don't know what to do any more. I wonder how my father died. Has Raoul ever said aught to you about him?'

'He died in England,' replied Jack, relieved that the moment of temptation had passed. 'There was some mystery about it and that's why Raoul went to Wales, where he had kin.' He added hastily, 'Don't look at me like that. I don't know any more than what I've said because I have not seen him since.'

She swallowed the tightness in her throat. 'Forgive me, Jack. I don't want to harass you—but surely you can understand why I am curious about Raoul? Can you tell me more about him?'

'We used to meet at numerous fairs throughout Europe and kept in touch by messenger through our agents,' he said, easing back on the keg. 'He was only eight years old when he inherited the title and scarcely remembers his father because he was seldom at home.' Jack really did not want to say more about Raoul. He was a reminder of happier times. 'Why don't you forget you were ever told the Comte was your father? Go on a pilgrimage,' he urged. 'That will keep your body and mind occupied and do your soul good. You'll meet new people and see sights that you've never seen before. You'll enjoy doing so.'

She looked at him in astonishment. 'You amaze me, Jack. I thought you were against my going on a pilgrimage. You said to do so without a trustworthy companion was a huge risk. Admit that I'm an embarrassment to you and, now you've discovered I've lied to you, you just want to be rid of me as soon as possible.' She paused for breath, but not long enough to give him time to interrupt. 'Yet, I suppose you still feel duty bound to protect me, so you will make certain you find that *trustworthy companion*. No doubt you're worrying about what Owain might say if aught were to happen to me whilst in your charge?' She shot him a challenging look. 'Well, you don't have to concern yourself about that. When I return to England, I will tell him that the blame was all mine, whatever happens to me.'

'Will you shut up, woman!' He glowered at her because so much of what she had just said was true. He had to get rid of her, but he did worry about her safety. He seriously didn't want any harm to come to her. The thought caused a wrenching in his gut.

'I'm right, aren't I?' Her chin quivered and she bit down hard on her nether lip. 'Just tell me one more thing, Jack, and I'll leave you alone.' She swallowed. 'Remind me again of the name of the town where Raoul lives?'

'Why?' he snapped.

'I think you know.'

'Vitré.'

'And is it in Normandy, too?'

'Brittany,' he said shortly, deciding he really must remove himself from her company before he made any rash commitments.

Anna looked thoughtfully. 'Then we are not far away from it.'

'It's miles away. At least two days' journeying.' He rose to his feet. 'I suggest you put what Hal said out of your mind and tell yourself that you are the Lady Anna Fenwick, née Anna ap Rowan.'

Anna gave him a glacial stare. 'It seems a waste of all my efforts to get here if I do what you say. I am half-French. I have a half-brother whom I would like to meet.'

Jack's expression was uncompromising. 'Give this up, Anna. I will not help you,' he said firmly.

She sprang to her feet. 'Did I ask for your further assistance? Although what harm it will do you, I don't know. Surely you want to know if your friend is alive or not? I know he might reject me, but if I could just see him then I will be content.'

Jack's jaw set. 'I doubt it. You'll want to speak to him about your father. You'll want to know what happened to him.'

She flushed and said softly, 'How well you know me, Jack.'

'I wish I'd never met you!'

Anna flinched. 'Obviously.'

He took a deep breath and his chest swelled. 'Why do you always have an answer? Do not think by goading me I will help you.'

'So be it,' she said, tilting her chin. 'I will trust to God and St Christopher to protect me. After all, you with all your knowledge and friends abroad managed to get yourself abducted by a fellow merchant, whilst Kate survived and returned home safe.'

Immediately, Anna knew that she had gone too far and shrank back as he brought his face close to hers. 'You know naught about why I was taken captive. It certainly wasn't by a fellow merchant, but was an act of revenge on the part of a man who wanted me dead. Unfortunately for him, I refused to die. You've made up my mind for me, Anna. Once Peter has set me down in France and taken on fresh water and stores, he will take you back to England.'

She was aghast. 'No! Please, Jack, don't do this to me. I have come too far to meekly return home. What if there is a storm in the Channel and the ship sinks and I drown? If I am to die, then I would rather it happened whilst I was trying to do what fate dictates.'

'Then you are a fool! I wash my hands of you.' He walked away.

She leapt up and grabbed his arm. 'If that means I can do what I want, then that suits me fine,' she said defiantly. 'Just set me ashore in France. I will seek out a religious house where I can lodge. I will ask the abbot or the reverend mother about making a pilgrimage but I will also ask directions to this town you mentioned: Vitré.'

Jack removed her hand from his sleeve and crushed it in his own, aware that his mariners were carefully trying to avoid looking at them. 'Why are you so set on having your own way without regard for anyone else's plans?' he hissed. 'Surely you realise that I cannot allow you to do this alone? Consider a moment if Raoul's mother is still alive. How is she going to feel if you arrive on her doorstep, saying you're her dead husband's bastard daughter?'

Anna suddenly felt sick. It really was remiss of her, not giving thought to Raoul's mother. 'You really believe in plunging in the knife, don't you, Jack? Why couldn't you have suggested that she is dead and Raoul is alive and married with children? You have a tendency to look on the dark side of life.'

A line of colour flushed along his cheekbones. 'Is that so surprising?'

She did not answer, but wrenched her hand out of his hold and walked away.

He stared after her, watching the sensual sway of her hips beneath the cloak. She was a stubborn, irritating woman and he half-wished he had not rescued her that day she had fallen from her horse. He could not deny she was driving him to distraction—but he could not afford to be diverted from his goal.

The only time he and Monique had quarrelled was when she had refused to leave France and go to England with him. He should have insisted, but had known he could not force her. She'd suffered enough from overbearing males in her life.

But Anna—it seemed they did nothing but quarrel. She was infuriating! She was also brave, generous and intelligent, but far too inquisitive. He feared that one day soon she would probe too far and, out of all patience with her, he would blurt out the truth to why there must be a parting of their ways. It occurred to him that she would never have submitted and done what Monique's husband had forced her to do for his masochistic pleasure.

'Where are you in your thoughts, Jack?'

He hadn't notice Anna returning. He blinked and stared into her flushed face and scowled. 'Here you go again: questions, questions.'

'I thought I'd best let you know that I will go ashore in France with or without your help, even if I have to swim ashore.'

He was incredulous. 'I don't believe you can swim.'

'I had three older brothers and—' She stopped abruptly and pain flashed in her face. 'Don't put me to the test, Jack.' Her voice was uneven. 'I have had two gowns already ruined by seawater. I don't wish to swim naked when I go ashore.'

Almost he could picture her. 'Have you no shame, my lady, making such remarks to me?' he growled.

Anna blushed a deep crimson. 'I said I didn't

wish to go naked,' she croaked, a stark expression in her eyes.

At that moment a crewman approached and, clearing his throat loudly, informed Jack that supper was ready and did he wish it to be served right away?

Jack nodded and signalled to her to sit down. He sat opposite her again. 'I don't know what I'm going to do with you, Anna.'

Her colour subsided. 'I do have a plan. One that might meet with your approval.'

'Is it feasible?' he mocked.

Her mouth tightened and several moments passed before she said, 'Let's presume that Raoul is alive and at home in Vitré. I will take two of my parchments and approach him about selling them for me.' She paused as if expecting him to speak, but he only stared at her from narrowed eyes. 'I know I allotted you that task, so I will see you do not lose out by my getting Raoul to sell them for me. What I want from you, Jack, is a letter of introduction. Then I will hand him your letter, making some excuse as to why you can't be there. You will say in your message that you have recommended him to me as a merchant to be trusted to sell them on my behalf.' She gave a hesitant smile. 'It means Raoul and I could become acquainted, purely on a business basis to begin with—I will soon know if I would be welcome into his family or not. If not, then I will not make known my relationship to him.'

'It's not a bad idea,' said Jack grudgingly.

'But not good?' She sighed. 'What's wrong with it?'

'You're an English lady. Why should you come all the way to France to sell your parchments to him? You could do it in York, London, Chester even…'

She said ruefully, 'You're right, of course. But I'm sure with your knowledge of people and merchandising you can think of a way of explaining that in the letter, Jack.'

'You don't have to try and sweeten me up with flattery,' he said, drumming his fingers on the plank table. 'Who is to escort you? Even if you were to travel with a band of pilgrims, if it became known you had such costly items on your person, then—'

'I am hardly going to boast about them,' interrupted Anna, surprised that he now appeared willing to allow her to have her way.

'Of course not. You do realise if you are to travel through France as a pilgrim you will need to have some knowledge about such shrines that a devout pilgrim would visit.'

She wrinkled her dainty nose. 'Kate told me of one or two, but I'm afraid they have slipped my mind.'

'You could mention Rocamadour,' Jack advised. 'Although it would take you out of your way.'

'Rocamadour?' she queried.

'When I first visited France with my father, he took me to see a cave where there were primitive paintings on the walls and—' He stopped short as their supper was brought to them. She would have pressed him to continue because she was interested in what he had to say, but it was obvious that he now wanted to eat instead of talking, so she gave her attention to her food and wine.

Once they had finished eating and were drinking more wine, she said with interest, 'I would hear more of Rocamadour, Jack. Tell me, was the cave you mentioned that of a saint?'

Jack was prepared to talk about the shrine. 'There is another cave where the hermit, St Amadour, lived that is closer to Rocamadour. Indeed, the town is named after him. Rocamadour is difficult to get to as it is built on a cliff face high above a gorge. To see it hanging there as the sun rises is a truly wondrous sight. The statue of the Black Virgin is said to have been carved by the saint.'

'And if I am to be a truly earnest pilgrim, are there any other shrines I should know about?' She smiled.

'The only other shrine of renown that I have visited is in Cologne, but that's another story,' murmured Jack.

Anna thought she'd like to hear that story some time, but it was obvious from his tone that he did not want to talk of that experience at the moment. No doubt he was tired after a worrying day with the weather. She was also weary and needed to rest. She felt oddly depressed at the thought of being parted from him. But surely she could manage without him? No doubt he would advise her what to do with her baggage and lute. If the pilgrimage involved a lot of walking, then she would be overburdened if she took her instrument with her. Although it might be possible for her to hire or buy a horse. Then she remembered that the only coin she had with her was English.

She glanced across at Jack and caught him looking at her. For a moment their gazes held and her pulse quickened. What was he thinking? Possibly that the sooner he was rid of her, then the quicker he could get on with the business that had brought him to France. Maybe she should leave asking if he could exchange her English coin for French until the morning.

Jack rolled over on his pallet, having woken from a nightmare. Images crowded into his head and he was concerned that Anna should have invaded his dreams again. He supposed it was not surprising, considering their conversation about pilgrimages. Attacks on pilgrims were not uncommon and women especially were considered fair game for the slave market by many ruthless and dishonest men. She was no flaxen-haired beauty but that reddish-gold shade of hair was unusual enough to be extremely attractive to an Eastern potentate. He had seen European women being sold in the market place in Arabia and knew that the fairest of them ended up in harems.

He groaned inwardly. How could he possibly allow her to travel through France without him? If aught were to happen to her, the family would never forgive him. Although, if he were dead, would that matter? But he did not want Anna raped and murdered or experiencing a living hell in an Eastern harem. So, he would either have to accompany her to Vitré or have to confine her to her cabin and set a guard over her when they anchored close to shore.

No doubt she would be furious with him and would try to reason with him when he refused to do what she wanted and sent her back to England. She would probably never forgive him. But why should that worry him? They might never meet again. Would she grieve for him if news of his death reached England? If she knew the whole truth, then perhaps she would decide that it served him right? He thumped his pillow. But why should he care what she thought of him? He would leave it to God to judge whether he had justice on his side, and eventually fell asleep.

Jack woke just before dawn. He rose and went to speak to the sailors on watch. Then he checked the wind's direction and the ship's exact location before having a word with Peter. The anchor was hauled up and they proceeded to sail north whilst keeping the coastline within sight. With God's good grace they might reach a cove a few miles south of St Malo, near the house of an old merchant mentor of Jack's.

Jack and his master mariner were both of a mind that it would be unadvisable to sail into the harbour at St Malo. At one time the port had been the see of Brittany's Archbishop and the church's rule had held sway; this was often in open defiance of the feudal Duke of Brittany. More recently the city had declared for the King of France, so it was likely that English ships could be St Malo's sailors' prime target for piracy. It made sense to keep the *Hercules*'s presence secret as long as possible.

Having decided not to worry her head any more about the dangers that might lie ahead of her, Anna slept heavily. But by the time she woke and came out on deck, it was to discover that the ship was under sail. She hurried to where Jack was sitting under the awning, quill in hand.

'What is happening? I thought we were going ashore,' she said.

He glanced up at her. 'We will eventually. We're heading for a landing place situated only a few miles from the road that leads to Rennes. Vitré is a few miles east of Rennes.'

'Oh!' Anna was so surprised by this information that she sank on to an upturned barrel without another word. She arranged her grey linen skirts to give herself time to think before she spoke. 'I thought you had almost decided to send me back to England.'

'I've changed my mind,' he said, without looking up from his task.

'So you are going to arrange for me to go to a religious house and then to travel to Vitré?'

'I'm going with you.' He glanced up at her. 'You were right. I would like to see if Raoul is alive and well. Master Dunn will to take the ship to Calais. Hopefully at least one of us will be able to rejoin the ship some time in September.'

She felt a flood of unexpected happiness and touched Jack on the shoulder. 'Thank you. I'm so glad you've changed your mind. I will feel so much safer in your company.'

Trying to ignore the warmth spreading through him from that brief, gentle contact, Jack gave the page his close attention and murmured, 'If Raoul is at home and prepared to have you stay with him, then I will leave you in his care and travel to Amiens to complete my business in France.'

'I see.' She was curious to what this business was, but did not ask. 'Shall we be walking to Vitré or shall we buy horses? How far is it?'

'I am hoping my retired merchant friend will either loan or sell me two of his horses.'

'That would make our journey so much easier and the parchments will be safer, too.'

'You still plan on asking Raoul to sell them for you?'

She hesitated. 'If his mother is still alive, I might need them as an excuse for my being there. She might have loved my father and I would not wish to disillusion her.'

'That is thoughtful of you, Anna,' he said, putting down his quill. 'I also had it in mind that you will need me to act as interpreter. Although Raoul speaks some English, he is not fluent in our language.'

'And you consider my French will be inadequate,' she said, without rancour.

'As I might have already said, I know what it is like to be a foreigner in a foreign land.' He smiled. 'Other foreigners always seem to talk twice as fast. Now why don't you go and see Cook? He's been baking this morning and there is fresh bread to be had.'

Chapter Seven

Anna was about to accept her dismissal when her curiosity overcame her. 'What is that you're writing?'

'It's a message for my brother. Hopefully Peter will be able to hand it over to a courier going to England when he reaches Calais.'

'I see.' She hesitated before asking was it possible for her to write a message to Owain and Kate to be delivered.

'If you wish. I cannot guarantee if it will reach them, but I could say the same about my own missive,' said Jack. 'You will tell them about Raoul?'

'Aye,' she said firmly.

Anna left him to get on with his message, whilst she went in search of breakfast. Afterwards, she packed her saddlebags and wished she'd had the time to pack more clothes. She would have liked to have presented herself in better style to Raoul, but there was naught she could do about it. At least the gown she wore was fresh and hopefully they would not be on the road too long. She spread her wet gown from yesterday on a keg in the hope it might be dry enough to take with her when they left the ship. Then she spent some time, composing and writing a message to Owain. This time she did not spare his and Kate's feelings, informing them of all that had happened the day her house had been struck by lightning. As she wrote she mourned the loss of the few items of furniture that she had chosen herself and spared a thought to having them replaced one day. She exempted Jack of any blame in her having made the decision to go to France, explaining that she had put him in a position where it would have been difficult for him to refuse to take her aboard his ship. She wrote about the voyage and told them a little about Raoul. She finished by saying that they must not worry about her and signed off with the words: *Anna, with love. May the Trinity keep you all.*

She frowned, hoping they could understand her script as she had written in the margins and on both sides of the paper. She took it to Jack and asked him to seal it for her as she did not have the means to melt wax. He did so and placed it with his own. She asked him whether she should leave her lute and the remaining parchments in the drawer beneath the bunk. He nodded, taking a key from his belt and handing it to her, telling her to lock them inside. She hoped to be able to recover her property some time in the not too distant future.

It was evening by the time the *Hercules* sailed into a small cove. They dropped anchor alongside a wooden jetty that jutted out into deep water. Jack slung his and Anna's saddlebags over his shoulder and jumped down on to the jetty. Then he turned and held out a hand to her.

She grasped it firmly and felt a tremor run up her arm. Such a reaction to his touch caused her to release his hand the moment her feet landed on the jetty. Her behaviour must be circumspect at all times and she had not forgotten how she had warmed to his touch in the cabin. To ease any constraint there might be between them because of their situation, she sought for something to say.

'Tell me, Jack, does this whole bay belong to your merchant friend?' she asked.

'Aye. He purchased the bay and part of its hinterland at a great price from the Duke of Brittany.' Jack kept his eyes fixed ahead as they trudged side by side up the beach towards the trees beyond.

'I presume there is a spring, or a well, nearby,' she said, noticing several of the mariners had come ashore with water containers.

'There is a spring. Its water is crystal clear and deemed sacred by one of the Celtic saints.'

'Which saint?' she asked.

'Her name has slipped my mind, but no doubt Henri will be able to tell you.'

'Is he married?'

'A childless widower. When last I stayed with him, he was planning on giving some of his money to finance a row of alms houses to be built for the poor of St Malo.'

'That was generous of him. I look forward to meeting him,' said Anna, smiling. 'He will not mind the ship mooring here overnight?'

Jack glanced up at the sky. 'It's going to be a fine night, so it has been decided that Peter will steer by the stars and put as much distance as he can between the *Hercules* and St Malo.'

'Do you deem that your friend will have heard the news that you're alive?'

'Possibly. He might also have news of Raoul.

Agents throughout Europe keep in touch with one another, not only about the availability and cost of merchandise, but anything that might affect their clients and the various markets.'

Anna considered asking Jack about the man who had wanted him dead, but one look at his serious profile decided her against it. They reached the trees and walked in silence for a while. Then a clack-clacking noise close by caused her to shrink against him as a large black bird flew over ahead. 'It's only a jackdaw,' he said, grasping her fingers and squeezing them reassuringly before releasing them.

She accepted his word for it, but kept close to him. 'Have we far to go?'

'A quarter of a mile or so. The trees will open out soon.'

It seemed to Anna that he had no sooner spoken than there was a lifting of the gloom beneath the trees. The dying rays of the sun slanted through the branches of oak and beech, lighting their path. After walking a little farther, the trees petered out altogether and they came to a meadow of tall grasses dotted with wild flowers of a variety of colours and hues. A couple of hundred yards farther on was a wall with a pair of closed gates set in it. Above and beyond the wall was what appeared to be a large stone building with a watch tower jutting out from one corner. As Anna gazed at the tower, she thought she detected movement.

'I think there's someone up there,' she said in a low voice.

Jack nodded. 'I remember Henri liked to keep a look-out. There's a marvellous view over the sea up there, so he can watch for ships coming and going.'

'Then he'll know we're here,' said Anna, glancing at Jack.

'Aye. But whether he realises it's the *Hercules* anchored in the cove, I can't say.'

'Is there a way you can signal to him, so he'll open the gate?'

'I intend shouting a halloo.'

She watched Jack cup his hands to his mouth and call up to the figure in the tower. She presumed he was shouting in French, although she could not understand a word of what he said. Apparently the man did because he vanished from their sight.

'You're certain your friend will help us?' asked Anna, hoping to enjoy the comfort of a decent bed now she was at last in France.

'Aye. Henri Lampaul knew my father and took me under his wing when I returned to France after he was killed.'

There was the sound of footsteps the other side of the gate and a male voice bellowed more words that Anna could not make head nor tail of. Then she noticed Jack's look of dismay. 'Henri is dead. It is his brother who was up in the tower.'

'I'm sorry, Jack.' She hesitated. 'Does that mean he won't let us in?' Even as she spoke there was the noise of bolts being drawn the other side of the door.

'He is honour bound to offer us hospitality. The trouble is I don't like Maurice Lampaul. We have met on several occasions and I couldn't take to the man. He has something of a reputation.' The gate swung open. Jack added hastily, 'Breton is spoken here, so you will have to trust me to say what is wise in the circumstances. If you feel you can't do that, there is still time to return to the ship and forget finding Raoul.'

'No. Let us go on,' she said.

Jack gave one of his rare smiles. 'I thought you'd say that. We continue on the understanding that you do exactly what I say. It is for your own safety, Anna.'

She nodded.

The gate had opened to reveal a stocky figure. It was obvious from his clothes that the man was a peasant for he was wearing a floppy straw hat, a smock and hose. When he opened his mouth to speak, they could see that most of his teeth were missing. Anna did not wait for him to finish speaking but swept past him through the gates and into a garden that consisted of rows of vegetables and fruit bushes. In the middle of this abundance ran a winding path constructed of flat stones of different shapes. It led to what appeared to be the back entrance to the house. A man of enormous girth suddenly appeared in the doorway.

Jack caught up with her and seized her arm. 'Slow down, woman! Walk more sedately so we can reach him together. I have been thinking. I suggest we pretend to be husband and wife.'

Anna stared at him in amazement. 'Why?'

Jack met her eyes squarely. 'I don't trust him.'

'Why? You mentioned he has a reputation. Is it that he has a bad reputation with women?'

'He is married but unfaithful and treats his wife and daughters like chattels.'

'I see. Are they here?'

'The servant says not.'

Anna almost said that they would go back to the ship, but what would that serve? She had her mind set on finding Raoul. 'You can't believe that he would come creeping into my bedchamber during the night?'

Jack gave a mirthless laugh. 'I'm not prepared to take that chance with your safety. If you find the notion of us sharing a bedchamber utterly repellent, then say so and we will return to the ship.'

'I would trust you before him. And at least we don't have to worry about a wedding ring as I am still wearing Giles's.'

Jack was glad she spoke so sensibly and he touched her cheek lightly with the back of his hand. 'I won't let you down.'

'I should hope not. Tell me if our marriage is one of convenience or a love match?'

He looked surprised. 'Does it matter?'

'Of course it does. It will affect the way we behave towards each other. Is Master Lampaul likely to know about your disappearance? If so, he will wonder how long we have been wed and that is something else for you to consider.'

Jack scowled as he rubbed at the scar on his face. She could tell he had not thought about that either. 'Obviously I should have given more thought to my suggestion instead of blurting it out the way I did. I'd best tell him that it happened recently, but that we'd had a fondness for each other for years; otherwise why would you marry one with such a scarred, ugly visage as mine?'

Before she could deny that he was ugly again, he added, 'Now we'd best make haste to greet him or he'll be wondering why we delay.'

Without more ado, Jack searched for Anna's hand and led her towards their host. She was glad of the reassuring pressure of that firm grip. When he relinquished her hand so that she could greet Maurice Lampaul, she had to steel herself not to show her revulsion when he slobbered over her hand. There was an expression in his unusual pale silver eyes that convinced her that Jack was right to be suspicious of this man.

'*Bienvenue!*' said their host.

'*Merci, monsieur,*' she replied, managing to resist wiping her hand on the back of her skirt.

As Maurice Lampaul led them into a hall he conversed idly with Jack in what Anna presumed was Breton. The room was furnished with heavy dark wooden furniture and there appeared to be porcelain statuary and objects of silver and enamel on most surfaces. Anna accepted the offer of a chair close to the fire and watched as Jack placed their saddlebags on the floor beside her chair.

There was a sound at the door and she looked up to see a middle-aged woman enter the hall. She wore a russet gown fastened up to her throat and her hair was completely concealed beneath a wimple. She carried a pitcher and, going over to a side table, she poured wine into pewter drinking vessels, before carrying them over on a salver. Anna wondered who she was, but their host did not introduce her, so Anna could only presume the woman was either his housekeeper—or possibly a lover. Unsure how to greet her, Anna remained silent.

Jack spoke to the woman and she answered him with a grave smile before turning to Anna and handing a goblet to her. She spoke softly in French, informing Anna that although Master Lampaul had already dined, food would be set before them whilst a bedchamber was being prepared for her and her husband.

Anna thanked her and then took a sip of what proved to be an excellent vintage. She tried not to think about their retiring for the night, but that proved impossible. It was more than two years since Giles's death and she felt a certain trepidation at the thought of sharing such an intimate space with Jack for a whole night. She presumed he would allow her time to undress and get into bed before he came upstairs. Doubtlessly he would consider it proper that he didn't share the bed with her. Hopefully there would be a truckle bed or at least a chair for him to sleep in. She sipped her wine and was glad when candles were lit in a silver candelabra that was placed at the centre of a table.

Anna and Jack were waved to chairs by their host and they sat down. A couple of servants brought in bowls of chicken, beans and onions in a wine-and-cream sauce and set them before them. Jack smiled at Anna across the table. 'I hope you are hungry, sweeting? Doesn't this food look appetising?'

His use of the endearment startled her. 'Very appetising, my love,' she said, with a flush on her cheeks. She was aware of Monsieur Lampaul's eyes upon her and was glad that her gown was of sober hue and fastened up to her throat. 'Does Monsieur Lampaul know I was a widow before I married you?' she asked in a low voice.

'I told him that I had known you since you were a girl and that I had promised to return and marry you after my next journey abroad. He asked whether you had remained faithful while I was absent.'

'And what did you reply?' asked Anna, her eyes bright with curiosity.

'That you were the kind of woman to remain true to one man,' said Jack smoothly. 'I said that you were a pearl amongst women.'

She was touched by his words, yet surprised that he had chosen to refer to her as such a rare jewel. 'And what did he say to that?'

Jack did not answer but, from his darkling expression, it was obvious to her that their host's comments had not pleased him. She changed the subject. 'Did you ask him about hiring horses?'

'Aye, but he refused in a charming way and said he could not risk their not being returned. He has offered to sell me one, but I'm not happy about his price so will need to bargain with him.'

At that moment their host spoke and Jack excused himself and turned to speak to him. Anna gave her attention to her food. Her thoughts drifted. She tried to imagine how her life would have been if Jack's words were based on truth. But she found it difficult. One couldn't go back and change life. Besides she would not have had Joshua if she had been betrothed to Jack and remained true to him. Her heart might have almost broke when she had lost her son, but she would always be grateful for those four short years he had been given to her.

But what of Jack? How different would his life have been? Perhaps he would have spent more time in England and might never have been abducted. She had spent enough time in his company to sense he was still deeply disturbed by his years as a slave. If only he was able to talk more about it. There was an air of mystery about him. He was not a man at peace with himself. She thought about how much of herself she had revealed to him. If she had not done so, then no doubt he wouldn't be helping her now.

Anna was aware that Jack was drinking his wine sparingly and she followed suit. Every few minutes he would slant her a smile and translate the men's conversation, which seemed to be mainly about the confrontation between the kings of England and France and how trade was suffering.

A dessert of crepes stuffed with sliced pears in a brandy liquor was served and, although that was sublime, Anna was beginning to wish the meal over. She was feeling sleepy and was also concerned about the saddlebags, which contained the two precious parchments. Her eyes kept straying to their baggage. It was a relief when the woman in russet reappeared and suggested that Anna might wish to retire and leave the men to their brandy liquor.

'I will see you to the bedchamber,' said Jack instantly, pushing back his chair. 'I will make the excuse of needing to visit the garde-robe,' he added in a low voice.

Anna thanked their host for such a delicious meal. He took her hand and placed a spanking kiss on the back of it and wished her a restful night. Whilst this exchange was taking place, Jack had fetched their saddlebags and hoisted them over his shoulder. He spoke to their host and then put an arm about Anna and they followed the woman out of the room.

Anna was glad of that helping arm. The woman led the way upstairs, carrying a lantern. She stopped outside a door on the first floor and opened it with a key. After pushing the door open, she was about to walk away when Jack stopped her. He asked for the key. She hesitated, but he insisted she give it to him. With obvious reluctance she did so. He enquired to the whereabouts of the garde-robe. She pointed along the passage. He thanked her and she hurried away.

Anna went into the bedchamber and she looked at Jack in dismay. A lantern on a small table threw out light, revealing a room that was simply furnished with a small armoire, a chest, a chair and a bed. Jack placed their baggage on the chair and gazed about him. 'It's not palatial, is it?'

'The chair doesn't look comfortable and there isn't much room on the floor,' murmured Anna.

Jack thought with a grim smile that told him exactly where she expected him to sleep. But when he had suggested their pretending to be man and wife, he had known if she agreed that there would be no soft bed for him that night. He did not have to remind himself that their words of endearment were but a pretence. 'I'll go with you to the garde-robe and then escort you back here,' he suggested.

'You really think there is a need for us to be so careful?' she asked.

He raised his eyebrows. 'You'd rather go along that dark passage on your own?'

She smiled. 'No.'

When they returned to the bedchamber, Jack insisted she lock the door behind him. 'You open it to no one but me,' he said firmly.

Anna slanted him a glance that told him she was no fool. And as soon as he had gone she turned the key in the lock. Then she went over to the bed and inspected it closely. It appeared to be a slat bed with a plain headboard and footboard with rectangular posts. She slid her hand down the inside of the box part and was relieved to find a palliasse made of straw, on top of which was a feather mattress. She turned back the covers and was pleased to discover that the linen sheets were spotlessly clean and bore the scent of dried flowers. In the absence of a comfortable chair or a truckle bed, it made sense to remove one of the mattresses and place it on the floor.

Despite her weariness, she set about trying to do so. But no amount of tugging on her part could lift the mattress high enough for her to get it over the side. This meant she would have to wait for Jack to return and help her remove it. In the meantime she decided to remove her boots and hose and unpin her braids. It came as a surprise to hear a knock at the door so soon after he had left.

'Is that you, Jack?' Suddenly her tiredness seemed to evaporate.

'Aye, let me in, Anna.' The words were slurred, but she decided the voice definitely belonged to Jack, so she opened the door.

He would have fallen into the room and crashed to the floor if she had not moved swiftly and managed to get her shoulder beneath his armpit.

'What has happened to you?' she gasped. Surely he could not have got drunk so swiftly?

'Not sure what happened,' he replied with slow deliberation, managing to straighten up. But when he stepped away from Anna, he went staggering backwards and fell on to the bed.

She hurried over to him, but then stopped and glanced back at the open door. Already suspicious to why he should be in such a state, she went and locked the door, before returning to him. 'How much brandy did you drink?'

He did not answer, but managed to get a grip on one of the posts and drag himself upright. He gazed at her from blurry eyes. 'Must get up an'— an' let you haf the bed,' he muttered.

'Never mind that now, Jack! Do you think Monsieur Lampaul managed to slip a sleeping potion into your drink?'

He shook his head, then nodded. His hands slipped from the post and he fell back on to the bed.

Alarmed, she cried, 'Oh, Jack! What am I to do with you?' She bent over and shook him but there was no response.

Anna straightened up. It was then she heard footsteps. She hesitated only a moment before tip-toeing over to the door and pressing her ear against the wood. The footsteps stopped. She was convinced that there was someone on the other side, who was listening exactly as she did. The question was, who was it? The woman or their host? The handle turned slowly, but when the door did not open, she heard a muffled curse.

Anna decided to let whoever it was know that she was awake. She moved away from the door and began to sing a French love song. She thought she heard muttering and then the footsteps move away. She was convinced it was their host outside and was glad she had locked the door. She returned to the bed and gazed anxiously at Jack. His breathing was laboured and he appeared uncomfortable. Noticing that he was still wearing his sword, she decided that he would be much more comfortable without it.

She climbed on to the bed and knelt beside him and managed to undo the fastening and slide the sword from its scabbard. The weapon was much heavier than she had thought and it fell from her hand and on to the floor. It made a loud clanging noise and she half-expected Jack to wake. He certainly reacted—sitting up and shouting out in his sleep. She could not understand what he was saying. The words were in no language that she had heard before. She wondered whether they were Arabic. By the light of the lantern she could see that his eyes were open, but he seemed oblivious to her presence.

'Jack!' she said loudly, waving her hand slowly

in front of his face. There was no response. 'Can you hear me, Jack?'

'Thirsty! Water! I want water.'

'I don't have any water,' said Anna.

'I must have water. Give it to me, you sadistic swine!' he snarled, reaching out and grabbing her wrist.

Anna cried out, guessing he was in the grip of a nightmare. 'Jack, wake up!'

'Who is that who speaks my name?' His eyelids flickered. 'Is it you? Or am I dreaming?' He drew Anna close and his arms went round her. 'I thought I would never see you again,' he whispered sleepily, planting little kisses down the side of her face. 'Where have you been?'

Despite her sense of shock, Anna's whole body tingled. Who did he think she was? Now his mouth was searching for hers. Their lips met. His breath smelt sweetly of liquor brandy that mingled with another odour that was familiar to her. Some form of poppy juice. Was she right in having suspected that he might have been drugged earlier? She swallowed his sudden sigh. Was that one of relief because he believed her to be the woman he wanted? Then he was kissing her with a hunger that spoke of a deep need.

It was so long since she had been kissed that her response was immediate and just as needy as his obviously was. She would not have struggled to free herself even if she could have done so. He was moving against her, so that the hard wall of his chest brushed her breasts, causing their tips to bud and swell as if about to burst into flower. Then he was unfastening her gown and drawing it off her shoulders and after that her kirtle. She really should stop him, thought Anna in a daze, as he caressed her breasts. His mouth skated over the curve of her jaw and his tongue licked the sensitive skin behind her ear. She shivered with pleasure and heard him murmur in his throat. Then, utterly unexpectedly, he began to sing a song. She wanted him to continue kissing and caressing her and could scarcely believe her ears. The words were in French, but she recognised the song as the one she had sung earlier.

'Jack, why are you singing?' Her voice was husky with emotion and her fingers caressed his scarred cheek.

His voice trailed off and he seized her hand. 'Who's that?' He sounded befuddled. 'What are you doing to me?'

Suddenly the candle in the lantern spluttered and went out.

'It's me. Are you all right, Jack? I think perhaps Monsieur Lampaul slipped a sleeping draught into your brandy liquor.' She knew that she should put some distance between them now and hastened to do so before he realised that he had begun to make love to her and was embarrassed and angry with himself.

'My head feels foggy and aches. I can't understand why you believe Henri should drug me. Am I ill?'

She felt a dart of fear. What was happening to him? Had he been given more than an ordinary sleeping draught and it was affecting his mind? Perhaps he might even die! 'Not Henri, but his brother,' said Anna, perched on the edge of the bed, tidying her clothing. 'Jack, do you remember his name? Can you recall us coming here?'

A further sigh escaped him. 'You mean Maurice?'

Relief flooded through her. 'Aye. I think he tried the door earlier.'

There was a long silence. Then Jack muttered, 'It's Anna, isn't it? Have I been dreaming?'

'Aye. You were asleep, but you shouted out in a foreign tongue. I wondered if it was Arabic.'

'It could have been. I can't remember now. I hope I didn't frighten you?' His voice came to her out of the dimness and she knew he was in his right mind and thankfully did not remember what had happened.

'Not really.' She hesitated. 'I think we'd best get some sleep now, Jack. But I'm surprised you were able to wake up so quickly if you were drugged. Perhaps you did not imbibe too much of the draught.'

'I didn't drink the brandy to the dregs.' He paused. 'I should be on the floor.'

'You fell asleep before I could take one of the mattresses off the bed.'

'There's no need to go to such lengths for my comfort.' His voice sounded strained. 'You say that Maurice Lampaul tried to get in here?'

'He tried the door, but I'd locked it as you told me to.'

She felt the mattress dip beneath her and saw his shadowy figure getting up from the bed and moving away over to the window. He picked up the chair and took it over to the door. 'What are you doing?' she asked.

'It's possible he might have a spare key and if, as we believe, he slipped a sleeping draught in my brandy liquor, then he might try again to get in here. By placing the back of the chair under the door handle, he'll find it difficult to do so without making a noise.'

Jack shoved the chair in place, angry with himself for allowing Maurice to dupe him. What if their host's plan had worked? He felt a chill of horror at the thought of Anna being raped by the swine. 'You get into bed and get some sleep while I keep watch.' His voice was rough, wondering how their host would have explained an assault on Anna the next morning. Or had he planned on getting rid of Jack if he had downed more of the opiate?

'If you're going to lie on the floor, you should at least have a blanket to keep you warm,' said Anna, getting off the bed. Immediately she stubbed her toe on the sword and let out a squeal.

'Are you all right?' asked Jack, hurrying around the bed.

'I tripped over your sword.'

'My sword?' His hand went to his scabbard.

'I thought you'd be more comfortable without it,' she said vaguely, nursing her toe.

'You mean you managed to remove my sword without my even being aware of it?' he asked, furious with himself and yet touched that she'd had such care for his comfort.

'I—I wouldn't say that exactly, you did stir when I dropped it. I didn't realise swords were so heavy. You must be really strong to be able to fight with it,' she babbled, hoping he would not remember what had happened next.

'Damn Maurice Lampaul to hell!' said Jack savagely. 'If I had him here right now, I'd—' He stopped abruptly. 'I've just remembered I paid him the price he asked for the horse without bargaining or seeing the damned animal. I must have been out of my wits.'

'Forget him, Jack, and help me up,' said Anna.

He begged her pardon and lifted her up and sat her on the bed. 'Which foot is it?' he asked.

'My left foot. But there's naught you can do about it.'

'I hope you haven't broken it.' He took hold of her foot and explored it with gentle fingers.

'You're tickling me,' she said with a giggle in her throat.

'I'm glad you can laugh.' He smiled himself as he released her foot. 'You get into bed.'

Anna was glad he could not read her thoughts, recalling his even more intimate caresses of earlier. 'I will, as long as you take one of the blankets and a pillow,' she said.

'I aim to stay alert,' said Jack, picking up his sword and thinking, *Fine protector I am.*

'You don't think you'll nod off?'

He did not answer.

Anna sighed and tossed him a pillow.

Jack managed to catch it and then removed one of the blankets. He sat on the floor with the pillow behind his back against the bed, so that he faced the door. It was not quite pitch black. He placed his sword at his side and draped the blanket about his shoulders. Some remnants of the drug made his head still feel fuzzy. Fortunately, the shutters had been left open and the unglazed window aperture allowed cool night air into the bedchamber. That should keep him awake, he thought, determined that Anna should not find him wanting as her guardian again.

Several moments passed and he wondered if she was sleeping yet. If they were to travel on in the morning, she needed her rest. He found himself thinking of some of the places he had travelled to and how she would have found them interesting. Yet it would not have been suitable for a lady such as her to sleep in the open or on a floor as he had often done. He wondered if it was one of those times that had figured in his dreams and caused him to shout out in his sleep. Yet normally when he woke from one of his recurring nightmares, he remembered it. Its sheer repetitiveness was stamped in his memory. Generally, he woke in a panic, angry and depressed. He could not remember being gripped by any of those emotions. In truth he had woken with an unusual sense of well-being.

A memory stirred in his mind. A French love song that he remembered singing in happier times. A favourite of Anna's, too, for she had sung it on the ship, igniting a torrent of emotion inside him. He wondered if the opiate was responsible for that sense of well-being or whether it was Anna's obvious concern for him. It seemed an age since he had shared a bedchamber with a woman. He groaned inwardly, wondering what Anna must have made of his allowing himself to be duped by their host. She had lightly brushed it aside, appearing not to hold him responsible. Yet, perhaps in her heart she had thought him some fool protector.

Monique had always expected him to be strong and in control, so as to take care of her and their son. She had called him *her handsome English roguish lover*. She would have hated his scarred face but Anna did not seem to mind it. But then she was not in love with him. His appearance was not important to her. Unless she only pretended not to care about his scar? He wondered where he was going with his thoughts. Suddenly he felt uncomfortable, comparing the two women. They could not be more different in appearance and ways. Monique had died for love of him. He must not find aught to criticise in her. Suddenly, he remembered making love to her in his dreams. Yet she had been invisible to him even then. Why did she not come to him so he could see her? 'Monique,' he groaned. 'Where are you?'

Anna shifted in the bed and was aware of a sudden chill about her heart. Who was this Monique whose name Jack muttered? Was she the woman he had dreamed he was making love to? Such sweet love, such delicacy of touch rousing in her pleasure and longing. Tears sprang to her eyes and trickled down her cheeks. What a fortunate woman this Monique was to be loved by a man like Jack. Sometimes he was rough and ill tempered but that was understandable in the light of what he had suffered but beneath that scarred exterior was a very troubled, sensitive man in need of the care of a loving woman. Now she thought she understood even more why he had refused to talk about his past. Perhaps when he was abducted he had left behind this woman Monique? Maybe his enemy had been his rival in love? Was she the unfinished business that had brought him back to France, risking his life by placing himself in danger from this enemy? He must really love her to do so. No wonder he had been so intent on distancing himself from Anna on the ship. No doubt he would continue to do so because neither could not deny that tug of bodily attraction between them. No doubt it would be a great relief to him to hand her over to Raoul. The thought caused Anna pain and she felt more alone than ever as the tears rolled silently down her cheeks.

Chapter Eight

What was happening? It sounded as if someone was breaking down the door. A familiar fury gripped Jack and he started up, reliving the moment when his master's men had dragged him out of the dark hovel into the blazing sunlight and forced him to his knees. It was not the first time he had been whipped, but now the lash was knotted and contained sharp pieces of metal.

'What's that noise?'

Jack started awake, realising he must have dozed off. He swore beneath his breath and berated himself for failing to stay alert.

'Jack!'

'Aye, I heard it,' he said, recognising Anna's voice.

Shrugging the blanket from his shoulders, he reached for his sword and stood up. For a moment the room seemed to whirl about him and he gripped the bedpost until everything steadied. He wondered if the dizziness was a result of the opiate. He looked at Anna and could see her face clearly in the pale light coming through the window. Her eyes looked puffy and he wondered if she had been crying. There was a sudden sinking feeling in the pit of his stomach. Had he failed her? Had their host managed to break in?

'That brute didn't get in here, did he?' he asked hoarsely.

'No! But look at the door!'

Jack did so, and he noticed that although the back of the chair was still rammed under the door handle, it had shifted. There was a slight gap between the door and the jamb. He tiptoed over to the door and stood listening a moment but could hear no sound of breathing outside. He guessed that if their host had attempted to enter the chamber, then he had left as soon as he heard them talking. Even so, Jack removed the chair and trod on a key as he did so. He picked it up before going outside and glancing up and down the passage.

There was no one in sight, but that was not to say that someone was not concealing themselves in one of the nearby bedchambers. He stood a moment, pondering what to do. He was in a mood for a fight, but guessed such a confrontation with their host would bring the servants running. Anna's safety must be his priority. He returned to the bedchamber and locked the door behind him.

'I'm of a mind to leave immediately,' he said in a low voice. 'I've paid for a horse, so we'll have the finest one in his stables.' He smoothed down his tousled dark hair and looked in her direction. 'From Lampaul's conversation, it would not surprise me if he provides information about shipping to those involved in piracy along this coast. Let's hope we can leave the house without meeting anyone on the way.'

Anna nodded. 'If you consider that the wisest course, then I will do what you say.'

He thought her voice sounded lacklustre and wondered if she had been crying because she regretted his having made the decision to travel to Vitré in her company. He felt sick inside thinking that she surely found him lacking in the attributes needed in the best of protectors. His plan had gone wrong from the outset. 'I'm sorry about what's happened,' he said stiffly. 'You'll have to ride pillion, but the sooner we're on the road to Dinan, the better I will like it.'

Anna nodded and climbed out of bed. 'I need to don the attire I removed last evening.'

'Of course.' Jack immediately turned away, so as to give her some privacy.

Anna gazed at his back and wondered why the thought of his loving Monique should so upset her. It was not as if she, herself, was in love with him. Yet it hurt to think that he must have believed she was this Monique when he had kissed her so passionately. She must try to forget these moments. Whatever Jack's relationship was with this woman, it had naught to do with why he was helping her and she must try to put her out of her mind. She fastened her cloak and whispered to Jack that she was ready.

'You must stay close to me, Anna. I don't want aught to harm you.' He hoped she was not thinking that he had already almost failed her and perhaps would do so again. He picked up their saddlebags and slung them over his shoulder. Then he unlocked the door and, with sword in hand, crept out into the passage.

Anna had every intention of sticking close to him. She wanted to get out of the house safely and continue their journey. Now she was aware of Monique's existence, the sooner their ways parted the better it would be for both of them. She followed him out into the dimly lit passage and was surprised when he headed in a different direction from that which they had used coming from the hall. She trod softly, almost on his heels, praying that their host or any of his servants were not lying in wait for them. Someone knew they were awake, but hopefully they would not suspect they would leave before daylight.

Jack stopped in front of a door and carefully lifted the latch and drew the bolt. The door swung open silently on to a narrow staircase. A question hovered on Anna's lips, but she kept silent, remembering Jack accusing her of for ever asking questions when they were on the ship.

Jack started down the stairway, glad that his eyes were now accustomed to the darkness. It would be terrible if Anna should slip, but at least he was there to break her fall if she did. His sharp ears caught the sound of her fingernails scraping the wall and he knew that she was following him closely. At least she trusted him so far and no doubt presumed that he knew of this back stairway from a previous visit to the house.

They came out into the yard and neither spoke as they made their way to the outbuildings that loomed dark against the sky. Jack glanced up at the half-moon, reflecting off the stable roof, and was torn between cursing and blessing its light. Certainly they would be able to see their way, but it also meant that if their host or his servants heard them escaping and decided to follow them, they would have no trouble doing so.

He handed Anna his sword and placed their saddlebags on the ground, indicating that she should keep watch, before gently lifting the latch and easing open the stable door. More than one horse whinnied as Jack entered the building, causing him to hesitate a moment whilst his eyes grew accustomed to the gloom. He had not liked leaving Anna alone outside, but it was necessary that he should have warning if someone should come. He made his way over to the nearest stall and soothed the horse there with soft words and gentle hands as he checked it over. Having made the decision that the animal seemed in fine fettle, he chose that one. It was not the first time he had visited this stable, so he had little trouble finding the horse's tackle. He also discovered a pillion seat on a bench alongside several saddles.

Concerned about Anna, he hastened to saddle up the horse. His actions were obviously disturbing the other horses because they whinnied and moved restlessly in their stalls. He was glad to lead the horse outside and even more relieved that she was still there.

The yard was not cobbled, so the horse's hooves made little noise on the ground. 'The gates?' whispered Anna.

'They were only bolted, but we'll not mount until we're outside,' Jack answered in a low voice.

He attached their saddlebags to the horse. Then they walked either side of the animal as they headed towards the gates. As he drew one of the bolts, the noise it made sounded loud on the night air and caused them both to look over their shoulders towards the house, but there was no one in sight. Once the gates were open, he placed his sword in its scabbard and helped Anna up into the pillion seat. He climbed into the saddle and she slipped a hand beneath his cloak and gripped the back of his belt.

Anna's heart was beating heavily; she was concerned that at any moment there might be a sudden shout of alarm. But all was quiet except for the screech of an owl that caused them both to start. Soon, they had left the gates behind and were riding towards the road that would take them to

Dinan, a little more than a league's distance away. Fearing her voice might carry on the still air, she refrained from talking unnecessarily. Besides, she had much on her mind.

Despite her decision not to think about the unknown woman in Jack's life, she could not help but do so. *Monique!* It sounded French, but was it possibly Arabic? Maybe she had been abducted and Jack had rescued her from one of these harems he had spoken about to Anna? Perhaps she had taken ill and he'd had to leave her at one of the religious houses in Europe until she recovered. Was that possible? She could not imagine Jack leaving someone he loved alone and in need. But no doubt wherever she was, it was obvious to Anna that he intended finding her. She told herself that Jack deserved some happiness after his sufferings; if being united with this Monique would make him happy, then she must pray that he would find her, however sorry, she, herself, might be at being parted from him.

She squared her shoulders, determinedly reminding herself that she had experienced a loving relationship with Giles. The past provided her with happy memories, even though Giles had always adhered to the church's ruling for married couples.

He had been strict about making love only on the days ordained by the church for husband and wife to beget children. When those days came round, more often than not their couplings were swiftly over. Days of abstinence had meant a swift kiss and a cuddle and then Giles would turn his back on her in order to resist temptation.

She had found it extremely frustrating, having realised early in her marriage that she was a sensual woman. Alas, when it came to the marriage bed, Giles had been unbelievably stubborn and resisted her wiles. On occasions, she had dreamed of a mystery man who swept her away on a tide of passion. She would wake afterwards, feeling pleasantly lethargic and filled with guilt.

Memories of Jack's caresses and kisses flooded her mind and she forced them away.

By the time they reached Dinan, the sun had risen and the gates were open, enabling them to pass through into the city. 'We'll give the horse a rest and stretch our legs,' said Jack. His head had cleared, although it still ached slightly. He prayed that Raoul would be there at the end of their journey because otherwise he visualised trouble ahead in fulfilling his vow for vengeance. Anna's safety was paramount. He felt a need to prove to her that she really could rely on him. 'We'll need to buy food and drink and then we'll be on our way again.'

He dismounted and helped Anna to the ground. She clung to his hand a moment and found comfort in its strength, then reluctantly withdrew it and walked by his side as they made their way along the half-empty rues of tall, half-timbered buildings. Jack purchased a flask of cider and some *galettes* from a bakery. As Anna ate her pancake stuffed with ham and cheese, she noticed a church ahead of them and her eyes lit up. Turning to Jack, she asked him could they spare a few moments to go inside.

'You can go on your own,' he said. 'I attended mass at St Sauveur's with my father years ago. It is a fine building and you must look out for the Byzantine influence in the ornamental decoration inside.' He offered the flask to her.

Anna took a drink of the cider and handed it back to him. 'Couldn't you come inside and point them out to me?' she asked reasonably. 'It would be so much more interesting if you could tell me about the architecture.'

He hesitated. 'I must take the horse to drink. Just look out for winged lions, sirens and a humped camel, bred for riding and racing. I have seen such beasts in Arabia.'

Her interest was immediately aroused. 'Did you race?' she asked.

'Aye, I did for my owner, the Lady Lydia.'

'So the time you spent in captivity was not all cruelty and loneliness?' she said, forgetting her vow not to pry into his affairs.

Jack expected another question from her and tensed. 'Don't, Anna,' he said harshly, and led the horse away.

Anna could have bitten off her tongue. Why did she always have to ask one question too many? She would know better next time, if there was a next time. No doubt if they found Raoul in Vitré, then Jack would not linger long in the town but go in search of Monique. It would be wiser if she concealed her concern about what had happened to make Jack the physically and emotionally scarred man he was now.

She went inside the church and discovered that it was all that Jack had said, and more. Looking at the humped beasts that she presumed were camels, she decided that he must have spent some time learning to stay mounted and race such a strange-looking creature. Had he won his race?

Perhaps he had not done so and that was why he did not wish to speak about it. And yet she could not imagine him allowing himself to be beaten.

Jack was vexed with himself. He could have told Anna about the camel racing, without revealing the secret he carried or aught of his plans, so why this reluctance still to speak of an experience that had done so much to raise his morale? Even as he asked himself that question, Jack knew the answer. He could not allow her beyond the barrier he had erected. If he were to do that, then it might weaken his resolve even further than it was already. He had made a vow and he had to keep it because he owed it to Monique and Philippe. Jack could only hope that their search for Raoul would be successful and his friend would accept Anna as his half-sister. He was a decent man, friendly, good natured and prepared to extend a helping hand to those in difficulties. If he offered Anna hospitality and ensured that she was safely escorted to the *Hercules* or another suitable ship if she wished to return to England, then Jack would feel he had succeeded in his role as her protector.

There was no sign of Anna when he returned to the church. He waited impatiently. This was another place with memories that would draw him back into a world where he had been happy and he was itching to get away.

Suddenly, Anna was there in front of him. 'I hope I haven't kept you waiting,' she said, smiling serenely.

'Scarcely at all,' he answered with a stiff politeness.

'It was so interesting.'

He nodded. 'Let's not waste any more time. We must be on our way.'

Her smile faded. 'I'm sorry if I've displeased you.'

He relented as he helped her into the pillion seat. 'It is not that you've displeased me. Only my father and I had a happy time here but within weeks he was dead.'

Anna was moved. 'I remember hearing Owain and Kate talking about his murder. I was so sorry, Jack. I remember your father being a kind man.'

He nodded and his eyes were moist. 'I saw him die. Three men came out of nowhere. It happened near a canal in Bruges one evening. As soon as they struck I knew that robbery was not their aim, but that they wanted Father and me dead. They went for him first. I tried to defend him when he fell to the ground, but I was only a youth with a staff and dagger. They were big strong men and one broke my arm. If it had not been for Mackillin arriving on the scene, they would have killed me, too.' His voice quivered. 'I have never forgotten that as he lay dying my father's last thoughts were of me and my sister, not himself. He made Mackillin promise to escort me home to safety and this he did. Since then I have tried to follow in their footsteps but there are times when I have failed.'

Anna gazed into his sombre face and, reaching out, touched his cheek. 'But you have succeeded, too. No wonder you are the man you are, Jack Milburn. I will continue to pray for your safety.'

Her words touched him and he held her hand against his face and found comfort in her caress. He felt proud that she should believe him a man such as Mackillin and his father. Then he remembered how he had failed to protect Monique and Philippe and how close he had come last night to failing Anna and his spirits drooped. He released her hand and climbed into the saddle and turned the horse's head towards the city gates. Her concern for him was suddenly a burden that he would be rid off. If de Briand should kill him then she would weep and there had been enough sadness in her life. He should not have come with her, but it was too late now to turn back and send her home.

She sighed. 'How long will it take us to reach Vitré?'

'By my reckoning, the town is a little more than ten leagues' distance,' replied Jack.

'Do you think we'll arrive there before nightfall?'

'It's still morning, so, unless the horse goes lame or a bridge is down or we fall in amongst thieves, I don't see why not.'

'You think it's likely that thieves will be lying in wait for the likes of us?'

He shrugged. 'It's a risk all travellers take, but the road to Rennes is a good one and well frequented, so we should be safe enough.'

'Tell me about Rennes,' she asked, thinking the town a safe topic for conversation to pass the time.

'It was founded when the Emperor Julius Caesar conquered this area before Christ's birth. It's situated at the configuration of two rivers, the Ille and the Vilaine. No doubt it was for that reason the Roman chose to make Rennes his regional capital. The rivers meant that communications were excellent for getting to the coast and the hinterland.'

'The Romans made Chester one of their bases in the north when they conquered England. I believe it was called Deva in those days. Have you ever visited Chester?'

'I don't remember doing so, although it's possible my father took us there when we were small.'

'You must visit Chester some time. If I were to choose a day that I could live over again, then it would be in that fair city.'

Jack knew he should resist asking her why, but found himself doing so.

'Because I spent such a happy time there. It was during the season of the mystery plays. Despite his being so young, Joshua seemed to find great delight in them. Perhaps it was the colour and the movement.' There was a catch in her voice.

'You still miss him very much?'

'I do! Once upon a time I could not even speak his name. Now I am beginning to believe that we *should* talk about those lost to us. It helps bring them alive again.'

Anna's words touched a chord deep inside Jack. Yet he could not talk about his son and Monique to her. She would consider him utterly immoral. He thought of his twin and how he had wrung a promise out of him to seriously consider making a sensible marriage such as his own when he returned. He had suggested Jack's house in

Kingston-on-Hull needed extending and had offered to keep an eye on the building work whilst Jack was away. To keep his twin from asking too many questions about his reasons for making a trip to France so soon after his return, he had taken up Matt's offer and agreed to such work being done.

'You must have seen mystery and morality plays on your travels, Jack,' said Anna, rousing him from his reverie. 'Is there one you favour?'

'Is there one you do?' he parried.

Her breath warmed his neck and a thrill ran down his spine. Her closeness was having its effect on him. As was the smile in her voice when she replied with the words, *'The Adoration of the Magi*! The Vintners' Guild finance the play every year. We were able to watch it from the Rows. In case you don't know, these are raised covered shopping walkways and they give an excellent view over the street.'

'I have visited the Shrine of the Three Kings in the cathedral at Cologne. Many pilgrims visit there for it is well worth seeing,' said Jack.

'I remember your mentioning Cologne when we were on the ship. I think I would like to go there one day,' said Anna. 'Disappointingly, the plays in Chester were cancelled this year, no doubt due to the guilds having to donate money for the king's war. I had to give *four pounds* to pay an archer's wages for six months.'

The reminder of Edward's war brought a frown to Jack's face. He wondered if the English army were still camped outside Amiens's walls or whether a battle had taken place. If so, it could make it more difficult for him to discover the whereabouts of the Comte de Briand. Little point in worrying about that now, he decided, for they had yet to find Raoul.

By mid-afternoon they had arrived at a large open space outside the walls of Rennes. 'This is the Place des Lices. I remember seeing a tournament here when I was with my father,' said Jack. 'Do you wish to rest for a short while or go on? We still have a few miles to go before reaching Vitré.'

'Let us go on,' said Anna.

Jack nodded, and so they continued with their journey. Both were weary by the time the turrets of the chateau of Vitré came in view. Jack pointed it out, wondering how soon he and Anna would have to part.

As for Anna, she was filled with apprehension. What if she had wasted Jack's time and Raoul was not here? Would Jack feel compelled to escort her to Calais when he was impatient to begin his search for Monique? Surely she could not allow him to do so when she had already taken up far too much of his time?

'If we don't find Raoul, I will stay at a religious lodging house in the city and ask for advice in making a pilgrimage,' she said firmly. 'Then you will be able to go about your own business, Jack.'

'Don't let's talk about that until it is necessary to do so,' he said roughly. It was obvious to him that now they had almost reached their destination she was regretting her gentle words to him and wanted to be rid of his ugly face.

So with the thought of finding Raoul very much in their minds, they came to the end of their journey. The sun was setting as they passed through a gateway flanked by two large towers into the town of Vitré. As the horse plodded along a street called the Rue d'Embas, Anna's nerves threatened to get the better of her. What was she doing here? Raoul might be her blood brother, but she did not know him! Surely Jack must consider her a foolish woman to have distracted him from his main business in France, just to meet with a stranger? She scarcely noticed that some of the buildings were built in the Gothic style, while others were typical of the timber-framed houses she had seen in Dinan. Instead her emotions were in a whirl and she no longer knew what she wanted.

Suddenly Jack turned to her and there was a gleam in his eyes. 'What is it?' she asked.

'Raoul is here!'

'Where?' cried Anna, gazing frantically about her.

Jack did not answer, but dismounted and told her to stay with the horse. She watched in trepidation as he crossed the street to where two men were deep in conversation. She noticed that one had a rich auburn hair and handsome face. He was well built and wore the clothes of a prosperous merchant. Was that Raoul? How she wished that she had with her one of her finer gowns. Her heart was thumping as she watched Jack approach the man. He looked up and his face broke into a smile. He spoke, but she did not catch his words, nor did she hear what Jack said in reply. The next moment they were hugging and the man kissed Jack on both cheeks. He must be Raoul, she decided with mixed feelings. His appearance was admirable and he looked so grand, she felt certain he would not wish to have aught to do with his father's English bastard daughter.

Jack pointed in her direction and she knew the moment had come. She must not make Jack ashamed of her. Taking a deep breath, she managed to climb down from the horse unaided and, stiff from spending so long on horseback, walked jerkily over to the two men.

Jack caught hold of her hand and drew her forward. 'Raoul, let me introduce you to Lady Anna Fenwick,' he said in English. 'Anna, this is my friend, the Comte d'Azay.'

She and Raoul stared at each other and she wondered if he could see that likeness to his cousin that Jack had noticed. 'So you are Anna.' He surprised her by speaking in attractively accented English and taking her hand and clasping it between his own. 'I thought I would never get to meet you, but I am happy to do so. Jack tells me that you came in search of me.'

His words startled her. He sounded as if he already knew about her. Just what had Jack told him? 'I am glad to meet you, too, and pleased that you speak such good English.' She flushed beneath the warmth in his eyes and noted that they were the same colour as her own. 'I must ask what you mean by saying that you thought you'd never get to meet me?'

'It is a long story and best told when we are comfortably ensconced in my house with a goblet of excellent wine and good food,' said Raoul firmly. 'I brought back with me a wife when I went to England six years ago and she will be glad to have another English lady for company.'

'You're married, Raoul!' exclaimed Jack. 'Who is this fortunate woman?'

Raoul smiled. 'Margaret is the daughter of a vintner I met in London. *Maman* had been berating me for some time about not having found myself a wife. But she did not expect me to bring one from England. I speak good English now, *oui*?'

'Aye,' said Jack, smiling faintly. 'How is your mother?'

'Alas, *Maman* died four years ago. It was a great grief to me at the time. But she saw her first grandson born and died content.' He beamed at them. 'So now you must come and meet my wife.'

'I'll be delighted to do so,' said Anna, amazed by what Raoul had told them. 'I hope our unexpected arrival will not interfere with her supper arrangements too much.'

'Margaret is a competent *chatelaine* and so you must not worry,' said Raoul, with a ready smile.

Jack fetched the horse and the three of them

walked along the street together. Now they had found Raoul, there was no excuse to prevent him leaving Anna with him and keeping his vow. Even so he felt depressed and had to force himself to speak and act naturally of their journey.

They had not gone far when they came to an archway at the side of a large house. Raoul led them along a covered passageway, which opened out into a large courtyard. Anna gazed about her at outhouses and a garden where a fountain played. Everything felt alien and she could not stop thinking that soon she and Jack would part. Maybe she would never see him again. Perhaps Monique would want him to live here in France and, if he loved her then he would do what she wished. As for Anna herself, she was realising more and more that she did not belong here.

Dusk had fallen and the courtyard appeared deserted. Raoul shouted a name and a man came out of the stable. Jack lifted their saddlebags from his horse and the man took charge of the animal. Jack glanced at Anna. 'Are you happy now we have found Raoul?'

'Of course I am,' she lied, pinning a smile on her face.

'Good,' he said, with a sharp nod.

Raoul led the way across the yard and through the garden to a door at the back of the house. Once indoors, they could hear voices. He smiled. 'That is Margaret. She is in the kitchen, arranging supper. I will tell her of your arrival.' He turned to Jack. 'You remember the way to the parlour?'

'I think I'll be able to find it,' he drawled.

'Make yourselves comfortable and I will join you shortly.' Raoul left them and went in the direction that presumably led to the kitchen.

Jack said, 'This way, Anna.'

'What did you tell him about me, Jack?' she asked, hurrying alongside him.

He frowned. 'I didn't mention his father, if that's what concerns you. Yet as soon as I mentioned your name, he seemed to recognise it and said that it would be a pleasure to meet you.'

Anna was bemused. 'But where would he have heard my name? Surely not in Wales or London?'

'Your husband had no contacts in London?'

Her brow knitted. 'I can't remember him ever mentioning anyone. He certainly never visited there during the time we were married.'

Jack gazed down into her shadowy face. 'Don't fret yourself about it. It's obvious he intends speaking about it later.' He stopped in front of a door and opened it. A fire burned on the hearth and there were several candelabras with lighted candles placed strategically about the room. Furniture glowed richly in the candlelight and he suggested that Anna sit down by the fire. 'You must be tired,' he said, feeling concern, for he sensed that she was not as happy as she had said.

'Tired and apprehensive,' she said with a light laugh, glad of the cushions beneath and behind her as she settled herself comfortably in a chair. 'But I've achieved what I wanted, haven't I? And all thanks to you, Jack. Although, what if, as soon as Raoul knows the nature of my visit, he becomes angry and tells me to leave? What should I do then?' she asked, looking up at Jack.

He hastened to reassure her. 'Raoul would not be so impolite. He has invited you here and, while you are under his roof, he will treat you with every courtesy. That is the kind of man he is.'

Jack's words should have eased some of the tension within her, but she could not relax. 'He does seem to be a kind man. Is he like his father, d'you think?'

Jack placed the saddlebags in a corner before sitting opposite her. 'How am I to know?'

She sighed. 'I do not wish to cause him any embarrassment.'

'Of course you don't.' He rested his head against the back of his chair and closed his eyes. 'You might as well sit back and take your ease, Anna. Stop worrying. After our disturbed night and the long journey we've had today, you can at least look forward to a good night's sleep.'

Anna thought that was unlikely, knowing that Jack would be leaving her soon. His casual mention of last night also reinforced the fact that he had no memory of kissing her at all. None of it should matter to her, but she knew it did.

The door opened and Raoul entered. 'Margaret will be along soon,' he said. 'She is having bed-chambers prepared for you and I have asked one of the servants to bring some wine.'

Anna thanked him.

'It is my pleasure,' he said, sitting on a settle a few feet from her and gazing into her face. 'No doubt you are curious to how I came to know your name?'

'I certainly am,' she answered politely.

He placed his hands on his thighs and leaned towards her. 'You are acquainted with a knight called Sir Richard Fletcher, I think?'

Jack started. Anna glanced at him and then Raoul. 'You mean Kate's half-brother Diccon?'

Raoul nodded. 'I believe he is also Jack's step-brother and he lives in London as part of the King's household.'

'So that's how you heard my name,' murmured Anna. 'Such a simple explanation. Yet what a co-incidence your meeting Diccon.'

'It was no coincidence,' said Raoul, his expression suddenly grave. 'I went there in search of him. Sir Richard was a witness in an investigation involving the murder of a knight called Sir Roger Miles.'

'I don't recognise that name,' she said, her brow puckering.

'No doubt that is because he was killed before you were born, Anna,' said Jack, his eyes intent on her face. He had a feeling that he knew what was coming. She would be hurt, but he doubted she would be put off by anything less than the truth.

Raoul darted him a thoughtful look. 'You must have been only a boy at the time, Jack. I was told it was hushed up and never mentioned in the family. In particular I was informed that Anna must never be told about it.'

A chill ran down her spine and she was filled with a sense of foreboding. 'I presume Diccon told you that, but why must it be kept from me? Was—was it to do with my mother?'

Jack and Raoul exchanged glances. 'What do you know, *mon ami*?' asked Raoul.

Jack hesitated.

'What is it?' demanded Anna. 'Tell me! What is this secret that has been kept from me? How could you be a party to this web of conspiracy after all I have told you about myself, Jack? Speak out honestly now, if you please.'

'I was no party to any conspiracy,' said Jack sharply. 'At the time I was but eight or nine summers old when I overheard a conversation between my father and stepmother. If I had listened more carefully, then I might have realised what it was about earlier, but it was just a jumble in my mind and I disregarded it as of no importance at the time.'

'What do you remember?' she croaked.

'A sense of relief on their part. A murderer had been found and just deserts had been meted out to him. The man responsible for bringing him to justice was one of the family and that was why their relief was so intense. There had been an investigation into the circumstances surrounding this murderer's death.'

'You seem to remember quite a lot. Yet you mention no names,' cried Anna, springing to her feet and going over to him. 'Tell me, Jack, how does this involve me? Was my mother the murderer?'

He stood up. 'She was not mentioned. Sit down, Anna! You're overwrought.'

She did not sit down, but asked in a bewildered voice, 'If my mother was not the murderer, then who was? And who in the family killed him?'

Jack hesitated and then said bluntly, 'I deem the murderer was the former Comte d'Azay and I know the man who brought him to justice was Owain. I wish you'd left well alone, Anna.'

Chapter Nine

The room seemed to shift. Anna did not want to believe it. Surely there must be some mistake?

'Sit down, Anna!' ordered Jack, worried that she might swoon. He seized her by the arms and forced her into the chair. Then he knelt in front of her and took one of her hands and chafed it.

'It can't be true,' she said hoarsely.

'It is,' said Raoul quietly.

Jack gazed into her ashen face. 'But what happened is in the past and you must not let it take such a hold on your life that it prevents you from living your life to the full now,' he insisted.

'But—but Owain killed my father. He deceived me,' she said in an impassioned whisper.

'I'm sure he kept quiet about it for your own good,' said Jack.

'How can you be so sure? If only I had known this when Will and Hal accused me of such terrible things…I don't know what I would have done.' Tears filled her eyes and overflowed.

Jack felt helpless in the face of her distress.

Raoul stood up and strode over to the door. 'I will fetch Margaret. Women can cope better with tears.'

He was almost at the door when Anna cried, 'No! Of your courtesy come back here and tell me what you know of this matter.' She wiped her eyes with her sleeve. 'I need to know all.'

Before he could speak, there came a knock at the door. 'That will be Georges with our wine,' said Raoul, opening the door.

The atmosphere was charged with tension, but the only sound in the room was the crackling of the fire and the glug-glug of the wine as the serving-man filled the drinking vessels.

Once that was done Jack took a goblet and held it out to Anna, 'Here, drink this,' he said.

She took hold of its stem and his fingers covered hers as she tipped the goblet and gulped down the wine. Only when it was empty did she relinquish her hold on the vessel. 'I will manage now,' she said with dignity.

There was relief in his face and he kissed her brow before moving away.

'See, Georges has also brought some special almond wafers,' said Raoul, smiling at her. 'You should have some of these.'

Anna thought if she ate one it would stick in her throat, but he was insistent that she had a couple, so she took them to please him. Jack had now moved and stood behind her chair.

Raoul placed another log on the fire and then took a sip of wine before saying, 'I barely knew my father. When I was a boy, he was never home. *Maman* and I spent most of the time at my *grand-père*'s house. When I became a man and had business in England and Wales, I was curious enough to want to know how my father died.' He fixed his eyes on her tear-stained face with a slightly anxious expression. 'I knew you were my half-sister before Jack brought you here.' She made an indistinct sound that he acknowledged with a lift of the hand before continuing. 'When making my enquiries into my father's death, I discovered that he had conspired with your mother to rob not only her husband, but also to murder Sir Roger Miles.'

'How?' she asked through stiff lips.

'A slow-acting poison.'

'But why did they want him dead?'

'A falling out of thieves where our father was concerned, but there was also talk that your mother wanted vengeance. She believed Sir Roger responsible for the death of Martin ap Rowan, whom she had loved.'

'Davy said Martin was buried at Domfront,' she said in a low voice.

'My father apparently planned to kill Owain ap Rowan, whom he held prisoner, but he escaped. There was a fight and my father was knocked to the ground and hit his head on a rock and died.'

Relief flooded Anna's body. 'So Owain did not murder him? Oh, I am so glad about that! But why did the Comte attack Owain?'

'It was to do with money that had been stolen from his father and the King of England.'

'I—I see. I understand now why Owain and Kate kept the truth from me.' She shivered at the thought that both her parents had cold-bloodedly conspired to deceive, rob and murder. No wonder Hal and Will had accused her of having bad blood.

Jack said softly, 'And you still belong to the ap Rowan family, Anna, so don't be thinking that you don't.'

'I am not so certain as you,' she said sadly.

'Believe me, there is more to belonging to a family than the blood that runs in one's veins,' he insisted.

Anna knew that later she would think about his words, but right now she wanted to know something more from her half-brother. 'How did you feel when you found out about me?'

He shrugged expressively. 'My father is not the first man, nor will he be the last, to deceive his wife and sire illegitimate children. William of Normandy, whom you English call the Conqueror, was a bastard son.' He smiled at her. 'You are not responsible for my father's wrongdoings and I am happy to make your acquaintance. You've had a long journey and now must take your ease. I'm certain Margaret will be happy to provide you with a change of raiment, and whatever else you may need whilst you are here.' He stood up. 'Unfortunately, I will have to leave shortly to go to Bruges for the Michaelmas Fair. But, in the meantime, Jack and I have much to talk about, so if you will excuse us.' He took his friend's arm and drew Jack apart from her, leading him over to the far end of the room.

Jack glanced back at her with a worried frown, but Anna had hung her head and appeared not to notice him. He hoped that she would take his words to heart and forget the past. She needed to be reminded how well loved she was by Owain and Kate. What a special, beautiful woman she was, inside and out.

Anna felt as if she had been dismissed now all had been explained. Was she wrong to feel hurt by the two men leaving her alone to wallow in her misery? She really did feel deeply unhappy about her parents' misdemeanours. Bad blood! Would Will and Hal's words continue to come back and haunt her for the rest of her life? She rested back in the chair and closed her eyes. What a fool she had been, not to have heeded Davy when he had told her to let the past remain in the past. Exhausted and sick at heart, she wanted to leave this place and hide away somewhere. But perhaps the only place she could find peace was in the convent where she had stayed before. Yet if she were to say to Jack that she wanted to return to England immediately, he would feel honour bound to escort her to Calais. And how could she allow him to do that, knowing he wanted to find Monique? Perhaps after he had left, then she would make her way to Calais. Hopefully, the *Hercules* would still be anchored there. Right now she felt sick and needed fresh air. Trembling, she rose to her feet and left the room.

For a moment she stood outside in the passage, uncertain which way to go. It was guesswork that led her out into the moonlit garden. She stood there, retching, praying she would not vomit into the flower bed. Slowly she began to recover and breathed deeply of the spicy scent of gillyflowers and the sweet perfume of a late-blooming rose. She could hear the tinkling of water and impulsively followed the sound to the pond. She gazed at the statue of a boy with a pitcher on his shoulder from which poured water and thought of her son.

How long she stood there with tears rolling down her cheeks when Jack called her, she had no idea. She did not answer him, hoping he would leave her to her solitude. She had to cut him out of her life, not cry on his shoulder.

'Anna, are you all right?' he called. 'Answer me!'

She wondered how he knew she was in the garden. A wild guess? Although, where else could she have gone if they had yet to be shown to the guest bedchambers? She could hear his footsteps moving about the garden and fatalistically knew he would find her. There was little sense in trying to hide. Why could he not leave her alone? Perhaps he felt guilty for having been the one to tell her that her father was a murderer. She sank down on to a bench, facing the pond.

Sensing when he stood behind her, she said, 'Please, go away, Jack.'

'I can't do that,' he replied, walking forward and standing in front of her.

She darted him a glance and then looked at the pond. 'Why not? You've done what I asked you to and soon you will be able to go about your own business.'

'That's what I intend to do, but I still feel some responsibility for you,' he said roughly.

'Why should you? You were against my coming to France and you were right. I should have listened to you. Then I would never have discovered that I truly do have bad blood in me.'

'That's nonsense,' he said angrily.

'It is the truth,' she cried, clenching her fists.

'You heard Raoul, you cannot be blamed for what your parents did.'

'I was born in sin! I am tainted by their evil deeds.'

'The sin was not yours! Look at Raoul, he is not evil, but a good man.' He moved so that he was silhouetted against the sky and loomed over her. 'We've spent a lot of time in each other's company lately. You'd never harm anyone. I know you, Anna.'

She sprang to her feet. 'Do you?' she fired at him, her eyes glistening with tears. 'Well, you didn't always give the impression that you wanted to know me better. In fact you couldn't wait to get rid of me. Now I know why. From the beginning you've had a suspicion about my parents. It was only your sense of duty that made you come this far, but now you are free to go.' She waved both hands at him. 'Go, Jack. Go find Monique.'

He drew in his breath with a hiss. 'What do you know about Monique?' His voice sounded raw. She was aghast; she had not intended letting him know that she knew his secret. 'Tell me, Anna, or I will shake the answer out of you.' He seized hold of her and drew her towards him.

She struggled. 'What does it matter? It is obvious that she fills your dreams so much that you mistook me for her last night.'

'What are you saying? How did I mistake you for her?' demanded Jack, shaking her. 'What did I do?'

'You kissed me,' she cried. 'Later you asked her where she had gone. Well, now you can go and find her. Obviously, she is the reason why you came to France.'

Jack was amazed that he could have kissed Anna and been unaware of it. His stomach clenched at the thought. 'I didn't go further than a kiss, did I?'

'If you're asking me whether…you…well, you…didn't,' she said.

He closed his eyes. 'Thank God! Forgive me, Anna, for taking advantage of you. It was not my intention. These days, I can scarcely remember what Monique looked like. I should explain that she is dead.'

'Dead!' Anna felt extremely odd. 'But you loved her?'

'Aye.' He could feel Anna trembling and guessed he had frightened her earlier. He wanted to soothe away her fears and take her mind off the foolish belief that she had bad blood. He stroked her face. 'Monique is lost to me now, killed by the same man who sold me into slavery.'

'What is his name?'

'The Comte de Briand. Davy brought me news of him. He is with King Louis's forces at Amiens.'

'Is he the reason why you are here?' she asked bluntly.

'Aye. But you must not worry about him.' All he could think about was the woman in his arms. His intention had been only to comfort, but now, feeling her so soft and warm against his body, he could no longer resist pressing a kiss against her petal-soft cheek.

'Jack?' Her voice was a whisper. She could feel his arousal and was amazed that she had such power to so easily arouse him. Was she a witch without realising it? She wanted him to make love to her, but it would be wrong to encourage him to use her as a substitute for Monique. Yet if he had not come here seeking her, then what was his business in France? A thought occurred to her and she experienced a different kind of fear. She forced herself to still his hand. 'Don't try to silence me with flowery words and a gentle touch. I want to know what is your business with this Comte de Briand?' Her voice was unsteady.

'It is none of your affair, Anna.' Jack dropped his arms and moved away from her. 'I was not trying to silence you,' he said emphatically. 'I fear you use that as an excuse because you don't want my ugly face close to yours.'

'You are not ugly!' she exclaimed in a vexed voice, drawing close to him again. Reaching out, she traced the length of his scar with the tip of a finger. He flinched. 'How did you come by this?'

'I cannot tell you! The remembrance shames me

and I deem you only say that I am not ugly because you have a kind heart.'

Anna shook her head. 'I am saying it because it is the truth!' Standing on tiptoe, she pressed her lips against his scarred cheek. She felt a tremor pass through him and experienced again that sense of power that her touch could so affect him. Shame filled her as it occurred to her that to enjoy such power was wrong. Maybe she was truly all those things that Hal and Will had accused her of being? She stepped away from him. 'But no matter—if you do not wish to believe me then it is your choice. I have made up my mind to return home. You were right in the first place, Jack, my wits had gone begging when I decided to come to France. I will make my way to Calais and seek out the *Hercules.*'

Jack had wanted to draw her back into his arms and kiss her, but now he wanted to shake her until the teeth rattled in her head. 'Don't be foolish! How many times have I told you about the dangers of travel for a lady on her own? Have you forgotten that the English soldiery is camped outside Amiens?'

'Of course not.' She frowned. 'Is that the road I must take to reach Calais?'

'Aye, but you must not think of doing so. Surely

it makes sense after your coming here to stay for a while? Rest, spend time with Raoul's wife when he goes to Bruges. I'm sure the Comtesse will be able to arrange for servants to escort you to Calais when you are ready to go home.'

'No,' she said firmly. 'I do not belong here. I will do what I please and leave on the morrow for Calais.'

He stared at her in disbelief and caught the gleam of her eyes and the faint shine of her moist lips in the moonlight. 'You can't do this. I will not allow it, Anna.'

'You cannot stop me! You go about your own business and leave me to sort out my own life. I am no longer your responsibility.'

'I saved your life,' he said, losing his temper and pulling her into his arms. 'Whilst I am alive, I will always feel I bear some responsibility for you.'

'Now, who is talking nonsense?' She struggled to free herself, but it was as if she was a butterfly imprisoned in an iron fist. Suddenly she wondered why she was trying to escape when she was where she wanted to be. She drooped against him and rested her head against his chest.

Her submission was so unexpected that Jack was suddenly at a loss what to do next. Really, he should release her and walk away, but instead he wanted to go on holding her. He wanted to stop hating and start loving, instead. Hatred and grief had held him captive far too long. He wished he could lose himself in her. He wanted the comfort of being held in a woman's arms and, most desperately, he wanted to kiss Anna and make love to her. Could he have really believed she was Monique last night? Before he could have second thoughts, he lowered his head and brushed his lips against Anna's. She did not pull away and he felt her quiver in his arms. He was aware of his own inner trembling, but could no longer pretend that kissing her was purely a test to see if he could tell the difference between her and Monique. If he was honest with himself, he had wanted Anna since he had pulled her up on to his horse. In a few days he could be dead and then he would never know what it would have felt like to have made love to the Lady Anna Fenwick.

He drew her even closer. Surely in the light of their parting and her recent suffering they could indulge themselves for a short while. He kissed her again and he felt her lips part to allow his tongue's teasing exploration. The heat in his loins was growing and he wanted to tear off her clothes and make love to her here in the secret darkness of the garden with the heady scent of flowers all around them. No ugliness, no hatred, no fear here. He could hear the tinkling sound of the fountain and it was like music in his ears. His fingers fumbled with the fastening at her throat and his mouth nudged aside the neck of her gown and down to her waist. His ears caught her gasp as he exposed her breasts, but he was too caught up in the heat of the moment to heed it. He gazed at their pale glowing loveliness and bent his head to caress their enticing peaks with his lips. This time he could not ignore her sighs of pleasure.

Suddenly she began to struggle and push him away. 'No, Jack. I will not have you believe me a wanton witch.'

'God's blood! Anna, I don't believe that at all,' said Jack, feeling all to pieces as he was dragged into the real world again. He had to exert iron control over every nerve, muscle and sinew to move away from her. He would have to leave her to fasten her gown; such finicky work was beyond him. He ran a shaking hand through his hair. 'The blame is all mine.'

'No. What happened between us just now proves how proud and yet also how mortally weak I am.' She did not look at him, but began to do up her fastenings.

Jack was about to argue with her when he became aware of whisperings. His senses had been trained to respond to the slightest hint of danger during his travels. Now he was warned of the possible approach of their host and his lady. He responded immediately by seizing Anna's hand and drawing her down on to the bench. She would have wrenched her hand free because she had not finished fastening up her gown, but he said in an undertone, 'Keep still.'

When she obeyed him, he realised that now she was aware that they were not alone. He fixed his eyes on the statue of the boy, which shone faintly in the light of the rising moon. Already in a highly emotional state, Jack was filled with a deep sense of despair. The boy reminded him of Philippe and the cost to his son of his past reckless behaviour. He could not deny the strength of his desire for Anna. But it was love she wanted and he could not give her what she needed. His lust might destroy her, convincing her that she was the temptress she had been accused of being.

The whisperings had ceased and it occurred to him that Raoul might have decided it might be wiser to leave his guests alone for the moment. Jack decided to wait a while before suggesting they return to the house.

Anna was also still in the grip of high emotion. She likened the shock of all that had taken place in the last hour to having been dropped into a rushing river and buffeted against rocks. Now she was struggling to find safe ground to stand upon. She waited for Jack to speak, but when he did not, she was unable to bear the suspense any longer.

'When will you leave, Jack?' she asked.

'You would be rid of me now? I don't blame you,' he rasped. 'You can have no part in the business that brought me to France.'

'You mean you plan to meet the Comte de Briand in battle? Isn't that foolish of you, Jack? Would it not be better to put the past behind you and go to Bruges with Raoul, instead? You've advised me to put the past behind me—why don't you take your own advice?'

There was a long silence. Jack gazed at the bronze boy in the moonlight and was instantly transferred to another time and another garden.

'I had a son once,' he said.

Anna thought she must have misheard him. 'What did you say?'

Jack took a deep breath and realised he wanted her to know the truth. Then she would understand why he had to face Briand. 'You judge yourself by what your parents did, Anna. But I carry the scars of a greater sin within me. I have never spoken of this to anyone else, not even my brother. Monique bore me a son, but we could not marry because she was the wife of the Comte de Briand.'

Anna was shocked by this revelation. How could the Jack she admired and respected commit such a mortal sin? The decent man she knew or thought she knew would never have committed such a sin and risked his immortal soul. She did not wish to believe him and wanted to scream that he was lying to her.

'I beg you not to judge me or Monique out of hand, Anna,' rasped Jack. 'Monique was a child when she was forced into marriage. Her husband was a widower in his forties and depraved. The acts he forced her to do with other men would turn your stomach. She ran away from him and we set up home together. Somehow he managed to trace her and killed her before I could prevent it. I managed to get the maid and my son out of the house. I fought the Comte and that is when I got this scar. It will always be a reminder that I failed my son because unfortunately Briand did not come alone and I became his prisoner.' Jack had spoken in a monotone, but now his voice rose slightly. 'For three days I believed the maid had managed to get Philippe to safety, but then my hopes were dashed when Briand told me that he had found them and my son was dead.' He ignored her gasp of horror. 'I wanted to die when he told me that Philippe was dead, but Briand wished me to suffer the agonies of guilt and a lifetime of slavery before ending my life in an alien land.'

'But you didn't die,' she said through stiff lips.

Jack smiled grimly. 'Nay. I managed to stay alive, fuelled by my hatred of him.' He glanced at her. 'Do you understand now, Anna, the kind of man I am? The depth of my sin? I am responsible for the murders of those I loved and must pay the price for what I did to them. You must not try to prevent me from avenging their deaths. If I survive, then we will meet again; if I don't, then pray for my soul.'

'You're a fool, Jack!' she cried, unable to bear the thought of him leaving her to go to his death. 'Put the past behind you and live!' She felt as if her heart was being splintered into pieces and knew what she must do. How could she allow him to face his enemy without proving to him that his sins were forgivable and there could still be pleasure in life?

She gazed up into his shadowy features and touched the fine line of his jaw before running her fingers up the side of his face. She felt his facial muscles tense and, remembering what he had said about his scar being a reminder of his shame, she reached up and pressed her lips against it yet again. For a moment he froze and then he moved his head, so that his mouth found hers. As they kissed her fingers searched for the fastenings on his doublet and she began to undo them. She had not finished doing up her own fastenings and within moments he had torn them apart and they were breast to chest, tantalising each other as their bodies slid against each other, kissing in a hit-and-miss fashion, whilst he removed her gown and she eased off his nether garments.

Hand in hand they hurried over to the lawn and dropped onto their knees, each gazing hungrily at the other's nakedness. All feelings of guilt or re-membrance of past loves had fled. Both trembled with desire. Then they were in each other's arms and rolling on the grass. His mouth blazed hot sensual trails over her skin, triggering pleasure that left her moaning. She longed for him to take her and she did not have long to wait. He slid on top of her and took possession of her in a passionate gallop that carried her to soaring heights of ecstasy and left her gasping for more. She heard the purr of fulfilment in his throat and believed that she had succeeded in her aim. She could only hope that he did not consider her wanton. If he did so then he had an odd way of showing it, for he continued to hold her in his arms as she came slowly down to earth, although the effects of that wondrous moment remained in her relaxed limbs and closed her eyes.

Never had Jack believed he could find such delight in pleasuring Anna. He had thought that her remembrance of her husband, and the shame she felt at being accused of being a wanton, might have made her resistant to his lovemaking. Instead, she had melted beneath his caresses in a wondrously thrilling manner. He felt good and could not deny the great sense of release and joy he had received from their coupling. He felt her stir in his embrace and she stretched and opened her eyes. Then he remembered where they were.

'We'd best make a move and get dressed,' he said in a low voice. 'Raoul and his wife will be wondering what's happened to us.'

For a moment Anna remained where she was and

then she sat up. 'I had forgotten about them. I had forgotten everything,' she said in a shaky voice.

'Me, too,' murmured Jack, getting to his feet and moving away from her.

She gazed up at him and marvelled at the strength and shapeliness of his legs and the masculine beauty of his body. Surprisingly, she felt no shame in looking upon his nakedness even now. Rising from the ground, she followed him over to the bench where they had left their garments. As she dressed, Anna considered how her misery had fled. She was now filled with hope, convinced that Jack would change his mind about having his revenge on the Comte de Briand. She and Jack might not love each other, but, having found pleasure in each other's arms, perhaps there might be a future for them together. She looked at him and saw that he was gazing at the pond and the statue of the boy in its midst. She remembered what he had told her about his son and felt an empathy with him. But all she said was, 'Are you ready to return to the house?'

'Give me a few moments. You go on ahead,' said Jack.

'If that's what you wish.'

'It is.' He sounded unlike himself.

Anna was suddenly filled with uncertainty and did not want to leave him alone. 'I'm sorry about your son. I do understand how you must feel.'

'I doubt it. Now go, Anna. I have much to think about.'

She was still reluctant to leave him and touched his arm. 'Jack!'

He turned on her. 'Go!' he roared. 'Am I not plagued by demons of guilt? I no longer know what is right and wrong! Please, go and leave me alone!'

She stared at him in disbelief and then turned and fled up the garden. She should never have given herself to him. Her intent had been to help him, but somehow she had failed and added to his guilt. She had tempted him into fornication, so adding to her own sin. She burst into the house, pausing in the passage way, and wondered where to go next. She leaned against a wall, trying to calm herself. Her pulses were racing and her head was throbbing. How was she going to face Jack across the supper table with them both feeling the way they did? She was aware of a deep pity for the dead boy caught up in Jack and Monique's affair. Suddenly she was raging inwardly at Jack for allowing an innocent child to suffer for his sin. How had he met Monique? How soon had they fallen in love and decided to risk all by having an illicit love affair? Was it so surprising that the husband had wanted to punish his wayward wife and kill the man responsible for taking her from him?

Rather a harsh punishment, though, said a reasoning voice in her head. *He killed the boy, too, remember?* Anna began to weep for that boy and her own son and strangely the two seemed to merge into one.

Suddenly a door opened and light flooded part of the passage ahead. A woman carrying a branch of candles came out of a room. She started when she saw Anna standing in the shadows. 'Is that you, Lady Fenwick?' she asked.

Anna wiped her eyes with her sleeve, knowing she could no longer remain skulking in the darkness. She forced herself to walk forward with a hand outstretched. 'You—you must be the Comtesse d'Azay?'

'Indeed, I am.' The other woman's eyes appeared to be searching the passage behind Anna. 'Master Milburn is not with you?'

'He said he will follow in a few moments.' Anna cleared her throat. 'It's a pleasure to meet you, Comtesse. It is kind of you to welcome me into your home.'

'Please call me Margaret.' She looked at her with concern. 'You don't look well.'

'I have a megrim, but it will pass. You must call me Anna.'

Margaret smiled. 'You will wish to go upstairs and rest. Your bedchamber has been prepared, so I will take you up there.'

Anna's body sagged with relief. To be alone and not to have to talk to anyone sounded bliss. 'That would be most acceptable,' she said.

As they climbed the stairs, Margaret asked her whether she planned on making a long stay. 'Unfortunately not this time,' answered Anna. 'I was unsure whether I would be welcomed here and did not come prepared. There are important matters I have to deal with at home.'

'You're a widow, I believe?'

'That is true. You have children, I believe?'

'Aye.' Margaret proceeded to tell her about her small son and daughter. Her descriptions about their appearance and cleverness lasted until they arrived at the guest bedchamber allotted to Anna.

The lighted candelabra revealed a well-appointed room, decorated in cream and pink draperies. There was a cherry-wood armoire, a box bed, a chair, a washstand and a carved chest on which had been placed her saddlebags. Margaret pointed out various items, such as the water pitcher and the drying cloth, then she went over to the armoire and flung open the doors to reveal the clothes within. She fingered a couple of gowns before turning to Anna. 'Please, help yourself to what you need and come down when you are ready.'

Anna thanked her. As soon as Margaret left her alone, she sank on to the bed. Her head felt as if it were splitting in half and that if she moved it, then it just might fall off. She could no longer think straight due to the pain, so she stayed where she was. After a while her back ached so much that she made the effort to remove her boots and outer garments. She washed herself and then rubbed herself dry on the extra-thick drying cloth. Taking out her silk night rail, she put it on and then blew out all the candles before climbing into bed.

She craved oblivion and closing her eyes, tried to relax. It seemed an age before she drifted into that state betwixt sleep and wakefulness. Now Jack filled her thoughts and she relived the moments of their coupling and prayed for God to forgive them and at the same time she asked him that it would not be for the last time. Snatches of their conversation echoed in her mind. She imagined he was standing nearby, watching her with sadness in his face, and dreamed that she was comforting him all over again.

Chapter Ten

It was the noise of someone moving about the room that woke Anna. Then a shaft of sunlight painted a bright lozenge of pale gold on the wooden floor. She could not believe it was morning. Another shutter was flung open and she realised it was Margaret in her room.

'Have I slept all the night through?' asked Anna, somewhat in a daze.

Margaret smiled at her. 'Aye. Master Milburn said you were exhausted and must be left to sleep.'

'When was this?' asked Anna.

'Last night. You must be famished. You missed supper.'

'Where is he?'

'He had to leave early. In truth, he did not even bid Raoul farewell.'

Remembering Jack's mood when she had left him last evening and also what he had said about confronting the Comte de Briand, Anna was filled with apprehension. She sat up. 'Has he gone alone?'

'He must have done. Raoul is vexed with him, for he left without saying where he was going or when he will return.'

Anna climbed out of bed. 'That's because he believes he might not return.'

'Why do you say that?' asked Margaret, looking startled.

Anna did not answer, but gazed about her for the garments she had taken off last night, but she could not see them anywhere. 'Where are my clothes?' she asked, frowning.

'I gave them to the laundress to wash. I thought you would appreciate some clean raiment.'

'I would, but I plan to go after Jack. How will I return them to you if I borrow some now?'

Margaret's eyes almost popped out of her head. 'Does he know you plan to follow him?'

'Not yet he doesn't,' said Anna, opening the armoire. 'But he must be stopped.'

Margaret shook her head. 'You really are the most unusual pair. Do help yourself to whatever you need, Anna. Don't worry about returning them. They belonged to Raoul's mother and I planned to give them away to a used clothes-dealer sooner or later.'

'Thank you,' said Anna, deciding to make the most of the offer and to pack a change of clothing just in case she should get wet. 'Where is Raoul?'

'In the parlour. Jack told him about your parchments and he's perusing them.'

'I see.' Anna was surprised that Jack should have remembered about them in view of what had happened last evening.

'I'll tell him to expect you down soon, shall I?' asked Margaret. 'No doubt he'll be eager to speak to you.'

'And I with him,' murmured Anna, giving her attention once more to the garments hanging in the armoire.

She removed a cream kirtle in soft linsey-woolsey and placed it on the bed. This was followed by a gown of green linen, embroidered about the neck, cuffs and hem in red and yellow silk thread. After a couple of years of wearing black or grey, Anna felt a lift of the heart at the thought of wearing such a gown. The fact that Jack was not there to see her dressed in such a fine garment grieved her, but she was determined to prevent him from getting himself killed. She'd had to cope with so much loss and sadness in her life that she did not wish to face any more grief. She took a shift of primrose yellow and a gown of blue from the wardrobe. Later, she would pack them in her saddlebags.

After performing her ablutions, Anna donned the fresh garments. They smelt faintly of lavender. Then she tidied her hair and covered it with a fresh wimple and veil, before leaving the bedchamber and going downstairs.

She had little trouble finding the parlour and expected to find Margaret and Raoul's children there, but he was alone in the room. He was sitting at a table gazing down at one of her parchments. She cleared her throat.

Instantly Raoul lifted his head and rose to his feet. 'Anna, you are much better this morning? You look delightful.' He held out a hand to her. 'Come and be seated. I must say that whenever I considered the possibility of meeting you, I did not think you would have with you such fine parchments as these.' He pulled out a chair for her. 'Your husband was a connoisseur.'

She ignored the chair. 'I am pleased to hear you

say that. Jack certainly thought they were fine examples of the period.'

'Ahhh, Jack!' Raoul grimaced as he picked up a silver bell and rang it.

A few moments later the door opened and a servant entered. Raoul spoke rapidly to him and then he left. 'I have ordered you a substantial meal, presuming you are very hungry after missing your supper.' He raised an eyebrow.

Anna thanked him. 'You must forgive me my bad manners last evening, but I fell asleep.'

'Jack said you were exhausted. I presume you know where he has gone if you intend following him.' He placed the parchments in their cloth wrappings and, putting them aside, stared at her.

'Indeed, I do. I must stop him from throwing his life away.'

Raoul frowned. 'I did not expect him to leave this morning without a farewell. My wife says you believe he might not return. Will you explain this?'

Anna hesitated. 'It is Jack's tale to tell. I can only say that his destination is Amiens and…'

'Ahhh, perhaps it has to do with the disagreement between King Edward and King Louis.' Raoul pursed his lips. 'I am still surprised that he did not mention this to me.'

Anna made a decision. 'Raoul, do you know the Comte de Briand and, if you do, do you like him?'

He seemed surprised by the question. 'Gaston and I have done business together recently. He is not a friend. Although, one cannot blame him for the kind of man he is. He has not had an easy life.'

'Jack told me his wife had a worse life at his hands.'

Raoul frowned. 'I did not know Jack knew him or his wife.'

'Apparently he did.' Her voice trembled. 'Is the Comte a strong man? A good swordsman?'

'He is a well set-up fellow and I should imagine he is as skilled at swordplay as the next man.'

'Jack plans to kill him or die in the attempt,' she said, pacing the floor.

'You must be mistaken!'

'You think I would say this if I was not sure of it?' she said passionately.

Before Raoul could reply, the door opened and Georges entered, carrying a tray. Her host sighed. 'You must eat now, Anna. You can explain what this is all about after you've done so.'

'But we must try to stop Jack before it is too late.'

Raoul looked at her sympathetically. 'You are overwrought because of what you discovered

about your parents. I cannot see what quarrel Jack
has with Briand. Calm yourself and eat.'

Anna gazed down at the slices of ham, fresh
bread rolls, butter and honey. 'What I feel has
naught to do with my parents. Jack believes the
Comte de Briand did him a great wrong and he is
determined to have his revenge.'

Raoul looked incredulous. 'I cannot believe this.'

'You must believe me,' said Anna forcefully. 'We
have to stop him.'

He sighed. 'Be silent. Eat whilst I ponder this
matter.'

Anna thought—how could she be silent when
she was seized by such a sense of urgency? She
managed to force a little food down, impatient for
Raoul to speak. Eventually he looked at her. 'Has
this to do with the years he spent in slavery?'

'Aye! But that is all I can say.'

Raoul looked annoyed. 'I cannot believe that
Gaston played a part in Jack's abduction,' he said,
shaking his head.

'Jack believes it. We must persuade him that there
is another way to deal with him,' she persisted.

'It is not so easy for me to drop everything and
follow Jack. There are arrangements I would
need to make. In the meantime, Anna, you will

do naught so foolish as to attempt to follow Jack on your own.'

Anna nodded, before sweeping out of the room and going upstairs. Raoul just did not have the same sense of urgency as herself, she thought. She fastened her saddlebags and hoisted them over her shoulder. Then she went downstairs and made her way across the yard to the stables. There she saw Raoul in discussion with one of the men and instantly she changed direction and went into the garden.

She sat on the bench overlooking the pond, reliving those moments of lovemaking again, wondering if Jack had felt something more than lust for her. If Raoul did not make up his mind soon what to do, then she would leave without him.

She gazed at the statue of the bronze boy in the pond and felt a familiar tightness in her chest and a stinging behind her eyes. She wondered if the sculptor had used a real child as a model or whether he had imagined those mischievous, boyish features. She thought of those moments spent here with Jack last night, when he had told her that he had once had a son. Possibly the moonlight shining on the statue had caused that explosive statement. Her mother's heart ached for the child and the man. She could so easily imagine Jack's anguish and guilt for not being able to save his son. Had she not felt the same when, despite all her attempts to heal Joshua with her potions, she had failed to do so? At least she had been able to kiss her son's eyes shut and prepare his body for burial. Poor Jack! She doubted he even knew where his son was buried.

She still felt shocked by what he had done and understood why he had kept it secret from his twin. Owain and Kate had been just as secretive where her parents were concerned and she knew that she must forgive them. She sighed. How many more secrets might be revealed before she could put the past behind her?

'Anna, where are you?' She started at the sound of Raoul's voice and rose to her feet.

'Ahhh, there you are,' he said, coming towards her from the direction of the stables. The sun shone on his bare head, burnishing his foxy hair so that it shone like copper. 'I have had word that the kings of England and France are about to make peace. I deem this a good sign, so we will ride for Amiens. Hopefully we will be able to prevent Jack from making a fool of himself.'

Anna's relief was intense. 'Thank you, Raoul. You are Jack's good friend.'

Raoul said ruefully, 'If he believed that, Anna, why did he not tell me it was Gaston de Briand who was responsible for his suffering?'

'He has his reasons.'

Her half-brother gave her a piercing stare. 'Yet he told you, Anna. That tells me something about you both.'

'Perhaps that we have suffered and grieve for the loss of loved ones,' she murmured, placing a hand on Raoul's arm. 'We must be on our way.'

'You feel strong enough to make this journey, Anna? I could go alone,' he said, as they crossed to the stables.

'I wouldn't have a moment's peace if you left me behind.'

Raoul nodded as if her reply did not surprise him. 'I have a fine little mare that will do you well.'

Anna thanked him. She had no notion of how far it was to Amiens, and dreaded to think what might happen if one of their horses threw a shoe or something else should happen to prevent them reaching Jack in time. She could only pray that they would find him before it was too late.

* * *

It was two days later that Jack woke to the sound of a trumpet blast. He threw back his cloak and prepared to face the day ahead. He had needed to stiffen his resolve on the journey several times, tempted to turn back and tell Anna that he was sorry to have shouted at her and to ask her forgiveness. He could not forget her passionate response to his lovemaking and longed to repeat the experience. Yet neither could he dismiss the vow he had made and he felt torn in two. He missed Anna's company more than he would ever have believed. Even when they had travelled miles without conversing, he had been conscious of her nearness and, without realising he was doing so, had drawn comfort from it. He exchanged greetings with a soldier before stepping out of the tent, and squelched his way across the sodden ground to the latrines. He had arrived too late the previous evening to enter the city, but after getting into conversation with a couple of English soldiers, he had been offered ground room in their tent out of the rain. But, more importantly they had provided him with information.

It was the first day of September and apparently the kings of England and France had recently met in Picquigny on the River Somme to make peace. Rumour had it that they had already come to terms and that Edward was to receive a lump sum of seventy-five thousand crowns to defray the cost of the English army here in France—as well as a yearly tribute of a thousand crowns. The latter depended on his withdrawing his demand to the throne of France, so bringing to an end the Plantagenet claim that had resulted in over a hundred years of intermittent fighting between the two countries.

Good news for trade, thought Jack, looking up at the sky. The rain had stopped and the sun was trying to break through the clouds. He lowered his gaze, to peer through one of the gaps between the tents, in the direction of the gates of Amiens. They were open. Whether he would find the Comte de Briand inside the city walls was another matter altogether. It was possible that he could have left Amiens for Picquigny. Suddenly, it occurred to him that he could take the peace treaty as a sign from God that it really was time he himself made peace with the past. He felt certain that Anna would see it as such a sign for him. He sighed; if he had any more such thoughts, he would be changing his mind about confronting Briand. Was that because Anna had taught him there was still much in life worth living for—music, beauty, friendship, good conversation, food and drink and the pleasure to be found in her arms?

A shadow crossed his face. He must stop thinking in such a way and remember his enemy's face twisted with glee as he had spoken of Philippe's death. Jack felt a curl of anger in his gut and his hand strayed to his sword, then dropped. He must get his horse and go into the city and break his fast. He needed to boost his strength for what lay ahead. He would go to an inn he remembered and eat and drink there.

The cathedral of Notre Dame towered over the streets of tall houses and, as Jack entered the city, memories flooded back of the sound of its bells waking him each morning. The house had been situated in the district of St Leu and he recalled Philippe playing with the wooden figure of a knight that the husband of a friend of Hortense's had carved for him. Tears pricked the back of his eyes and then his mouth set in a harsh line. His son's death must be avenged. After he had eaten he would visit the house where he had last seen his son in the hope of feeling a sense of his presence. Then he would go in search of his murderer.

* * *

It was a short while later that Anna set eyes on Amiens. The English camp was in disarray. Tents were being folded and put in carts; campfires were being doused and men and horses were milling about all over the place. Obviously now the hostilities between the kings of France and England were over and the peace treaty signed, the English soldiers would be leaving in droves for the port of Calais. But that was of little interest to her, concerned as she was about Jack. Raoul had shown less concern and she had sensed that he believed that she had got matters confused somehow. Any qualms she might naturally have felt at travelling alone with the half-brother she scarcely knew had been allayed by Raoul's overriding good manners and protective attitude towards her.

As they entered the city, Anna gazed about her, hoping to see Jack. Raoul led her through the bustling streets directly to an inn and they went inside. There followed a rapid exchange between Raoul and the innkeeper to which Anna listened carefully. She had been practising her French on Raoul during the journey and he'd told her that she was improving. Yet he had often seemed secretly amused by what she said, without explaining why.

Now he turned to her with a smile. 'You can stop fretting, Anna. Jack was here only a short while ago. According to the innkeeper he spoke of visiting a house in the St Leu district where he had once stayed.'

Anna wondered how he could be so cheerful. 'Could it not be the house where de Briand is staying?'

'That is highly unlikely, Anna. Gaston is a man of means and it is not the most salubrious of districts.'

Anna was puzzled. Then it occurred to her that the house might be the one where Jack had lived with Monique and Philippe. 'Can the innkeeper direct me to this St Leu?'

Raoul spoke to the man and then turned to Anna. 'We will stable the horses and leave our baggage here. Apparently the area is only a short distance away.'

Anna was relieved. 'I cannot delay, Raoul. Please, if you will deal with such matters, then I will go in search of Jack now.'

Raoul sighed. 'If that is what you wish, Anna, then who am I to prevent you? If you are not back here with Jack in the half-hour, I will come in search of you.'

They went outside and Raoul pointed in the direction she must take. She thanked him and set out for the district of St Leu. After the manner of their parting, she prayed that Jack would not be angry with her for getting Raoul to chase after him. But it was too late to worry about that now.

Jack was aware of a feeling of *déjà vu* as he turned a corner into the street where he had spent so many happy times. The street seemed unchanged by tragedy. Late marigolds bloomed in a tub outside the door of the house that he had rented and a dark-haired boy with his back to him was sweeping the step.

Jack dismounted from his horse and wished the boy, *'Bon jour.'*

The lad glanced up. His gaze fixed on the man's scarred face and his eyes widened in trepidation. Jack swore inwardly. He had seen expressions bordering on curiosity, fear and distaste often enough. Only Anna had reacted differently, even touching his scars with such gentle tenderness. Not wanting to scare the boy, he turned his face so as to present his best side to him.

'There is no need to fear me,' said Jack in French. 'I mean you no harm. I am only curious as to how long you and your family have lived in this house. Can you help me?'

Instead of answering, the lad dropped his broom and hurried indoors. Jack sighed and was about to climb back into the saddle and leave when he heard the lad talking. A woman answered him and her words instantly turned Jack's world upside down. With a pounding heart, he was to about to mount the steps when a crone appeared in the doorway. She was carrying a stick in a threatening manner and the boy hovered behind her.

Jack realised that he recognised her and was swift to reassure her that he intended her no harm. 'I once lived in this house. My name is Jack Milburn,' he said hoarsely, his heart in his throat. 'Am I right in believing that you are Hortense's mother and this is…this lad is my son, Philippe?'

She screwed up her face and, followed by the lad, came down the steps and peered up into Jack's face from rheumy eyes. Then she let out a shriek, dropped the stick and, turning to the boy, spouted forth a torrent of words, before giving him a push in the back that sent him scurrying past Jack.

Jack shot out a hand, but the boy managed to evade him, only to stumble and land at the feet of a woman in a green gown. She bent over him and helped him up. 'I hope you are not hurt, young man?' she asked.

The lad gazed up into her concerned face and appeared to be dumbfounded by the sight of her. Then he glanced at his father and hung his head.

'Anna!' cried Jack, staring at her in amazement. 'How did you get here?'

'I rode, of course.' She smiled. 'I came to stop you throwing away your life.'

'What!' He felt in a daze and could do no more than stare at her and his son. Her hands rested firmly on the lad's shoulders. 'Are you all right, Jack?' asked Anna, her smile fading. 'You look…'

Jack found his voice. 'Shocked? I am. But not for the reason you might be thinking. Anna, this lad is my son, Philippe.'

Anna blinked. 'How is this possible?'

'De Briand lied! That is the only answer! He lied, knowing it would intensify my suffering.'

'If this is true, then…' Anna's voice trailed off. She was struck by the wonder of it and what this must mean to Jack. She gazed down at the boy and, taking a deep breath, said gently in French, 'Look up at me, Philippe, I want to see you properly. I am Lady Anna Fenwick and a good friend of your father.'

Slowly Philippe lifted his head and stared at her. The fearful expression in his dark eyes touched her deeply, and she smiled to reassure him. She was aware of a tingling sensation in the nape of her neck and down her spine. 'By the Trinity, Jack, he has your eyes and your mouth.'

'Does he?' said Jack, feeling a sudden dampness behind his eyes. 'I didn't get a proper look at him. My face frightened him and I looked away.'

'You're not frightening, Jack,' said Anna calmly. 'He just doesn't know you. Besides, it is what one is like inside that is important and you are good.'

Jack shook his head. 'I don't know how you can believe that, Anna, after all I've told you about myself. Philippe is certainly not going to believe it. He'll be asking himself where I've been all these years if I care about him.'

'Then you will tell him,' she said firmly.

Jack continued to stare at her over his son's head. 'Tell him I was defeated by his mother's murderer and spent years as a slave?' His voice cracked. 'I can't do it.'

'You'll have to, Jack, if you are going to be a proper father to him and take him to England as your son,' said Anna, turning the boy round to face his father.

The stunned expression in Jack's eyes told her that he had not got as far as thinking how his son being alive was going to utterly change his life.

Jack swallowed to try to ease the sudden tightness in his throat. He took a step forward. The boy shrank back against Anna and his hand fastened on the skirt of her gown and he gripped it tightly.

'He's scared of me,' whispered Jack. 'Do you really think it's right in the circumstances to take him away from all that's familiar and take him to England?'

'There's only one question you have to ask yourself, Jack. What is best for his future? Can you provide him with a better life than he has here?'

Jack did not answer, but she could tell from the change in his expression that she had given him something to think about. She felt the boy stir beneath her hands. He tugged on her arm and spoke to her in French, saying that the grandmother had told him to fetch Hortense. She bent over him and replied in the same language.

'Philippe, your father and I will come with you to speak to Hortense.' She glanced at Jack. 'Is that all right with you?'

'Of course.' He removed his hat and ran a hand through his hair, unable to take his eyes off the pair of them. 'I have to thank her and there's questions I need to ask her. She'll want answers from me, too. No doubt she told Philippe I was dead. It will be a tremendous shock to her, knowing I'm alive.'

'*Non,*' said Philippe. 'Hortense say my papa alive,' he said in English.

'You speak English!' said Jack, in continuing amazement. 'I would not have believed that you could remember the little I taught you.'

Philippe shrugged bony shoulders. 'The English soldiers—I learn a leetle from them.'

'That is good,' said his father.

'I'm puzzled,' said Anna. 'How did Hortense know you were alive, Jack?'

'She not know...but...have faith.' Philippe placed his hands together as if in prayer. 'She say one day Papa come for me.'

'God's blood!' muttered Jack, shaking his head. He was scarcely able to believe what he was hearing.

'Where is Hortense, Philippe?' asked Anna.

'She has gone to Antoine's shop.'

Jack's face lit up. 'I remember Antoine. He is a wood carver, who had an ailing wife, a friend of Hortense. He struggled to take care of her and make a living. I know where his shop is.'

'Then let us go there,' said Anna.

The words were no sooner said than there was the clattering of sabots. Philippe looked relieved. 'Here is Hortense!' He tore himself from Anna's grasp and ran towards the approaching figure.

Anna felt a moment's anxiety when she saw a woman who was possibly six summers older than herself. She wore a brown homespun gown and was plain-faced. Perhaps she would not want to part with Philippe now his father had returned and would cling on to him. Anna watched her greet the boy with a smile and listen to what he said. Then she looked at Jack and Anna and her hands flew to her face in shock.

Immediately he hurried towards her. 'Hortense! It is I, Jack Milburn. Say you recognise me!'

The woman recovered swiftly, raising her hands joyfully into the air, smiling broadly. '*Monsieur*! I knew you would return one day for him. I felt it in my bones that you were still alive. Every day I prayed to St Jerome and Our Lady that you would come. God has granted my prayer.' She squeezed the boy's shoulder. 'Philippe, this really is your papa.'

The lad lifted his head and peered at Jack. 'He has a scar.'

She nodded. 'Remember what our neighbour told us? They saw him being carried away by evil men.

Remember that his face was covered in blood, but they knew he was alive because they heard him groan when he was thrown on the horse?'

Jack smiled with relief and bent and kissed Hortense on both cheeks. 'My thanks for keeping faith and taking care of my son.' He touched his scar. 'This was given to me by de Briand. It has been a constant reminder of what happened the last time I saw you. De Briand told me that Philippe was dead. He sold me into slavery. I was only freed a short while ago. I returned to France to avenge Philippe's death and that of his mother.'

Hortense's eyes were filled with sadness. 'I am sad that you have suffered, but it explains much.' She glanced down at the boy. 'See, did I not tell you there would be a good reason why your papa delayed in coming for you? Now he will take you in his ship to England. You will learn to be a merchant venturer like him and have adventures. This is God's will for you, Philippe.'

The lad looked none too happy.

His expression was not lost on Jack. 'If I am to take him with me, will you come, too, Hortense?' he asked in a rush.

She shook her head. 'Alas, I cannot. I have promised Antoine to marry him. He is a widower now and for the past year he has wanted me to be his wife. The wedding is to be soon. Now the English are leaving, he is making lots of money.'

Jack could imagine how that could be. The soldiers would want keepsakes and gifts for their women at home. But he was dismayed at the thought of taking an unwilling boy home to England with him. Yet take him he must, this son who had haunted his dreams. Despite their being strangers to each other, he could not possibly desert him. It was his duty to take care of him. Besides, it was obviously what Anna and Hortense expected of him.

He looked down at Philippe and thought about how he had clung to Anna and her warmth of manner towards the boy. He remembered what she had said about preventing him from throwing his life away. Perhaps…

Before he could follow his train of thought further there was a sudden commotion in the street that drew their attention. It was Raoul and he was greeting a well-dressed man in a loud voice. Jack glanced at Anna.

'You didn't think that I came here unaccompanied, did you?' she said, with a twinkle. 'Not after all your warnings about the dangers to a woman travelling alone. I left Raoul stabling the horses at the inn. We were told by the innkeeper that you had mentioned visiting this district, so I came to find you.'

'I see.'

Raoul suddenly broke off from what he was saying and looked towards them. He murmured something to his companion, who nodded and then hurried off. Raoul came striding towards them.

'No doubt you are surprised to see us, Jack,' he called. 'But we came to prevent you from making a fool of yourself by challenging Gaston de Briand to a fight to the death.'

Jack shot Anna a startled look. 'What did you tell him?'

Raoul answered for her. 'That you wished to revenge yourself on the man who sentenced you to six years of slavery. What more is there to tell? Are we to presume, Jack, that you haven't met with Gaston yet?'

Jack's eyebrows shot up. 'I have no quarrel with the Comte de Briand's son. There's been some mistake.'

Raoul nodded. 'Indeed there has, for Gaston is the Comte de Briand. His father died five years ago, stabbed in the back by an unknown assassin.' He looked thoughtful. 'Now the old Comte, he had many enemies. A most unsavoury character, accused of the most unspeakable deeds. I should have guessed it was he to whom Anna referred when she told me that you were determined to kill the Comte de Briand.'

Jack felt as if a weight had fallen from his shoulders. 'All this time I've nursed a deep hatred of the old Comte. I can scarcely believe that he's been dead these past five years.'

Raoul smiled. 'Believe me, my friend, it is true. No longer do you need to risk your life, avenging yourself on a man who has been duly punished. Hopefully, he is now rotting in the fierce flames of hell. So now you can come with me to Bruges.'

'Much as I would enjoy your company,' said Jack, swiftly recovering from the shock of this welcome news, 'I cannot accompany you to Bruges. I will be returning to England as soon as I can. There is something I must tell you, Raoul. This boy here…'

Raoul glanced at Philippe. Then he gave the boy a second glance before looking at Jack. 'You will explain?'

'I was about to…this boy is my son, Raoul. Monique de Briand was his mother.'

There was a stunned silence from Raoul. Then

he took a deep breath and said, 'I am beginning to understand. There were rumours when Monique de Briand went missing that either her husband had secreted her away and kept her a prisoner in a dungeon, or that she had a lover and had fled with him. Not for one moment did I think that you could be that lover, Jack.'

Jack said wryly, 'You knew the Comte, so you can guess why I couldn't chance the affair being gossiped about even by my friends in their cups.'

'I wish you could have trusted me. I could perhaps have been of help to you,' said Raoul seriously.

'And risk your life?' snapped Jack. 'As it was, someone betrayed us and Monique paid with her life.'

Raoul frowned. 'He was a wicked man.'

'Enough said.' Jack looked down at his son. 'Philippe, this man you see before you is my friend, the Comte d'Azay. You will make your bow to him.' His son gave him an uncertain look, but a nudge in the back from Hortense was enough to make him obey his father.

Watching father and son, Anna felt something twist in her heart. 'Is Jack not fortunate, Raoul, to have a son to share his home? I am certain that once they grow accustomed to the change in their circumstances they will find pleasure in each other's company. They will be able to share so many pastimes. Music, fishing…'

'It is possible that it will turn out that you are right, Anna, but this situation needs consideration,' interrupted Raoul. 'How is Jack to cope single-handedly with the boy? Unless this woman he is with…'

'Hortense took care of him for me,' said Jack. 'But she cannot come to England with us.'

Raoul frowned. 'Then I can see trouble ahead for you, Jack. It is a lot to expect a boy brought up in France to settle in England amongst strangers, not knowing a word of the language.'

'He does speak some English,' said Anna, annoyed with Raoul for creating difficulties. 'And Jack will be able to converse with him in his own tongue, as well as improve his English.' Her tone was confident. 'He will want him to be part of his family. I'm sure he will adapt.'

Jack wished he felt as certain of that as Anna did. 'He's going to come as somewhat of a surprise to them,' he said, expecting verbal explosions from his family when they set eyes on his son.

'It appears to me, Jack, that what you need is a little more time to consider matters,' said Raoul.

'You would be better leaving the boy here with your having no wife at home to be a mother to him. You could pay this woman to continue to care for him.'

Anna looked at Jack in dismay. Surely he would not agree!

Chapter Eleven

'I couldn't do that,' said Jack. 'Anna is right. My family will accept him once they have got over the initial shock and it will be for his sake as much as mine.'

Raoul shrugged. 'If that is your decision.'

'It is.' Jack hesitated. 'Have you eaten yet?'

'*Non*! We arrived but a short while ago,' answered Raoul. 'But we are staying at the inn where you breakfasted. What will you do? Stay here with your son or return to the inn with us? Have you bespoke a chamber there? If not, you can share mine. I have arranged to meet a friend.'

Jack hesitated. Then he turned to Hortense and said, 'I need to speak with my friends. I will return later and we will discuss my plans for Philippe.'

'The English lady, she will be returning to

England with you when you take him to your home?' asked Hortense.

'Why do you ask?' queried Jack.

'She is pretty and has a kind face. Philippe will need kindness shown to him in the days to come.'

'He will receive it,' said Jack firmly, placing a hand on his son's head. 'I will see you shortly, Philippe. You must not be scared of me.'

The boy made no answer, but only looked at him.

Jack sighed. 'I shall fetch my horse and then we'll return to the inn,' he said.

A relieved Anna bid Philippe and Hortense, *'Au revoir!'*

Then she began to make her way back to the inn. She wanted some time alone to think about the miraculous change in Jack's life and what it could mean to her.

Jack and Raoul followed her a few moments later. 'You should marry Anna, my friend,' suggested Raoul. 'Despite your scandalous behaviour, I am certain she will have you.'

'The thought had occurred to me,' said Jack, leading his horse by the reins. 'Although I am not so certain as you that she will accept me.'

'She is fond of you, Jack. Why else do you think we are here? I am sure she would consider a proposal from you. Her self-esteem is not high after what she discovered about her parents. The boy needs a mother and it is time you took a wife. I deem it a highly sensible solution to the problem that faces you.'

'She told me that she would prefer to enter a convent rather than marry where her heart was not involved. She will *not* make a marriage of convenience.'

'*L'amour!*' exclaimed Raoul, rolling his eyes. 'Besides, her heart is engaged. Did you not see her face when she gazed down at your son? She is already half in love with him.'

Jack made no answer. He guessed what Raoul said was partly true. He sensed that his son would be more willing to come with him if he knew that Anna would be living with them. But how to voice a proposal to Anna needed some thought.

They came to the inn and saw her waiting for them outside.

'I will see to your horse,' said Raoul, 'whilst you arrange for the hire of the parlour and a meal to be served there for yourself and Anna.'

'Thank you for your consideration,' said Jack stiffly. 'But what about you?'

'I will visit my friend Jules and dine with him. I

haven't seen him for several months and he is a collector of parchments; it's possible he might be interested in buying Anna's. That is if you, both, are agreeable to my broaching the matter with him?'

'You'd best ask her yourself,' said Jack drily.

So that is what Raoul did.

'I don't see why not,' said Anna, pleased at the possibility of making a sale so soon. 'Some French coin would be very useful.'

Jack turned to Anna. 'Are you willing to eat alone with me, Anna—or would you rather forgo my company after my show of ill temper at Raoul's?'

She thought there was a strained expression about his eyes and mouth. Not surprising in the circumstances. She smiled. 'Of course I will break bread with you, Jack,' she replied, slipping her hand through his arm. 'It seems an age since we dined together on the ship. Although, of course, we were never completely alone then.'

'And our circumstances were very different,' he said, relieved with her answer.

'Aye. The direction of our lives has changed in the short time we've been in France. We've both discovered truths about our pasts that, whilst very different from what we expected, nevertheless, mean...' Her voice trailed off.

'Mean what?' asked Jack, remembering the feel of her in his arms. It would be extremely pleasant waking up every morning with Anna beside him.

She hesitated. 'That we both now must consider the future.'

'That is true. Perhaps we can discuss it over a meal?' he said, despite there being little time to mull over what he was going to say to her.

He had words with the innkeeper about a private parlour and a light meal and in no time at all they were being shown into the inn's private parlour. A fire crackled on the hearth, sending shadows dancing round the limewashed walls. They sat opposite each other at a small table. Jack waited until drinks were poured before saying, 'Are you sure you want to return to England, Anna?'

'Indeed, I do,' she answered, removing her gloves. 'I have had enough of travelling for a while and consider it time to sort out my affairs at home.'

'Then you are willing to travel to England with me and Philippe on the *Hercules*?'

'Of course.' She smiled. 'He's a fine boy, your son. He might be a little scared of you at the moment, but no doubt he will get over that once he knows you better. You will take him straight to your house in Kingston-on-Hull?'

'Aye. I hope you don't mind?'

'Of course not. I understand why you wish to see him settled into your home as soon as possible. I presume you will be able to provide me with an escort to Rowan?'

'Of course. If that is what you want,' he said gravely.

'I have nowhere else to go.'

'You have changed your mind about entering a convent?'

She did not immediately answer him, remembering her stay there almost a year ago. It was true that she had found peace behind the convent walls, but it was not where she wished to remain for the rest of her life. If her journeying had taught her anything, it was that she had more to offer than prayers and piety.

'Anna?'

She looked at Jack. 'Aye. I deem that God did not intend me for the devotional life after all. I believe the gifts that he has given me would be more useful out in the world.'

Jack felt some of his tension evaporate. 'I am relieved to hear it.'

She smiled. 'Have you any suggestions about what I should do with the rest of my life, Jack? I would appreciate your advice.'

He marvelled that she could be so forgiving and willing to seek his help. 'You are a constant surprise to me, Anna. How can you ask my advice, knowing what you do about me?'

'Perhaps it's because of what I know about you that I can ask. You have suffered and have seen life as I will never see it. What do you consider will make me feel useful and happy?'

Jack did not immediately answer. He was thinking over what Raoul had said about Anna being already half in love with his son. He felt a stab of envy. Was it possible that she would accept a proposal of marriage from him solely in order to be a mother to his son? He was not as confident as Raoul that she would accept him. He certainly had not forgotten how she had responded to his lovemaking.

'You're deep in thought, Jack. Is it that you deem me useless?' she teased.

Jack reached for his wine and took a mouthful, 'I do have a suggestion to put to you.'

'What is it?'

Before he could reply a serving-woman entered, carrying a tray. Both waited impatiently as she set before them two bowls of creamy mushroom soup. As soon as she departed, Anna picked up her spoon and dipped it in the soup. She did not wish to appear too eager to hear what he had to say, so supped the soup and broke off a chunk of bread from the loaf. Slowly, she lifted her eyes and gazed at him. She thought he appeared oddly unsure of himself. He was fiddling with his spoon and gazing at a point somewhere over her shoulder.

Then suddenly he said, 'Knowing you were homeless, I once suggested that you might like to stay at my house in Kingston-on-Hull. That offer still stands. I know you need to sort out your affairs, but surely you could leave matters to Owain a little longer? I wondered if you might like to live with me and Philippe?'

'In what capacity?' asked Anna, her heart increasing its beat.

'I need a woman to keep house for me and to be as a mother to Philippe.' He reached across the table and placed his hand over her free one. 'I know you are a good woman, much too good for me.'

'Nonsense.' Her fingers trembled in his grasp. 'You know what I am.'

'Indeed, I do. I admire you more than I can say, Anna. You are brave and true.'

The colour rose in her cheeks. 'You flatter me, Jack.'

'It's true,' he protested. 'You have all the qualities that I admire in a woman. I deem you would make an ideal *chatelaine.*'

'Chatelaine?' said Anna slowly. 'What do you mean by that word? It's French, isn't it? Raoul used it, I think.'

Jack nodded, wondering what was holding him back from asking her to marry him when it was eminently sensible to do so.

Anna wondered why he hesitated so long. After the flattery, was he now reciting to himself all the traits that made her unsuitable to be a mother to his son? She could not bear the silence any longer. 'You don't have to answer, Jack. I know a *chatelaine* is the mistress of the house. She holds the keys to every cupboard and chest. You could say that she *is* the key to the smooth running of the household.' Her tone was brittle. 'But whether she is the master's concubine or his wife depends on his commitment to her.'

He paled. 'It's exactly for that reason I'm making a pig's ear of this proposal. My intention was to ask you to marry me.' His fingers tightened over hers. 'I know that I might not be the husband you would prefer, but it's possible that we could still make a good match of it.'

'You mean you believe that we can support each other for fairer or fouler, for better for worse, for richer for poorer, in sickness and in health?' she demanded.

'I would swear it before God, and, once having made such a vow I would do all in my power to keep it.' He realised he was crushing her fingers and begged her pardon. He raised her hand to his lips and kissed each finger. 'I will protect you from those curs that insulted you. I will also provide for you from my own wealth, so that you can keep Fenwick Manor for your own. If we were ever to have a son, then you could give it to him.'

It was a generous offer in the circumstances; a bride or her father or brother was expected to give a dower to her future husband. Yet Anna would have preferred him to make a promise to give her his love. Instead, Jack was being eminently sensible and so must she, even though she tingled with each tiny kiss he planted on her crushed fingers. No longer a green girl with romantic dreams, it was best that neither she nor Jack deceived themselves into believing their marriage could be aught else than one of convenience. A contract that bound them together. She was suddenly filled with doubt. Could either of them really settle for less than they'd had with their previous lovers?

'You truly tempt me to accept your proposal, Jack,' she said in a low voice.

'Do I? Then say aye.'

His smile was one of such charm that she almost agreed there and then. But she told herself that she had acted hastily so often in the last few weeks that this time she must give more thought to such an important decision. A sigh escaped her. 'Your offer is honest, generous and fair. I have no doubt that I could fill the role you have in mind for me, but I cannot decide such an important matter without giving it more thought,' she said.

Her answer was a blow to him and he dropped her hand. 'Of course! It was foolish of me to expect an immediate answer,' he said in clipped tones. 'How long do you think you will need to make a decision? I have it in mind to leave Amiens as soon as possible.'

'I will sleep on it and give you my answer in the morning.'

'Then I will hope your answer is the most sensible one,' he said with chilling politeness.

'Indeed,' she murmured, thinking there was that word sensible again. She set aside her soup bowl for the serving maid to remove. Realising that if she did not make conversation it was likely that the rest of the meal might pass in an uncomfortable silence, she forced herself to say, 'Tell me about your house, Jack.'

For a moment she thought he was not going to answer, but then he looked across at her and said, 'At the moment that is all it is: a house. I would like you to turn it into a home where a young boy, who is bound to be a little frightened and bewildered once in England, will in no time at all stop feeling an outsider and start feeling this is where he belongs.'

His words touched the mother's heart within her and she questioned if that had been Jack's intention. She did not blame him if it was, because she would have done all in her power to provide for her son's needs in such circumstances.

There was a knock at the door and Jack called, '*Entrez!*'

The serving maid entered with their next course and took their bowls away. After that they ate in silence and to her disappointment he made no more mention about his house. She wondered if he was regretting his proposal, but could not see why he should do so. He needed her help.

When she had finished eating she asked Jack to excuse her, saying that she was tired. He agreed that it must have been a tiring few days for her and asked how she had got along with Raoul. 'Better than I expected,' she answered. 'He was all kindness. Now if you'll excuse me, Jack?'

She left him alone and was shown upstairs by one of the maids to a bedchamber. She had not lied to Jack. After two days' travelling she was weary, and due to her concern for him she had not slept well in the inns where she and Raoul had spent the two nights on the road. So she undressed and climbed into bed.

She lay on her back, gazing up at the ceiling, thinking over Jack's proposal and the days spent in his company. They had been filled with the unfamiliar, interesting sights and excitement, as well as fear, sadness, pain and sensual pleasure. She would carry away with her many memories, but most of all she would never forget that it was here that she had learnt so much about herself and what was important in her life. If she married Jack, there would be pleasure to be had in the marriage bed and she felt confident that she would be able to organise the household to his satisfaction. She had been in his company long enough to know they shared certain similar interests which boded well for their future. Most of all she could give his son the love he needed.

She rolled over on to her side and closed her eyes. She would accept his proposal. It would have given her much joy to have Jack's love, but she must be content, knowing that she was doing what she believed to be right for the three of them.

When later she rose and went downstairs there was no sign of Jack. She presumed he had gone to visit Hortense and Philippe. For a moment she was tempted to go to the house, but knew that she must allow father and son this time together without her. She must also leave it to Jack to decide matters concerning their departure without her interference.

That evening Anna and Jack had supper with Raoul. She asked her half-brother what his friend had had to say about her parchments.

'He showed great interest and made an offer.'

Jack looked surprised. 'You have the parchments with you?'

'Aye. When I knew we were coming to Amiens, I thought it possible that an opportunity might arise to find a buyer. So, what is your opinion?'

'You haven't told us the sum he offered,' said Jack.

Raoul lowered his head and brought it close to theirs and whispered an amount. Jack whistled and even Anna was impressed. 'Accept it,' she said. 'I would like some of the money in French coin, the rest can be paid by banker's draft into one of Jack's banks. I'm sure he has one somewhere in Europe.'

Jack said curtly, 'I cannot accept.'

'It's the most sensible answer,' insisted Anna. 'I cannot carry such a large sum of money on my person.'

'You're very trusting of this knavish fellow,' said Raoul, a twinkle in his eye.

'Indeed. And I have not forgotten your commission, Raoul,' said Anna hastily.

He protested. 'It is a pleasure to be of help to you, Anna.'

She smiled and wagged a finger at him. 'Just because we are related, it does not mean that I expect you to work for me without being paid.'

She glanced at Jack. 'I deem I could get very interested in trading if it is this profitable and exciting.'

'Printing is where it's going to be worth invest-ing your money in the future, Anna,' said Raoul. 'Would you not agree, Jack?'

'Certainly,' he replied, toying with the stem of his goblet. 'But it is not for the faint-hearted and requires patience, cunning and a great deal of tact with some customers.'

Raoul agreed.

After that the conversation was conducted by the two men. It was about the new printing presses and a Londoner called William Caxton, who had held the position of Governor of the English Nation of Merchant Venturers in the Low Countries until recently. Jack had made no mention of Hortense or Philippe and Anna wondered why, but did not like to interrupt the men's conversation by asking. So, instead, she excused herself and went to bed.

The following morning Anna woke early and dressed and went downstairs. She was relieved to find Jack alone in the parlour. He was pacing the floor, but stopped as soon as he became aware of her presence. He did not beat around the bush, but said, 'Have you made your decision?'

She nodded. 'Indeed, I have. I accept your

proposal, Jack.' His face lit up and she smiled. 'It seems to me the most sensible course for both of us to take. As long as you have no more secrets up your sleeve. For instance, I would like to know how matters went with Hortense and Philippe?'

'Of course. It went pretty much as I expected. The boy is still nervous of me and so I told Hortense that I had asked you to marry me. I thought that might make Philippe easier in his mind if he believed that you were to stand in place of his mother. I hope you didn't mind my doing so?'

'Of course not! I want to make both you and Philippe as happy as possible.'

Jack brought her against him and pressed a hard kiss on her mouth. 'Thank you, Anna. So shall we make our vows?'

'You mean now?'

His face fell. 'I thought it would be most sensible. Will you agree to take me as your husband from this day forth?'

Of course it was sensible, she thought, so agreed. 'I will. Do you agree to take me as your wife from this day forth?' she asked, her lips humming from his kiss.

'I do. It will make our sleeping arrangements so much simpler on the road.'

'Of course, you're right. It is eminently sensible,' she said with a sigh.

Jack sensed he had made a mistake. 'Unless…?' He stopped abruptly.

'Unless what?' asked Anna, gazing up at him.

'You would prefer to wait until we reached England?'

'That certainly would not be sensible,' she said, realising just how much she wanted to share his bed as soon as possible. 'But why do you ask when we have already agreed and have taken each other as husband and wife?'

'It suddenly occurred to me that you might want to have Kate and the family present to witness our vows. Perhaps you would like to have a proper ceremony with a new gown and women to attend you. To have flowers in your hair?' He touched a stray red-gold curl. 'To have bride cakes baked. If that is so…then I am prepared…to wait…on your convenience.' His voice came to a haltering stop.

Anna had not given thought to any of those things, but now she did and hastened to reassure him, adding, 'If we waited until we get to England, who is to say how long it might take to gather all the family together? I think we should invite them to a celebratory feast and I should like to have a priest bless our union, but right now that is out of the question. But we should have someone to witness us take our vows.'

Jack surprised her by seizing her by the waist and swinging her up into the air. 'Well said, Anna! Your words prove to me that I made the right decision in asking you to marry me.'

She laughed. 'I am glad you think so. Now put me down. You are making me dizzy.'

He did what she asked, but did not instantly set her free, just stood gazing down at her. 'I will make certain you won't regret your decision, Anna,' he said softly.

'I pray, too, that you have no regrets.'

'I'm certain that I won't. Now let us break our fast; as soon as Raoul makes an appearance, we will tell him our news and repeat our vows in his presence.'

She nodded.

Jack would have liked to have drawn her close and kissed her again, but already she was separating herself from him. She walked over to the table. 'Will you now accept the money for the parchments being paid into your bank?'

'I suppose I must.' His eyes were thoughtful. 'But you must have my ring to wear on your finger, Anna.'

She nodded, realising this would mean removing Giles's ring. She took it off without any show of reluctance and placed it in a concealed pocket in her gown.

Jack looked relieved. 'I will buy you a new one this very day.'

There was a sound at the door and Raoul entered the parlour. 'You have not yet broken your fast?' He stifled a yawn.

'As you can see,' said Jack. 'We will eat soon, but first, *mon ami*, I must tell you our news. Anna and I have agreed to be husband and wife. We hope this meets with your approval and ask if you would witness our vows?'

Raoul's eyes lit up. 'I am delighted to hear such wonderful news. From the moment I saw you both together, I decided that you would suit.' He clapped Jack on the back and kissed Anna on both cheeks.

'We will ratify our agreement with a blessing ceremony and a lawyer once we are settled back in England and can gather our family together,' said Jack.

'It would be good, Raoul, if you could join us,' said Anna, smiling at him.

'I am not as certain of that as you, Anna. I am my father's son and I doubt I would be welcome.'

'You consider us less gracious in England than here in France?' she asked in a sad voice.

'The circumstances are different, Anna. Besides, am I not here now to witness your vows and will I not share a wedding breakfast with you?' His face eased into a smile. 'I presume in the circumstances you will not be needing me for the bedding ceremony?' he said with a wicked gleam in his eye.

'Definitely unnecessary,' said Jack, remembering those heart-racing moments in his friend's garden. He turned to Anna. 'Shall we now repeat our vows?'

She nodded.

He took her right hand in his own and repeated the simple vows that he had made to her earlier. Then she did the same before they exchanged a kiss and smiled at each other. Her smile reminded Jack of the carefree girl he remembered from years ago. Whistling cheerfully, he left the parlour to order breakfast.

Anna followed him with her eyes and found herself praying that one day their marriage would be a true union of body, heart and soul.

Over breakfast, Jack and Anna agreed that they must visit Hortense and inform her of their marriage. 'I shall tell her that we will be leaving on the morrow,' said Jack. 'I see little point in delaying our departure.'

'You do not think he should have time to get to know us better?' asked Anna.

Jack hesitated and then shook his head. 'He will get to know us better by spending whole days in our company and he might as well do that as we journey home. Being parted from Hortense and his home was always going to be difficult for him.'

Anna did not argue with his reasoning. She could only do her best to be there to comfort Philippe. So after they parted from Raoul, who was to meet with his friend Jules to arrange the transfer of monies in exchange for Anna's parchments, they set out for Hortense's house. Anna guessed that it would be just as painful for the Frenchwoman to part with Philippe as it was for him to say goodbye to her.

Soon after they had arrived at the house and informed Hortense of their marriage—news that she appeared to be delighted to hear—Jack told her to pack Philippe's belongings ready for the journey to England the next morning. Anna could tell that news came as a shock to her.

'So soon!' she exclaimed.

'I have been away from my home six years, Hortense,' said Jack gently. 'There is much work for me to do there.'

'I understand,' she said, sighing. 'But I tell you now there is little in the way of clothing for me to pack for Philippe. He has only one other set of clothes, for he grows apace.'

Jack stared at his son who had been sitting listening to them and noticed that he looked ashamed. He was dressed plainly in a well-worn linen shirt, a darned homespun woollen tunic, hose and wooden sabots.

'He must have some new clothes,' said Anna.

Jack agreed. He felt shamed by his son's obvious embarrassment and wanted to explain that it was not Philippe's fault. 'But where can we get new clothes for him at such short notice?' he asked.

'True. Perhaps Hortense knows of a used clothes-dealer, then you can provide her with coin to purchase some decent garments for him. He will also need boots. When we reach England he can be measured up for some new ones,' said Anna.

'An excellent notion,' said Jack, pleased.

Turning to Hortense, he told her of Anna's suggestion and handed over a purse and told her to buy what was needed. He was aware of the change in his son's expression as he listened to his words. Hortense beamed at Jack. 'I know of an excellent dealer. I will take Philippe to see him immediately. I will make you proud of him.'

'We're already proud of him, aren't we, Jack?' said Anna in French, smiling at the boy.

He nodded. 'We will come for you in the morning, Philippe. This day we thought you might like to spend with Hortense or your friends.'

'The lady is to be my new *maman*?' blurted out Philippe, looking at Anna.

'I am,' she said firmly. 'You will like being on the ship and living in England, Philippe. You will see.'

Philippe shot his father an uncertain glance and then he lowered his head and mumbled, 'I have never been on a ship before. What if it were to sink—who would save me?'

'It's not going to sink,' said Jack, startled.

'But if it did?' persisted Philippe.

'Then your papa would save you,' said Anna, bobbing down so that her face was on a level with Philippe. 'He is a brave man. He saved me when I fell from my horse and a man attacked me. More than once he has rescued me when I was in trouble.' She brushed back the boy's brown hair. 'I know you will be brave like your papa. You are going on a big adventure and there will be lots of exciting sights to see.'

He squared his shoulders. 'I will be brave.'

'Good.' She smiled and kissed his cheek before straightening up. 'Then we will see you on the morrow.'

Philippe nodded. Jack hesitated, then kissed his forehead and took his leave of Hortense.

As Anna and Jack walked through the bustling streets they were silent. The enormity of what lay ahead was giving them both cause for much thought. 'We should buy Hortense a bride gift from Philippe,' said Anna suddenly. 'Do you know of a goldsmith's shop where we could do so?'

He nodded. 'How thoughtful you are, Anna. I forgot to thank you for boosting my image in the eyes of my son. Do you really consider me as brave as you said?'

She laughed. 'Of course I do! You think I would speak falsely to your son? He needs to know the kind of man you really are.'

'I am not always brave, Anna,' he said with a sigh. 'But I will try to live up to your belief in me.'

'I should have also told him that under that stern exterior of yours beats a generous heart.' She squeezed his hand. 'Now Hortense. I thought she might like a bracelet or a brooch. A keepsake from Philippe.'

He grinned. 'Is it that you speak of my gene-rosity so as to get me to spend lots of money?'

Anna's eyes twinkled. 'Of course.'

Jack lifted her hand to his lips and kissed it. 'We both jest. But there are several goldsmiths here in Amiens and we will do what you say. I will also give Hortense a sum of money in appreciation of what she has done for me in keeping my memory alive so Philippe did not forget me.'

Holding Anna firmly by the hand, he led her through the city streets to the goldsmiths' quarter. Inside one of the shops they were shown a variety of brooches. Jack asked her opinion of several of them and she picked one that resembled flowers and leaves.

'You have excellent taste, Anna,' he said. 'The goldsmith tells me that the lords and knights of the English army frequented his establishment and admired pretty pieces like this one.' He turned back to the vendor and spoke rapidly in French. The man smiled and went and unlocked a display case and brought forth a tray of ready-made gold rings. 'Now, Anna, it is your turn. You must pick a wedding ring,' said Jack firmly.

Thrilled that he had remembered his promise, she gazed down at those rings displayed on the tray. Three were made of plain gold and one was patterned with grapes and leaves. The fifth was intricately designed and reminded her of a Celtic ring made of silver that she had seen in Caernarfon, formed of flowing knots. 'I like this one the best,' said Anna, pointing to it.

Jack gave a nod to the goldsmith and the ring was handed to Anna. 'If it doesn't fit, then I am sure it can be altered in time. You must have the one you want,' he said.

'It is very pretty,' she murmured, inspecting it more closely and musing on what the knots symbolised. Yet she hesitated to put it on.

'Is something wrong, Anna?' he asked,

She lifted her head and gazed from beneath her eyelashes at him, feeling suddenly shy about voicing what she wished him to do.

'Here,' he said, plucking the ring from her fingers. He took her hand and slid the ring on to the third finger of her right hand. 'There, it is a perfect fit.'

Indeed, it was and that, for Anna, was symbolic. But she did not speak her thoughts aloud, only hoping that they would come true.

Chapter Twelve

Jack paid for the purchases and they left the shop.

'Where next?' she asked.

He raised an eyebrow. 'Where do you wish to go?' She gazed towards the soaring towers of Notre Dame Cathedral, but did not speak. Jack sighed. 'If we must.'

'Why do you say that, Jack?' she murmured. 'Is it that you blame God for what happened to you?'

He did not answer. 'We will go to the cathedral and then we will return to the inn and eat. Hopefully we will see Raoul there. I must pay him for your horse.'

'I can pay for my own horse,' she retorted.

'Indeed, you will not,' he growled. 'You are my wife now and I will provide for you.'

She opened her mouth and almost blurted out that he had not bedded her since they made their vows so their agreement could be dissolved.

Immediately, she was ashamed of herself. How could she think such a thought when she wanted to be with Jack and to have him make love to her? She also wanted to see him laugh more.

Once inside the cathedral, Anna gazed with interest at the cathedral's painted walls and was struck dumb by the soaring magnificence of the nave. Jack had been inside the cathedral before, so he was looking for something else. It was here that Monique had wept over her sins and he had tried to comfort her. Eventually, he had persuaded her to walk the labyrinth with him, but she had given up halfway. He went over to the design in the floor and, whilst Anna was gazing up at the roof, Jack was staring intently at the tiles.

Suddenly, she became aware that he had wandered from her side, and looked about her. Then she saw him and watched, wondering what he was doing as he traversed this way and that, his eyes fixed on the floor. She walked over to him and noticed a strange pattern in the tiling and was curious as to its meaning. 'Jack,' she called in a low voice.

A moment ago he had appeared completely absorbed, but now he lifted his head and gave her a smile. 'Have you seen one of these before, Anna?'

She shook her head. 'I was about to ask you its meaning,' she whispered.

'It's a labyrinth, similar to a maze. Betwixt Milburn and my home in Hull, there is an ancient maze out in the open. It is believed to have been used to trap evil spirits during ritual dances. Matt and I were caught out there during a storm one afternoon. He swore he felt a presence that sent shudders down his spine.'

'Did you feel it, too?'

Jack grinned. 'Of course I did. Later, I believed it was only because he had put it in my mind and that the heaviness in the air was caused by the storm.'

'But surely this labyrinth set in the floor is not meant to trap evil spirits?'

'No. It symbolises the Christian life and the hard path to God. Most folk cannot go on pilgrimage to far lands, so by meditative prayer whilst walking the labyrinth, one tries to reach God. I came in here with a demon riding on my back and then I remembered this being here.' He touched his cheek. 'This scar—do you hate it?'

She wondered why he should choose that moment to ask such a question. She reached out and traced its snaking length with a gentle finger. 'I thought I had already made clear that it does not bother me. It is part of the Jack I know now, so why should I hate it?'

He pressed her hand against his cheek and held it there. 'It's ugly. Covered it's invisible, so I could pretend it's not there,' he rasped.

'But it won't go away, Jack. You have to accept it and stop worrying about what others think of you.'

'But Philippe, he—'

'He will become accustomed. I said earlier that it is the inner man that is important. You must show him that man more and more.' She took his hand and placed it against the tiny scar on her face. 'I deem you would persuade me that this tiny scar does not matter. Yet it reminds me that there are those in England who still believe me to be a witch. I have to try hard not to let what they said about me matter.'

He stroked her cheek. 'But you're not a witch.'

'Of course not. But my mother was a wanton and my father a murderer. I do have bad blood.'

He scowled. 'Nonsense. We have touched on this matter before and you are not like them.'

'I—I enjoyed you making love to me and we were not wed,' she whispered in his ear. 'Does that make me a wanton?'

'Not in my eyes. It is a sign of your...' His voice trailed off as he became aware that they were being watched. 'Come, let us get out of here.'

Anna wondered what he had been about to say. A sign of her what? But she could not ask him. Once they were outside, she said, 'I don't know what I might have to face if I return to Fenwick. Despite my belief that Owain is capable of sorting out matters there for me, I cannot be sure that he will be able to do so.'

Jack frowned. 'There is no need for you to fear, Anna. You will not go alone. You are my wife and I will protect you with my life. Now let us go from here. I still have arrangements to make.'

That evening as Anna undressed ready for bed, she wondered what Jack had been going to say. To him her enjoyment of his lovemaking was a sign of...what? He must know that she was fond of him, just as she was certain he was fond of her. So they were not in love, but fondness was a fair basis on which to build a marriage. Yet they were only setting out on their married life and much could go wrong. If aught was to happen to Jack, how would she cope? She felt a sudden shiver of fear and then told herself she was being foolish. Jack was having a final few words with Raoul but she wished her husband here now.

She was gripped by a nervous excitement as she stood naked, fingering her old darned silk night rail. Then she set it aside and reached for the primrose silk shift that she had taken from the armoire at Raoul's house. The garment had spent two days and nights in her saddlebag, but fortunately the scent of lavender had so impregnated the garment that it overrode the smell of horse. As she pulled the garment over her head and let it fall, she enjoyed the sensual feel of the silk against her skin. Suddenly she heard footsteps outside in the passage. Despite her quickening pulse, she resisted the urge to leap into bed and conceal herself beneath the bedclothes as she had done on her first wedding night. Instead, she sat on the side of the bed and began to remove the ribands that fastened her braids.

There was a discreet knock on the door, then it opened and Jack entered the bedchamber. He paused momentarily just inside the doorway and watched her. She tugged at a riband and it came loose, slipping from her fingers and falling on to the bed. 'Is—is all arranged with Raoul?' she asked.

'Aye,' said Jack, approaching the bed. 'Here, let

me do that.' He sat beside her and took hold of one of her braids, pausing to kiss the nape of her neck before swiftly unravelling first one plait and then the other. The red-gold curtain of her hair rippled down over his hands and arms. 'What lovely hair you have, Anna.' His voice was husky. He could not resist lifting the waving mass and burying his face in its scented beauty.

'You think so?'

'I would not say so if it were not the truth,' said Jack, gathering the massed strands of hair in one hand and moving it to one side. He planted tiny kisses down the side of her neck and Anna felt a delicious lethargy creep over her. 'You have beautiful skin, too,' he murmured.

'I'm glad you deem it so,' she said in a throaty whisper.

His fingers had found the bow of the drawstring that gathered the neck of her shift. She felt the ribbon tighten and then loosen before the garment slipped from her shoulders and fell in a huddle about her waist. Her senses were heightened as he slid a hand up her spine and round her waist to lightly touch her breasts. Her breath caught in her throat as his teeth grazed her neck and he slowly turned her around to face him.

'I want to make you happy, Anna.'

'And I you.'

'Then let us join together now.' He blew out the candles and began to remove his clothes.

Anna would have liked to have watched him and was disappointed. 'Why did you kill the light?' she asked.

She sensed his hesitation before he said, 'I thought you might have preferred it. You need not worry about my finding you in the dark. I have an excellent sense of direction.'

'No doubt,' she said drily. 'You are a traveller, after all.'

A light laugh escaped him. 'You would still hear my tales, Anna?'

'Of course. But only when you are ready to speak of them. I would hear of the time you raced camels.'

'I was matched against the finest riders in the city and I won my race. One of my rivals said it was more by luck than any great skill.'

'Of course, you denied that,' she said firmly, delighted that he was opening up to her.

'Aye. Although he would have ground me down if it had not been for my lady. She was jubilant and said that I had the ability to become a great rider. She wanted me to race again, but I had proved my point that I was their equal. Besides, within weeks of that race, she sadly died of an apoplexy. Fortunately for me she left instructions in her will that I was to be given my freedom, saying that I had proved my worth. She left me several jewels of great price. Immediately I sold one and took ship to Alexandria and thence another vessel to Venice.'

'How kind of her. I am so glad that you were not prevented from leaving that country.'

'It was not as easy as I make it sound,' he said ruefully. 'But I had learnt the language and made contacts whilst labouring in her service.'

Anna felt the bed give and the next moment he was lying beside her and had drawn her into his arms. 'Now enough of talking. I want you, Anna,' he murmured against her ear. His tongue darted out and licked her earlobe. She felt a sensual thrill uncurl inside her and then her arms went up round his neck and she was offering him her lips and her body.

This time their lovemaking was a more leisurely affair and she took time in exploring his body with gentle hands and sweet kisses, having in mind his belief that he was ugly. So it was that she felt the scars on his chest and back. The temptation to ask what had caused them was overwhelming, but his tension was such that she resisted and surrendered instead to his caresses that proved to be deliciously satisfying. Afterwards they both fell into a deep sleep.

Jack woke suddenly. He was perspiring and filled with fear, having dreamt that Anna had been snatched away from him and he could not find her. Then he felt her stir against him and his relief was enormous, causing him to question the depth of his feelings for her. He would have liked to have made love to her all over again, but told himself that he must let her rest. He pressed his lips against her naked shoulder and experienced a flood of tenderness. She had given him so much and he was grateful. He turned away from her and lay on his back, planning the day ahead.

Several hours later Anna woke to the realisation that she was alone in the bed. Suddenly she was frightened. Where was Jack? She called out his name. 'I didn't mean to disturb you when I left the bed,' he said, coming towards her.

'It doesn't matter. Is it time to rise?'

'Soon. We will have to make an early start.'

She stretched and yawned. 'How far is it to Calais?'

'Twenty leagues or more. We will need to break our journey. There is an inn in Arras where I stayed years ago.'

'On business?'

'Aye. I had a commission to buy a wall hanging for a very rich customer back home, whilst delivering bales of woollen cloth to sell on behalf of my brother at the fair there. I came along the river in a flat-bottomed boat from the sea. The city is well worth a visit. I am certain you will enjoy seeing it. Hopefully, so will Philippe.'

'I'm sure we both will. Tell me more about it.'

'It used to be in the domain of the Dukes of Burgundy during our wars with France and is well fortified. It has a fine cathedral and the town grew up around the abbey of St Vaast. You will be pleased to know that English is commonly spoken due to the city being close enough to Calais for our countrymen to make their homes there.'

Anna felt the mattress dip as he climbed back into bed. She wondered if he would want to make love again. She had her answer in no time at all, as he drew her towards him. She relaxed, reassured that he had found her satisfactory earlier.

As the light of dawn filled the bedchamber, she

noticed the scars on his back and this time she guessed what had caused them and was horrified.

'Were you whipped as a slave, Jack?'

'To my shame,' he rasped, turning his face away.

'Why should you be ashamed?'

'They treated me as if I was worth less than a dog. You can't imagine what that does to a man, Anna.'

'Oh, I think I can. But you endured, Jack. And I for one am proud of you.' The sight of his back truly shocked her and she wanted to weep for him. 'Did no one anoint them with salve for you?' she murmured, touching the scars lightly.

'Salt! The first time I was beaten they rubbed salt in the wounds.' The words burst from him.

'The pain must have been agonising!' She wrapped her arms round him and let her tears fall.

'Please, don't cry, Anna.'

She rested her face against his poor back and sobbed.

'Anna, please,' he said desperately. 'Don't cry! It's the past. Over and done with. As you say, I endured. I'm here to tell the tale.'

She gained control of her emotions and wiped his damp back with her hair. 'So you are. I'm glad you can see it in that light now.'

Jack turned and took her wet face between his

hands and kissed her gently. He felt far too emotional to speak of his feelings. Instead he said roughly, 'Shall we rise and make an early start?'

She nodded.

They dressed. She donned the blue gown taken from the armoire in Raoul's house. He offered to comb her hair for her. She thanked him and he brought her against him. 'Surely you do not unbraid your hair every night?' he asked.

'No. It is cooler and more convenient when braided.'

He began to bring some order to the red-gold mass of hair. 'Then you did so last night for my pleasure?'

'Aye.'

Her words pleased him and he told her so. She felt appreciated and sensed they had drawn closer. He braided her hair and she coiled it about her head. They did not speak but it was a comfortable silence.

Later they shared a last breakfast with Raoul, who had decided to visit Paris before travelling on to Bruges. Afterwards, he went to the stables with them and watched their horses being saddled. 'You will sell the horses in Calais, Jack, or will you take them to England with you?'

'I will sell them. There is little enough space on

my ship for us and the cargo, without concerning ourselves with horses,' said Jack.

'You should have a bigger ship built,' said Raoul firmly. 'Can I look to see you in London in the spring?'

'I have not thought that far ahead, but maybe in May when the winter storms are over,' said Jack, attaching the saddlebags to his horse.

Raoul took hold of the bridle of Anna's mount and led the horse outside. She followed him out. For a moment they stood, gazing at each other. 'So this is farewell, dear sister,' he said. 'It was a very short visit. But perhaps next time…'

Anna did not know what to say, for she had no idea of Jack's plans. Raoul bent his head and kissed her. 'God grant you a safe journey and much happiness. Do not fret yourself about our father. One must live in the present.'

She wished him Godspeed. He helped her into the saddle and stepped back. He waved to them as they departed in the direction of Hortense's house.

Anna was aware of Jack's gaze upon her and she wondered if he considered her even a little foolish for having come all this way to find her half-brother. Yet if she had not done so, then she and Jack would not be married, so all had turned out well. She wondered what Owain would think when he heard the news. One thing was for certain—he would need to look for another husband for Beth.

Philippe was sitting on the doorstep waiting for them when they arrived at the house. He was neatly dressed in a cream linen shirt, a doublet of brown fustian, black hose and boots. On his head he wore a soft velvet brown hat and fastened about his thin shoulders was a cloak. Beside him on the step was a bundle. He looked on edge and started when Jack dismounted. He called for Hortense.

Slowly, she came out of the house. Her dark hair was wispy about her tear-stained face. 'So you have come for him,' she said.

Jack placed both his hands on her shoulders. 'I cannot thank you enough, Hortense, for all you have done for my son. If you were not marrying Antoine, I would have taken you and the grand-mother with us.'

'*Non*! Impossible.' Hortense gave a watery smile. 'She would never leave Amiens. Besides, you have your wife to be a mother to Philippe now. But take your leave quickly and don't allow him to look back. He cried in his sleep last night.'

A muscle in Jack's throat twitched and for a moment he felt a sense of helplessness as he looked down at his son. Was he doing right taking him away from here? Then he caught Anna's eyes on him and was encouraged.

'It is natural that he will be sad to leave you, Hortense, and you must believe I will bring him to visit you when I can. But before I go, you must have these.' From a concealed pocket he took two pouches. 'One is payment for your provision for Philippe and the other is a bride gift from him.'

A smile broke out over Hortense's face and she opened the smaller pouch first. As she removed the brooch her eyes almost popped out of her head. She kissed it and, seizing hold of Jack's doublet, she kissed him, too, before babbling almost incoherently her appreciation and gratitude.

Watching them, Anna hoped that gift would go some way to ease Hortense's grief. And soon she would be married herself and hopefully have children of her own.

Then Hortense kissed Philippe. 'Go, go, and be happy,' she said in heavily accented English.

Philippe scrubbed at the spot where she had kissed him and did not speak. His father lifted him on to the pillion seat. A sob broke from Hortense and she turned away.

'Let us go quickly, Jack,' urged Anna. 'This is so painful for them both.'

With a final *'Merci et au revoir!'* Jack and Anna rode away from the house. Anna's eyes were on Philippe, who hung his head, not looking this way or that, as they made their way to the city gate. Once outside the walls of Amiens, Anna drew her horse alongside Jack's. He was looking stern. She wondered if he was thinking of Monique. Perhaps there would be times when he looked at Philippe and was reminded of her. Anna knew that she must not be jealous of her memory or it could wreck everything good between them.

Despite the earliness of the hour, some of the English soldiery who had delayed leaving Amiens were on the march. Jack exchanged greetings with two or three of them and whiled away an hour, listening to some of their soldiers' tales. Then their ways parted as Jack wished to make better time. They had travelled some distance before Philippe began to call out questions to Anna in French. She was relieved that the boy had come to life at last, but could not answer all his questions and told him so. 'You must seek answers from your father.' He hesitated to do so, but Jack had already heard the questions and flung answers over his shoulder.

As they approached Arras they could see the cathedral and the towers of several buildings soaring into the sky inside the city walls. It was late afternoon and their journey had passed without incident. Jack wasted no time taking them to an inn that overlooked a large square called Grand Place. Although the innkeeper did not immediately recognise Jack, he appeared to do so after a short conversation and he offered them a bedchamber overlooking the square. 'It is my finest one,' he said.

'Can I have some hot water sent up?' asked Anna.

The man smiled and nodded and handed Jack a key. Immediately he gave it to Anna and told her to go upstairs, whilst he stabled the horses. Philippe hurried after Anna and they were shown to their bedchamber by a serving maid. Anna was pleased to see that the room was as finely appointed as the innkeeper had boasted.

Hearing music, Anna went over to the window and then she beckoned Philippe to join her. 'Come and see,' she said, noticing that a couple of musicians had struck up a tune with pipe and drum in the square. 'Do you like music, Philippe?' she asked.

He nodded, his eyes lighting up.

She watched his thin face. He seemed absorbed in the music as they listened to the men's playing. Then one of them began to sing. When he had finished his song, the music stopped and there was clapping from the passers-by who had stopped to listen. She also clapped and after a moment so did Philippe. Then the other musician began to speak. He spoke in several languages, one of them English. She understood that they belonged to a group of travelling players and were to perform a play that night. A very familiar tale: *Le jeu de Robin et de Marion.*

'Could you hear what was said, Philippe?' she asked.

'*Oui*! I would like to see this play. Do you think Papa would allow it?'

'We will ask him. I do not think he will say no.'

'You ask him,' said Philippe promptly. 'He will say yes to you.'

She knit her brow. 'And you believe he will say no to you?'

The boy shrugged his shoulders.

'But why, Philippe? You are his son and he was very sad when he believed you were dead.'

'He was away a long time.'

'But surely you know now why that was?'

He nodded and turned away, wandering round the chamber with a faraway look in his eyes.

Anna felt that for the moment she had lost him in a similar fashion to that in which she lost Jack at times.

Later when her husband entered the bedchamber, she told him about the musicians performing a play that evening. 'I thought you might consider it suitable entertainment for the three of us to enjoy,' she said, smiling.

Jack nodded. 'If it will help occupy Philippe's thoughts, so that he does not miss Hortense and the grandmother too much this first night, it can only be the good.'

'I had forgotten about the grandmother,' said Anna.

'I don't think she could bear seeing Philippe depart. She had the care of him when Hortense was working at her sewing,' said Jack, gazing across the room to where his son was taking something out of his baggage. 'What has he there?'

She looked and saw that he held a carved wooden manikin.

'Obviously a parting gift from the wood carver,' murmured Anna.

'Perhaps a replacement for the one I bought him when he was small,' said Jack in an odd voice.

Hearing them talking, the boy brought it over and showed it to them. Its arms and legs were jointed so that they could be moved. 'Antoine is very clever,' said Philippe, admiringly.

'I agree,' said Jack, watching him. 'If I'd thought about it I would have commissioned several of these from him. I'm certain my nephews and nieces would enjoy such a plaything.'

'It is still worth bearing in mind, Jack,' said Anna. 'And I don't solely mean as gifts for them. Surely there must be a market in England for these and it would enable us to keep in contact with Hortense. I wonder if he has ever thought of making a Noah's ark with tiny wooden animals? I am certain I have seen such somewhere.'

Jack gazed at her in surprise. 'You're really taking this seriously, aren't you, Anna? But you have not thought about the costs of transporting such playthings. A good English wood carver would prove cheaper.'

Her face fell. 'You are right. I had not thought about that.'

Jack felt uncomfortable for having dampened her enthusiasm and relented. 'It is a sign of your

willingness to please. But there are those customers who would be willing to pay the extra for such
skilled work and to boast to their neighbours that
their children's playthings had come from France
at great cost.'

Her eyes brightened and he thought how easy it
was to make her happy and experienced that tenderness he had felt towards her early that day.

'So it is a notion worth thinking about for the
future, Jack?' she said, her eyes bright. 'I can see
Philippe when he grows to be a man, travelling
here and—'

'You must not plan too far ahead for my son,
Anna,' warned Jack. 'You more than anyone
should know that. Let us live one day at a time.'

She knew he was right, but his use of the word
my in relationship to his son made her only too
aware that Philippe was not *her* son. She was not
a real wife and mother. Her happy mood evaporated and she was subdued as they went downstairs to eat a meal of lamb in a red wine sauce
with onions, beans and mushrooms. She noticed
that Philippe ate with a good appetite and was
thankful for that at least. A lost appetite would
have meant he would lose weight and be more
inclined to sickness.

* * *

Afterwards, they went outside and wandered about the town for an hour or so before returning to the Grand Place in time to see the travelling players setting up their mobile stage on a two-tiered wagon. Philippe stuck close to Anna, but spoke not at all. She realised that he was probably feeling insecure and pining for Hortense and the grandmother.

The musicians struck up a tune. The two she had seen earlier were now joined by a man with a stringed instrument. She thought of her lute left behind on the *Hercules* and prayed that the ship had safely reached Calais.

Philippe surprised both Anna and Jack by beginning to clap his hands in time to the music and his thin boyish features were alight with glee. Jack smiled at Anna over his head and she felt better. She prayed that from now on, they would draw close and could become a real family.

Philippe was half-sleep by the time the play came to an end and, despite his protestations, Jack carried the boy back to the inn on his shoulders. But he left it to Anna to undress his drowsy son and put him to bed. She told herself that it made sense to place the lad in the middle so that he would not fall out. So, with Philippe acting as a buffer between Anna and Jack, there was naught for them to do but to turn their backs on each other and go to sleep.

Hours later, Anna woke to discover she was curled up on the edge of the bed. But it was not her precarious position that had woken her, but Jack talking in his sleep. 'Go quickly! *Allez vite!*' he said loudly. There was a pause, then, *'Ne pas demander aux questions.'*

Anna felt the mattress shift beneath her and a sleepy voice, say, 'Hortense, where are you?'

'Courez! Courez vite!' said Jack.

'Hortense, *Grand-mère!*' called Philippe, sounding frightened.

A knee dug into Anna's back and she fell out of the bed, hitting the floor with a thump. She heard the boy's voice rise to a worrying pitch. She managed to lift herself off the floor and feel around to the other side of the bed.

'Jack, Jack, wake up!' she cried, kneeling at the side of the bed and shaking him.

She heard Philippe yell in French, 'Who is there? Hortense, where are you?' He began to weep.

Jack groaned. 'Philippe!'

Anna had hurt her elbows and knees and winced as she dragged herself up on to the bed. It was plain to her that neither father nor son was aware of what had happened to her. 'Jack, are you awake?'

'Of course, I'm awake. I heard Philippe shouting. What are you doing out of bed?'

'You were shouting. You woke us up,' she explained.

He reached out and drew her close to him. 'Are you all right?'

'Aye. Were you having a nightmare?'

'The one where Philippe is taken away from me.'

'Well, there is no need for you to worry about that any more,' said Anna softly. 'Isn't he here with us?'

'I know that now,' said Jack with a grimace. He was a breath away from kissing her, but knew that once he started doing so he would not want to stop. 'I suppose you'd best comfort Philippe. He's asking for Hortense.'

'I want to go home,' sobbed Philippe.

'Of course you do, sweeting, and you will.' She crawled over Jack and took the boy in her arms.

Jack envied the boy. Yet he understood his uncertainties and the need for reassurance. He realised that he was going to need all the diplomacy that he had learnt in trade and during his years of enslavement in the coming weeks if all was to work out the way he wanted.

An hour or so later Jack was bidding his wife and son to get dressed. 'We must be on our way soon if we want to reach Calais today. Pray God the *Hercules* will be anchored in the harbour. If the weather holds fair then we should be able to set sail on the morrow.'

Chapter Thirteen

It was a relief to both Anna and Jack to find the *Hercules* anchored alongside one of the quays at Calais. Master mariner Peter Dunn's face showed surprise and pleasure at seeing Anna again. 'It's good to see you so soon, Lady Fenwick,' he said.

'And I to see you, Peter,' she replied, accepting his help aboard.

She decided to leave it to Jack to inform him of her changed status and about his son. She took a deep breath of the sharp salty air and watched Jack lift his son aboard and then climb on the deck himself. Philippe looked sullen. She knew that he felt that she had tricked him by saying he would go home. Home to Philippe was still Amiens and she sympathised with him. She overheard Jack asking whether his missive had been sent to his brother and the lady's to Master ap Rowan. Peter nodded. Only then did Jack inform him of his marriage and introduce his son to him.

The mariner did not look as surprised as Anna might have expected. But she reasoned that perhaps Jack was not the only merchant venturer or mariner to have had a woman and children in a foreign port. But she doubted few had sons that they took home with them or introduced another woman to the crew as his wife. Turning towards her, he gave her his hearty congratulations, adding, 'All the crew were expecting you both to come back wed.'

'I'm glad we didn't disappoint them,' she replied, laughing.

Jack said to Peter, 'I need the cabin in the fo'csle tidying up and rearranging for my family, if you don't mind taking the deckhouse cabin.'

'That's fine with me, Master Jack. Is there aught else you want sorting out?'

'Of your courtesy, Peter, if could you bring me my lute and parchments from the drawer in the deckhouse cabin?' asked Anna, looking to Jack to provide him with the key.

'Of course, my lady. I mean, Mistress Milburn,' said the mariner.

Anna was hoping that some music might lighten Philippe's spirits on the voyage. In the meantime she was glad to relax on deck whilst the fo'csle cabin was made ready for them. She bid Philippe to come and sit by her. With a show of reluctance he did so. 'So what do you think of your papa's ship?' she asked. He raised his shoulders almost to his ears and then let them drop. She smiled. 'You're withholding judgement until you have sailed in her?'

He looked puzzled and she realised he had not understand what she meant. 'I mean you have not made up your mind.'

'I thought she would be grander,' he muttered.

'Ahhh! You think that if your papa is rich then he would have a great galleon. Maybe he will one day.'

Philippe's expression changed. 'He would need one if he were to sail west across the Great Ocean,' he said.

'What do you know of the Great Ocean, Philippe?' asked a voice behind him.

They both started and looked up at Jack.

'Well, Philippe?' he enquired.

The boy flushed and lowered his head.

His father frowned. 'Am I an ogre that you are frightened to answer me?'

Anna glanced at her stepson. 'He will not

bite,' she whispered, 'but can tell you many tales about the sea.'

A sigh escaped the boy. 'My friend Tomas says that the earth is flat and if you were to sail west the ship would fall off the edge. But my other friend Pierre, he says that his uncle, who is an apothecary, believes that the earth is round and spins round the sun. If that is so, then what is it that keeps us from flying off?'

Jack drew up a keg and sat down opposite him. 'An interesting question and one that has plagued many a mariner.'

'Have you an answer, Jack, other than it is by God's good grace?' asked Anna.

Jack pulled a face. 'Even with God's good grace the earth, planets and stars must surely follow certain rules.' His steely-blue eyes narrowed. 'As for whether the earth is flat and one could sail west and eventually come to the end of it and fall off, I do not believe it.'

Philippe said eagerly, 'Where would all the water go? It would need an enormous pail to catch it all and who would hold it?'

Jack nodded, managing to keep his face straight. 'Aye. But these are serious matters for a small boy to ponder on.'

Philippe's mouth tightened and he looked very like his father. 'I am not so small,' he said gruffly, springing to his feet and hurrying away.

Jack exchanged grimaces with Anna. 'He's as prickly as a hedgehog,' he said.

'He'll get over it,' said Anna, disappointed that the conversation had come to such an abrupt end.

'You'll have to keep your eye on him,' said Jack. 'I don't want him running away whilst we're tied up here.'

She nodded. 'He mentioned friends. He is going to miss them.'

'So he will. But there is naught we can do about it if he is to sail with us. It's interesting that he has been in discussion about the Great Ocean.'

'The thought of sailing off into the unknown probably appeals to him. Did you never want to discover what lies further west beyond Ireland?'

'There was a time, but that desire has passed.' He smiled at her. 'I am ready to settle down and to leave such ventures to the next generation.'

'Now who is planning Philippe's future?' said Anna, returning his smile.

Jack sighed. 'It is good to look forwards after not allowing oneself to believe that one had a future, never mind considering that of my son.' He stood up and walked away.

Anna thought about what he said and was glad he felt like that.

It was a relief to her when she was told the fo'csle cabin was ready for them to move into and, although it was not much bigger than the cabin she had occupied previously, at least their small family would have some privacy. They were to sleep not in bunks but on pallets in a kind of wooden framework a foot or so high. Their clothes went into a great seaman's chest attached to the floor and a smaller chest swallowed up the rest of their baggage. Peter had handed her lute to her and she plucked at the strings before stowing it away with her parchments. On the morrow she planned on inspecting them and showing them to Philippe, knowing she would find pleasure in doing so. Her own son had been too young to take any real interest in them. It occurred to her that perhaps she should give Philippe one of the parchments for his own to enjoy and keep as an investment.

When she and Jack finally retired to the cabin, they found Philippe asleep and there were tears on his cheeks. She sighed and tucked a blanket in beneath him, hoping that he would not wake until morning. The ship would sail on the early tide.

Jack blew out the candle in the lantern before they lay down to rest. 'No regrets, Anna?' he whispered, facing her.

She could not read his expression. 'About what?' she asked in a low voice.

'About returning to England as my wife and mother to my son?'

She shook her head. 'How do you feel, knowing you are going to have to face your twin with the news? Do you think he will welcome me as his sister?' she asked in a voice barely above a whisper.

'Why should he not? You have much to recommend you.'

She murmured, conscious of Philippe a few inches away. 'I am glad you think so. He might consider it extremely unseemly of me to have persuaded you into taking me aboard your ship.'

Jack shrugged. 'Whilst I am extremely fond of my twin, I do not live under his dictate. Having said that, I want the family ties between us to remain close. It is a shame that his children are younger than Philippe.'

'The Mackillin boys aren't. Perhaps once we

are settled back in England, we can take him on a visit to see them.'

'That's an excellent notion. Do you have any other suggestions to make?'

'I have thought of giving Philippe one of my parchments if you approve,' she said.

'That is extremely generous of you, Anna,' he said, sounding startled.

'I want Philippe to know that I regard him as a son.'

'That is what I want, too,' said Jack, drawing her into his arms and kissing her. 'But leave it until we reach home,' he murmured, longing to make love to her, but not wanting to wake the boy.

Anna guessed what was on his mind. She looked forward to reaching England and sleeping in a proper bed with him, just the two of them, once more.

The voyage to Kingston-on-Hull was very different to the outward journey to France. The sea was much rougher and Philippe showed a worrying tendency in a future merchant venturer to succumb to the *mal-de-mer*. Anna tended him, but he was miserable and several times was convinced he was going to die. Jack assured him that during all his time spent at sea he had never known anyone to die of seasickness. She played her lute and bid Jack tell tales to the boy of his travels and so she learnt of how he had been shipped to Africa and crossed a mighty desert there in chains to be sold in the market place of Arabia. He spoke of the Venetian ship he sailed on and of a battle with pirates. But, of course, that was not the only story that Jack told his son. He spoke often of the markets of Europe, of people and the legends of the various countries, of saints and sinners.

But, although storytelling helped pass those stormy days when they were blown off course, it was a relief when the weather changed, the sun came out and the air was tempered by a light breeze that blew them towards the English coast. With better weather conditions everyone's temper improved and Anna and Philippe were able to spend more time on deck.

Jack expressed concern that his son could not read French, never mind English. 'A condition that must be remedied,' he said, frowning down at the boy.

Philippe jutted his chin, obviously displeased to be found wanting by his father. Even so, he proved willing to learn and soon a start was made on improving Philippe's grasp of the English language and teaching him the alphabet, a task in which Anna helped the boy. Now the sea was calmer and

Philippe had his sea-legs, he also took an interest in the sailing of the ship and navigation. Jack was secretly pleased with his progress, although sometimes his son got into places where he had no right to be and received a scold. This resulted in him muttering that he wanted to go home. Jack and Anna decided to ignore such mutterings.

More than two weeks after leaving Calais, the *Hercules* sailed up the River Humber and into Hull and tied up at one of the quays. Anna was so thankful to see her own country again that she could not wait to set foot on English soil. She brought her baggage on deck and left it there until Jack told her what to do with it. Then she hurried ashore, followed by Philippe. It seemed an age since she had left England. So much had happened that she felt a different person, once more able to cope with the problems that faced her. She gazed about the bustling waterfront, noticing goods piled up on the quayside. She presumed they were there to be inspected, taxed and then removed by cart or wain to warehouses or their owner's homes. The port was larger and busier than she had imagined it to be and she was looking forward to becoming acquainted with the town. Suddenly she felt a hand on her shoulder and looked up into Jack's serious face.

'I'm going to have to leave you, Anna. I must speak to the harbour master and I don't know how long I'll be.'

'Do I wait here for you?'

Jack hesitated. 'No. You could go straight to the house if that's what you'd prefer. I'll have Joseph show you the way.' He turned towards the ship and bellowed an order to the nearest mariner. Then he added, 'Take Philippe with you. I don't want him getting into mischief whilst I'm busy.'

'You're too late,' said Anna with a wry smile. 'Look over there!' She pointed to some piled-up crates.

Jack swore when he spotted his son climbing up them. He shouted to him to come over here. Anna was thankful that Philippe's understanding of English had improved and so he had no excuse for acting as if he did not understand the simplest instructions. In the last few days of the voyage he had learnt some of the mariners' more salty phrases and Jack had had to discipline him for swearing in Anna's company. Naturally, the boy had resented his father's actions and had been prickly towards him ever since.

When Philippe made no move to do as he was told, Jack went along the quayside and fetched him. Anna watched him drag the boy from the top of the crates by the scruff of his neck and scold him. A man suddenly appeared and Anna guessed that he was the owner of the cargo. There followed a brief heated dialogue before the two men shook hands and Jack hustled his son towards Anna. Philippe's expression was sulky as his father thrust him towards her.

'Will there be someone at the house to let us in?' she asked, holding Philippe firmly by the hand.

'You should find William there. He's a retired sailor and I left him in charge. It's likely that you'll find men still working on an extension to the house.' He took a key from a pocket. 'But in case no one is there, here is the key to the house.'

Anna took it and thanked him, saying she would see him later. He gave her a nod before hurrying away. Joe joined her and Philippe. He was carrying their baggage, including her lute. Anna looked down at the boy and indicated that Joe should hand the musical instrument to him. 'Why don't you carry this, Philippe?'

The boy's face brightened and, wrenching himself free from Anna's grasp, he took hold of the lute. When Joe moved off, Philippe walked alongside him. Anna followed them, curious to see the house and hoping that Philippe would settle down soon here in Yorkshire.

They had left the port some way behind them when Joe pointed to a greystone house standing on a knoll. The building backed on to fields. 'That there is Master Milburn's house,' he informed. 'Good view of the river, but yours is a goodly way from the rackety goings-on at the waterfront. Near enough to town, though, to call in every day if needs be.'

Anna gazed at her new home with interest, but could see no sign of labourers and presumed that was because the extension to the building was out of sight on the other side of the house. She was impatient to get there, so quickened her pace. Joe called to Philippe to keep up. Anna paused and looked back at the panting boy and realised he was having a struggle to carry the lute now. Her face softened, for he had not complained.

'Shall I take it now, Philippe?' she asked, reaching for the instrument.

He shook his head and clutched it against his chest. She'd had experience of male pride from a young age, but did not want to risk his dropping her lute.

'Philippe, please give it to me.' She put her hand

on the shaft of the instrument, but he refused to surrender it and muttered something in his own tongue. No doubt he was cursing her, thought Anna, frowning.

She tugged and suddenly he let go of the lute. She did not have a firm enough grip on it and it slipped through her fingers. She let out a cry of distress and bent and picked it up. Part of the decorative wooden inlay round its rim had been damaged and one of the pegs had broken off, so that a gut string hung loose. 'Oh, no!' she cried.

Before she could say anything else, a frightened Philippe ran off after Joe. She gazed mournfully at her precious lute, then picked up the broken peg and hurried after the man and boy, wanting to reassure Philippe that it was just an accident and the lute could be mended. By the time she reached the front gates, Philippe and Joe were out of sight. She pushed the gates wide and went up the path leading to the front door. She immediately became aware of men's voices coming from the rear of the house. She decided to go round the back and see what was going on. The sight that met her eyes filled her with dismay.

There must have been a garden of sorts once, but it had been trampled down. The stable yard was partially concealed beneath blocks of stone, wooden planks, piles of tiles, sand, cement and buckets. Joe and Philippe were standing next to a grizzled-haired ancient with a peg leg. Those three were gazing at a group of men who were arguing. To Anna's surprise she recognised one of them as Jack's twin, Matt. He carried more weight than Jack and looked older, but there was no doubting it was him. It gave her an odd feeling coming upon him so unexpectedly like this. She scarcely knew Jack's brother and, not knowing exactly what her husband had said to him in his missive about her, she was uncertain how to approach him.

Suddenly she noticed that one of the men was looking at her. He nudged the man next to him, who stopped in mid-sentence. It was then that Matt became aware of her presence. She saw his eyebrows shoot up and then he dismissed the men and came over to her.

'Are you who I think you are?' he asked curtly.

The lack of welcome in his voice made her feel as if an icicle had been slipped down the neck of her gown and slithered down her back. 'Who do you think I am?' she asked.

'The Lady Anna Fenwick. What are you doing here? Where's Jack?'

'He has matters to deal with regarding his ship down at the harbour,' replied Anna, tilting her chin. She decided Matt had no right to speak to her in that tone and she was not going to wither beneath it. 'Jack told me to go on ahead. Did you receive his missive? I presume you must have from your mentioning him and me in the same breath.'

Matt looked surprised. 'I received no missive from my twin. When did he send it?'

'The same time as I sent one to Owain. Jack told me that his explained to you some matters he had kept from you, but wished you to know about if aught should happen to him,' she said.

Matt looked baffled. He squared broad shoulders beneath the fine wool of his doublet. 'I know that Owain received your letter. I had a visit from his brother, Hal, and Sir Giles's nephew, Will.'

'What!' Anna paled. 'What did they say to you about me? For I tell you now that they have borne false witness against me before. Their accusations are untrue.'

Matt's expression was uneasy. 'They were worried about you. Concerned about your state of mind because of the depth of your grief after you lost your husband and son. They feared that you were in danger of harming yourself and bringing shame on the family. The only accusation they made against you was that you set fire to your house.'

Anna was astonished. 'I don't believe it! Why should they come to you and tell you this?'

'They said that Jack had taken pity on you and helped you, ignoring their warning that you were a danger to yourself and him. They wanted to seek my help in protecting Jack, suggesting that I come immediately to his house in the hope that he had returned home. I was coming here, anyway, to see how the men were progressing with the building work. So now you know all.'

Anna's mouth fell open. For a moment she did not speak, but then she gathered her wits together and her eyes flashed with annoyance. 'They are both crafty and evil. They hate Jack for coming to my aid and spoiling their plans. Will wanted me dead, believing then he would get his hands on Fenwick Manor. He was furious because Giles had made it clear in his will that if aught happened to our son then I would inherit. I think it was because the dowry that Owain gave to him on our marriage was an extremely large one. Giles left his nephew a goodly sum, but Will was not satisfied.'

Matt's brow knitted. 'Jack can vouch for this? You appear to me to be in your right mind. I just wish I had received Jack's missive.'

'You will be seeing him soon, so he will explain all to you,' said Anna, relaxing a little. 'I only wish that you had consulted with Owain. He would have explained to you the kind of men Hal and Will are. I told him all when I wrote to him.'

'They said your beauty had bewitched Jack.'

Anna laughed. 'Do you believe your twin to be so easily led astray?'

'Jack has a warm heart and an over-developed sense of chivalry,' said Matt seriously.

'I would not deny that,' said Anna, glancing down at Philippe and placing her hand on his shoulder.

Matt stared at the lad and his mouth dropped open. 'That boy! He's the image of Jack! Where did he come from?'

'His name is Philippe and he has come from France,' said Anna. 'But do not ask me any more, for it is up to Jack to explain.'

Matt could not tear his gaze away from the boy. 'So he is the secret that my twin has been keeping from me,' he said angrily. 'I have known for a long time that Jack was troubled in his mind, even before he went missing, but I never thought it would be a child. Come here, lad!' he commanded, holding out a hand.

Philippe did not move, staring at him apprehensively.

Matt made a move towards him. Philippe ducked from beneath Anna's arm and, avoiding his uncle's outstretched arm, ran.

'He's frightened,' said Anna, making to go after him, only to get her lute tangled in her skirts and went tumbling over.

Joe dropped the baggage and both he and Matt bent over Anna and helped her to her feet. 'I must go after him,' she said, freeing herself from their hold.

Anna wasted no more time, but picked up her skirts and ran round the side of the house. She paused a moment on the front path, her eyes searching for the boy. Then she saw him. He was already out of the gateway and had crossed the track towards the river. She hurried through the gates and went after him. He had disappeared into the undergrowth, but she guessed most likely that he would follow the course of the river. But in which direction? Towards the town or away from it?

Then Anna heard a twig snap behind her and she turned. She could scarcely believe her eyes when she saw Hal. She would have run, but it was too late. He moved and cut off her way of escape. Straight away, she realised what he and Will's intention had been in seeking out Matt's help. They had wanted to know where Jack lived and his twin had led them straight to him.

'No mask, Hal? What are you doing here?' asked Anna, scared but playing for time in the hope that Matt and Joe would come after her.

'I saw you arrive. I never thought we'd be so lucky as to have you land on the doorstep so soon,' said Hal, smirking. 'Owain wore the mask, you know. I was with him on the raid to rescue your mother and Kate's brother.' A giggle escaped him. 'You've no idea how exciting it was, hiding in trees with our bows and arrows and all the masked figures below intent on worshipping old Nick. When Owain suddenly appeared out of the Devil's Graveyard, it caused quite a stir. Your mother put a blade through his shoulder, but she received an arrow in the back for her wickedness. She died in his arms. Despite his losing so much blood, he insisted she was taken home to be buried at Rowan.'

'So that is how my mother died,' said Anna, feeling as if everything was unreal.

'Owain killed your father, you know.'

'I know.'

'Oh!' Hal looked disappointed. 'How did you find that out? Did Davy tell you?'

Anna shook her head. 'My half-brother, Raoul, discovered the truth. He was curious to find out how his father met his death.'

'So you have a real half-brother.' Hal did not look pleased. 'I suppose you found that out in France? I wasn't pleased about what you wrote to Owain about me, Anna.' His eyes glinted danger-ously. 'That's when I decided that you and Jack had to pay for what you did. I'm an outcast. I can never return to Rowan.' His hands curled into fists. 'Jack should never have interfered in our plans. I aim to marry you, so I can inherit Fenwick. Will's in favour of it. But he still wants to see you burn. He's even found a place for you. A labyrinth up in the fells, supposed to be a trap for evil spirits.'

'A labyrinth! He must be crazed!'

'It's the sort of place Will gets really excited about. But don't you worry, I won't let him burn you. Once we're married…'

Anna clamped down on her fear and said lightly, 'You're too late to marry me, Hal. Jack and I are married. If aught were to happen to either of us, then his son will inherit Fenwick. You didn't know he had a son, did you?' She smiled.

Hal's expression turned even uglier. 'I don't believe you're married to him and he has a son. You're only saying that to make me change my plans,' he snarled, lunging towards her, only to trip over a tree root and land heavily on the ground.

Anna gazed about her wildly for a weapon. Then suddenly Philippe appeared. He looked scared, but was carrying a broken branch that he handed to her. 'Hit him, *maman!*'

She brought it down on Hal's head. He tried to get up, so she hit him again. The branch snapped, but he had slumped to the ground. She bent over him. Then suddenly she heard Philippe give a warning cry. But before she could turn round she was blinded by a cloak. A knee dug into her back and she was forced to the ground. She yelled to Philippe to run, adding in French, 'Tell Papa, the labyrinth!' She heard Philippe cry out again and then silence. A cord swiftly pinioned her arms to her sides and then she was kicked to one side. She could hear heavy breathing and then a noise as if something was being dragged along the ground. Then there came a splash before she heard the thud of feet again. Terrified that

Philippe had been thrown into the river, she struggled to free herself, but it was useless. She was dragged upright and then slung over a shoulder and carried away.

Jack had finished his business with the harbour master. Doubting there would be much in the way of food and drink in the house and making the decision that Anna was going to need a woman to help her in the house, he decided to go in search of both. So Jack busied himself, hiring servants, a wagon and horses and buying in provisions. It came as a shock to him to be hailed by his brother just as he was setting out for home.

'We've got trouble, Jack,' said Matt, stern faced, reining in his horse next to the wagon.

'What are you doing here, Matt? And what kind of trouble are you talking about? Haven't the men finished? Is Anna vexed with the state of the place?' fired Jack.

'It's not that kind of trouble. It's Anna and your lad. What a secretive fellow you are, brother,' drawled Matt. 'But never mind that now, you have to come quickly.'

Jack said grimly, 'What's happened to them?'

'I'll tell you on the way. Can you get some speed

out of those horses? I don't suppose you can leave the wagon here?' asked Matt.

'God's blood, Matt. Will you explain?' cried Jack, whipping up the horses.

'I suspect Anna's been abducted.'

Jack's heart banged with fright. 'Hal and her husband's nephew, Will?' he croaked.

Matt looked at him in surprise. 'How did you know?' he asked.

'Who else would take her?' Jack felt sick at heart. Only now did he admit to himself just how much Anna meant to him and that he would be lost without her. He had to rescue her. 'Tell me what you know,' he said.

Matt did. Soon the wagon was rattling along the track that led to the house at a fair lick. The passengers clung tightly to the side of the wagon. Jack was heedless of the danger that such speed presented if they hit a pothole or a large stone. Fortunately he drove into the stable yard without meeting with any mishap and jumped down from the wagon as soon as it drew to a halt. He ignored the builders and, flinging a command to Mistress Wainwright, the new cook, to climb down and go into the house and to the manservant to unload the wagon, he left them to it.

He hurried through the opening in the unfinished extension, sparing no glances for the wooden struts overhead that awaited a roof, but crossed the floor of beaten earth to a passage that led to a large, untidy kitchen. Chairs were placed higgledy-piggledy about the room and there were only a few pots and platters on the shelves. A plain scrubbed wooden table had been pushed up against a wall and on it stood a barrel and several tankards. The air struck chill as there was no fire on the hearth and there was dust everywhere. He was followed by his brother. Jack left the kitchen and came out into a passage. He noticed the baggage placed on the floor in the passage and a muscle quivered in his cheek. He passed several doors on his way to the front of the house and threw open another door. The sunlight that poured out of the room almost blinded him and he put up a hand to shield his eyes. Then he saw his son slumped in a chair, looking the worse for wear.

'Philippe, are you all right?' Jack hurried over to him. His son slid from the chair and ran over to his father and flung himself into his arms. His grasp of English had deserted him and he babbled away in French.

Without realising what he was doing, Jack

brushed twig and leaves from his son's clothes and when his boyish tones finally petered out, Jack kissed him. 'You are intelligent and very brave and I am proud of you.'

His son's eyes shone with tears. 'You will find her, Papa. You will rescue *maman* from the wicked man?'

'I will,' said Jack, praying that he would be in time. One word his son had kept repeating: *labyrinth*. Jack had to believe that was where Anna was being taken.

'Can I come with you, Papa?' asked Philippe.

Jack shook his head. 'You must rest. Your uncle will take care of you.' He glanced at his twin.

'You don't want me to accompany you?' asked Matt.

'No. This I have to do alone,' said Jack grimly.

He kissed his son once more before he left him in his brother's care and hurried outside. He saddled up one of the horses in his stable and knew he was going to have to ride like the wind if he was to save Anna.

Chapter Fourteen

Anna was trying to put on a brave face, but she was sick with fear. She had prayed for rescue, hoping Jack would come. She had put her faith in Philippe hearing what she had said and recovering from the blow on his head. At least there was a full moon. She struggled against her bonds. Unfortunately, Will had knotted the cord so tightly there was no give in it. But as soon as they had arrived here at the maze, he had slashed a hole in the material covering her head so she could see what was happening. He had spared her no details as to how he planned to get rid of her, as if she didn't already know he wanted to see her burn. He had told her that Hal was dead. She had wondered aloud if she had killed him. But Will had admitted that he had never been in favour of Hal's plan to marry her and gain possession of Fenwick.

'But Hal, being a big man, I wasn't going to argue with him. I'd come off the worst,' he'd said. 'So when I saw you'd knocked him out, I seized the opportunity to get rid of him.'

'How?' asked Anna hoarsely.

'I dragged him to the river and pushed him in.' Will had laughed. 'He'd have cheated me out of seeing you burn. He wanted you and wouldn't have let you go. Bewitched him, you did.'

'I did not,' cried Anna.

But Will had not been prepared to listen to her. She had asked after the boy and he had shrugged and told her that he'd given him a blow that had stunned him. It did not seem to matter to Will that the boy was Jack's son, unless he was unaware of it. He had gone off collecting wood and had, making torches of kindling, but begun to build up his fire.

Anna was alone with the silence of the fells seeming to press in on her. She could see the bonfire clearly by the light of a couple of flaming torches, for night had fallen by the time they had reached here. Then she heard the squeal of some wild creature and jumped out of her skin. She looked to the torches and their light cast flickering shadows over the maze cut in the turf.

Suddenly she realised that there was something moving out there. Her heart began to thud. If only it could be Jack. Then she heard a sound to her right and Will appeared. He began to come towards her. She could not see his face clearly and he dropped what he carried on the pyre. Then he took a torch and tossed it into the piled-up wood.

The moment she feared had come. Tears blocked her throat as she thought of Jack, wishing that she had told him how much she loved him. Will drew something from his pack. But only when he approached her did she realise he was wearing that devilish mask. Anna screamed.

'You'll burn now,' sniggered Will.

'I think not,' said Jack, riding into the light as the kindling and dry wood burst into flames.

Anna watched in wonder as Jack leapt from his horse and drew his sword. Will gave a muffled curse and produced a dagger. With one swipe of his sword, Jack forced him to drop the dagger. Then he tossed his sword aside and with a roar, went for Will. Pummelling him with his fists, left, right and centre, he finished him off with an upper cut to the jaw. The force of the blow caused Will to spin and, with arms flying, he fell face down on to the fire. She watched in horror as his clothes began to smoulder and tiny flames appeared. His screams were muffled by the mask.

Jack was tempted to let him burn, but, with a curse, hurried forward and, reaching out, dragged him to safety. He smothered the flames with his gloved hands and rolled him over on to his back.

Anna was unable to tear her eyes away as the screeching Will tried to rid himself of the burning mask. The heat from the fire had caused the oil in the paint to melt and then ignite. Jack swore and, reaching out, tore off the mask. She let out a strangled cry. The mask had burnt its devilish impression into Will's face and there was little left of his skin.

Jack dropped the burning remains of the mask in the grass. Picking up Will's dagger, he went over to Anna and slashed her bonds. She fell into his arms and clung to him. Only after a couple of fraught moments did she suddenly become aware that he was holding his arms out straight and not hugging her. Was he furious with her for getting herself into such a dangerous situation? But his kiss rid her of that idea.

A sudden cry brought the kiss to a speedy end. They turned as one and to their amazement saw Will, who had somehow risen to his feet and tried to stagger towards them with his dagger in his hand, felled by Matt. 'You didn't really think I would let you ride into danger without me this time, did you, Jack?'

Anna was speechless. But her husband said, 'Is he dead?'

'I thought I'd best put him out of his misery,' said Matt, wiping the blood off his blade on the grass. 'Besides, imagine the looks he'd get with a face like that, the swine.'

Anna felt Jack's hand brush her side and she thought she knew what he was thinking. 'I love your face,' she whispered.

'I'm glad to hear you say that, but it's not that which is bothering me right now,' he said, wincing.

'What is it?' she asked, taking hold of his wrist. Then her gaze took in the smouldering and half-burnt gloves and, with a cry of dismay, she began to ease it from his hand. Jack gritted his teeth as Anna removed his other glove. She inspected his hands. 'There are several blisters, but hopefully there will not be any lasting damage,' she said in a trembling voice. 'I will anoint them with salve once we get home.'

'Home!' A smile broke over his face that was covered in smuts. 'Our home and that's exactly where I want to be with you, sweetheart.'

Somehow, he managed to place an arm round her and bring her against him.

Anna thrilled to his use of the endearment and lightly touched his cheek. 'What would I have done if you'd fallen into the fire? I would not have wanted to live.'

Jack kissed her fingers. 'I must have been crazed to have dragged the cur from the flames.'

Anna knew exactly why her husband had done what he did. 'It is that warm heart of yours concealed beneath this tough exterior.' She poked his chest.

'I'd say he's crazed,' interrupted Matt. 'I will not mourn him. By the by, what's happened to Hal?'

Jack turned to him. 'I forgot you didn't understand a word Philippe said. He helped Anna knock out Hal, but then Will turned up. He bundled up Anna and prevented Philippe from escaping by hitting him over the head. I don't know what happened to Hal, but he was missing when Philippe regained consciousness and staggered back to the house. He kept repeating *labyrinth* and I put two and two together. He wanted me to save his *maman*.'

Anna felt the warmth inside her grow. 'Like father, like son. I owe my life to you both. Will confessed to me that he pushed Hal in the river.

He only went along with Hal's plan to marry me to gain Fenwick Manor because he was so much stronger than him.'

Jack swore. 'Hal always had his eye on you.'

'He went crazy when I told him we were married.' Anna sighed. 'You don't think he might have regained consciousness and swum ashore?'

'He would have had to do so fairly swiftly. Do you think Will would have allowed that to happen?' asked Jack.

'He left me only for a few moments,' she answered, feeling partly responsible for Hal's death. He had wronged her greatly, but she felt a little sad that the man she had once regarded as a brother had met such a fate and died unshriven.

Jack seemed to read her thoughts. 'You had no choice, Anna. You had to defend yourself,' he said firmly.

There was a silence.

'So what are we going to do with Will's body?' asked Matt.

Jack stared at his twin. 'I suggest you take charge of it. I'm for home.'

Matt sighed. 'Me, too.' He looked down at the dead man. 'I suppose it would be wrong to leave him here for the crows and the foxes, so I'll tie him to his horse and see to his burial.' He glanced at Jack and Anna. 'When can I expect to see you two again? You're welcome to stay at Milburn Manor whilst the building work is being done at your house.'

Jack looked at Anna and she shook her head. 'I'll send a messenger, Matt, when we're ready to come,' he said. 'There are matters we need to sort out.'

Matt nodded. 'I guess you two want to spend some time alone.'

Jack grinned. 'You guess right.'

The twins hugged each other and Anna kissed her new brother. They said their farewells to Matt and watched him ride off, leading the horse with Will's body tied to it. Then they mounted Jack's horse with Anna upfront. She insisted that she take the reins. Jack protested, but she was firm with him. 'This is one of those times when you must allow me to override your command, Jack. It would be foolish to damage your hands further; besides, it would be painful for you.' He submitted to her will and, with his arm looped about her waist, they set off on the return journey.

Jack prayed that Anna had truly meant it when she had indicated that she was prepared to stay in his house and put up with inconvenience of the building work in progress. Perhaps in the coming weeks she might change her mind and prefer to travel south and spend some time in the Palatine of Chester. Whatever her decision, he would agree with it. Besides, they had a lot to discuss with Owain and they would have to arrange a meeting with Anna's man of business to decide what to do with Fenwick Manor.

There was also the matter of the legal side of their marriage to be sorted out, arrangements to be made for the Church's blessing and a celebration with the family. The difficulty about such a gathering was not only getting them altogether with winter drawing near, but the unfortunate matter of Hal. Despite what Jack had said to Anna about the unlikelihood of Hal surviving being pushed into the river, he would not feel easy in his mind until his body was found. Only then would he be able to accept that the threat to Anna was finally lifted.

The house appeared to be slumbering in the early morning sunshine when they arrived back at the house. They rode into the stable yard and dismounted. Jack frowned because there were no men working on the extension and all was quiet.

'Perhaps they've taken a day off or they might be in the kitchen,' suggested Anna, leading the horse towards the stable and thinking she had yet to see the interior of her new home.

Suddenly they heard a door open in the house and a moment later Philippe came out into the yard. His face was alight with relief. 'Papa, it is you! And you have my lady mother with you.'

Anna gave Jack a pleased look and then smiled at her stepson. 'Aye, your papa came to my rescue.'

'He is brave, yes?' said Philippe, grinning.

'Extremely brave,' said Anna, glancing at Jack's hands.

'Where's Joe, Philippe?' asked Jack, considering the conversation boded well for their future.

The boy's expression altered and he informed them in a mixture of French and English that Joe had found a body lodged in the weeds in the river and he had gone to report it to the constable in the town. 'I like Joe. But I prefer it that you two are here with me. Do you know there is a *grand-mère* here? She makes apple tarts and they are delicious.' He licked his lips. 'Also, there is William— he tells me stories about when he was a mariner. He speaks French.' Philippe looked at Anna and then at his father. 'What happened to the other bad man? You kill him with your sword?' he asked with relish.

Jack said with a wry smile, 'What a bloodthirsty boy you are. But, aye, he is dead. Now tell me, where are the men who were working on the house?'

'Two are inside and two others have gone to keep an eye on the body.' He gazed up at his father and said eagerly, 'Will you be going to see it? May I come with you?'

'Certainly not,' said Jack with a faint smile. 'You are a ghoul, lad.'

'I suppose I should have a look at it,' said Anna. 'After all, it might not be Hal.'

Jack said, 'I think it's more likely to be him than not, sweetheart. You go inside with Philippe and wait for me there. I'll go and look.'

She did not move. 'I'd rather come with you, Jack. I want to see for myself if it is Hal.'

Anna thought he was going to refuse her. But then he nodded. 'All right. Come with me.'

'Let me come as well?' asked Philippe, holding his head to one side and pulling a face.

Anna laughed. It seemed the wrong thing to do in the circumstances, but she could not help it. The boy looked so comical. 'You can come, but you must stay at a distance,' she said.

He smiled and slipped his hand into hers. 'I am sad that your lute was broken. But we fix your lute,

Papa and I. In the house there is a fine miniature sailing ship. William, he tell me that Papa made it.'

Anna glowed at Jack. 'Can you fix my lute?'

'I'll have a good try and, if I can't, then you shall have a new one from Venice,' said Jack.

He headed towards the river, followed by Anna and Philippe.

They found the labourers, sitting on the bank a few yards from the body. Anna could scarcely believe her eyes when she saw that one of them was fishing with a hand line.

'I won't pay you for doing that,' said Jack, frowning. 'It doesn't need two of you to watch a dead body. Get back to work. I want the roof on and a door to the extension by the end of the month.'

'But that's only a week away,' protested one of the men.

'I'll pay you all twice as much if you get it done,' said Jack. He turned to his wife. 'Now, Anna…'

She nodded, and taking a deep breath, walked over to the body. Her face blanched as her eyes gazed down at Hal, then she averted her face. 'May God have mercy on his soul,' she said, crossing herself.

Then she hurried away.

Philippe glanced at the body and then at his

father before rushing after her. The boy helped Anna unsaddle the horse and she gave him the task of fetching the beast some water and fodder. Jack entered the stable and gazed at her.

'Are you all right?' he asked, looking concerned.

She nodded, although she was feeling unlike herself. But that was understandable in the circumstances. Jack put an arm about her shoulders, 'Come on, Anna, let's get you inside the house. You need to rest.'

She allowed herself to be ushered indoors. The first room she entered was the kitchen. She expected to see building dust, so she made no comment about it to the woman of middle years, who introduced herself as Mistress Wainwright. Philippe's so-called grandmother, she presumed.

Jack watched with a mixture of anxiety and pride as Anna asked after the woman's health and then discussed what they were to eat for dinner before ordering that warm water, drying cloths and bandages be sent up to their bedchamber. Then he hurried his wife out of the kitchen and to the room that he considered the best in the house, glad that the sky was not overcast. He so wanted her approval of his home.

The parlour was full of light and Anna felt her

spirits lift. She realised the brightness was due to there being three windows in the room. She walked over to the largest and gazed through the glass and thought she caught a glimpse of the river in the distance. The other two windows were set in the side wall and were also glazed. She reckoned the glass was of the expensive Flemish kind, worthy of a rich merchant venturer's home. There were shutters outside and she imagined them to be very necessary during the winter storms.

'What do you think of this room?' asked Jack.

She looked at him and saw the need for reassurance in his eyes. She remembered her house at Fenwick and thought how different it was from this one. Her gaze roamed the room. A fire burned on the hearth, giving out a goodly heat. She noted that the walls were limewashed and hung with several charts and sketches of seascapes. It was comfortably furnished with a settle and cushioned chairs, as well as a polished table and side cupboards with shelves above. On top of a seaman's chest stood the model of a sailing ship that Philippe had mentioned. She went over and lightly touched a miniature sail.

'You have skilful fingers, Jack,' she said. 'Which reminds me…'

'Your lute?' he said.

'No!' But she had spotted her broken lute on a window sill. She went over and picked it up, waking the sleeping cat curled up beside it. She placed the instrument on a different window sill. Her green-brown eyes met Jack's steely-blue ones and she smiled. 'I like this parlour, but now I need to see our bedchamber...and I need my saddlebags.'

'Most likely they have already been taken up,' said Jack, leading the way out and along the passage and upstairs. 'You will probably wish to make changes, Anna. It is very much a man's bedchamber.'

Anna smiled. 'That will not come as a surprise to me, Jack. Be careful of your hands,' she said, touching his arm lightly as he stopped in front of a door.

It was she who flung it open. The bedchamber was not as filled with light as the parlour, but that was because there was only one window and the room was naturally not as large. Even so, she liked what she saw. Despite what Jack had said, she could find few faults with its furnishings of light oak. As for the bed, she had never seen one so large. Of course, the room needed a few feminine touches, but they should not prove difficult to obtain.

To her relief, she saw that her order had been in-

stantly obeyed for there, on a small table, were
bowls, hot water and cloths. She noticed their saddlebags in a corner and went and opened one and
removed from it a jar of salve. She ordered Jack
to sit down on the bed.

He raised a dark eyebrow. 'My clothes are filthy
and so are yours.'

'So they are,' she said with a saucy smile.
'Perhaps we should remove them.'

'Anna!'

She blushed. 'You deem me forward? A wanton?' she asked anxiously.

He grinned. 'No. It's just that I might have difficulty taking mine off.'

'Of course,' she murmured.

Without more ado, she first removed her own
boots and hose and then she proceeded to remove
his. She pretended to be unaware of his arousal,
but even so she could not resist trailing her fingers
down the length of his naked thigh. She felt the
long, strong muscles quiver and caught the sound
of his indrawn breath. She guessed that if his
hands had not been blistered and sore he would
have pulled her on to his lap. Swiftly, she removed
his doublet and then unfastened his shirt to fling
them in a corner. He was still wearing a garment

that covered his manhood and she told him to sit
down on the bed again.

He did so, watching her intently with a faint
smile on his face. She poured water into a bowl
and dampened a cloth. As she cleansed his hands,
not a word of complaint passed his lips. Yet it was
obvious to her that he was in pain. That task done,
she wasted no time in anointing the blisters with
dollops of salve and then bandaging his hands. No
sooner had she done so than he reached out and
seized her skirt. He drew her back towards him
and pulled her on to his knee.

'Now you must behave sensibly, Jack,' she teased.

His lips twitched at the corners. 'I don't see
how I have any other choice.'

'I suppose not.'

He tickled her bare foot with his big toe.

'Jack, you're distracting me.'

'From what?'

'I must find us some clean clothes.'

'Later,' he said. 'Now remove the rest of your
clothes.'

'We must be sensible, Jack,' she said with a
sparkling glance.

The look in his eyes caused the breath to catch
in her throat and she leaned forward and kissed

him. He returned her kiss with such passion that it immediately set her whole body on fire. She had to force herself to bring the kiss to an end. 'We must desist. Your hands…'

'You started it, sweetheart.'

'I know, but…'

He tickled the side of her face with his tongue. 'Where there's a will, Anna, there's a way. I confess that from the moment you set foot on my ship, you undermined my resolution. You showed me there was still so much to enjoy in this world and you gave new meaning to my existence.' He took her hand and raised it to his lips. 'I was a fool not to realise how much you meant to me earlier than I did. I made a mess of asking you to marry me, because I didn't want to accept that I could love you as much as I do. That you could love me.'

'You don't have to explain to me, Jack. I felt the same,' she said earnestly.

'I wanted you for so much more than as a mother for Philippe.' His voice was raw with emotion.

'I didn't marry you because I wanted another son. I wanted to be so much more to you. That evening in Raoul's garden was a revelation to me. I never thought I could experience such delight.'

He grimaced and gazed at his bandaged hands.

'I suppose you consider yourself safe from my attentions with my hands bound.'

'Safe?' she murmured. 'I always feel safe when I am with you, Jack.'

She could not have made him feel better about himself. 'Take your clothes off, Anna, and remove my last garment. I'm going to place myself in your hands.'

She instantly undressed and stood unashamedly naked before him. She could tell from his eyes that the sight of her pleased him. But she was willing to comply with his wishes further, so she removed the last of his nether garments.

After the manner in which they had spent the last twenty-four hours, she expected neither of them to be filled with vigour. She found delight in exploring his body with slow sensitive fingers, kissing his scars and caressing that most manly part of him.

'You are an exceptional man,' she breathed softly.

'And you, a most excellent wife.' He stilled her hand by pressing one of his bandaged ones over it. 'Now perhaps I can prove to you just how exceptional I am,' he said with a chuckle.

He proceeded to do so in ways that revealed to her that he did not need the use of his hand to bring her to a pitch of pleasure that had her crying out for more. More was exactly what he gave her before joining with her and carrying them both to the realms of such exquisite delight that even when they lay in each other's arms afterwards, their bodies still glowed with the remembrance of it.

'I deem I'm going to be happy here,' said Anna.

Jack said anxiously, 'You don't want to go and live elsewhere while the men finish the extension? There'll be noise and dust and inconvenience.'

'No,' said Anna, smiling. 'I have you and Philippe and a home. What more could I want?'

Jack knew what he wanted for her. He could never replace the son she had lost, but they could have a child of their own. A brother or sister for Philippe. He looked forward to that day.

Epilogue

August, 1476

Jack popped his head through the bedchamber doorway. 'Are you ready, Anna?'

She had her back to him and raised an arm, fluttering her fingers at him. 'I won't be long.'

He came further into the room and closed the door behind him. He moved into a position where he could see his wife placing their daughter in her cradle. 'I wonder why we never thought of having a daughter,' he mused, perching on the bed.

Anna smiled at him. 'I suppose we had it fixed in our heads that she was going to be a boy.'

'You weren't disappointed, were you?' he asked hesitantly.

'Were you?'

He shook his dark head and, leaning forward,

planted a kiss on his wife's mouth and then on Tabitha's reddish-brown hair. 'She reminds me of her mother.'

Anna laughed. 'How can you possibly say that? I doubt if I was ever as pretty as she is. Besides, she has your eyes.' She rubbed her cheek against her daughter's rose-petal soft skin. 'I'm glad Philippe approves of her.'

'He adores her. A sister is special. He's already boasting about her to the Mackillin boys,' said Jack. 'I'm glad they were able to come.'

'And the rest of the family. It's a pity Raoul can't be here,' she said.

'We did see him in London in the spring.'

That was true. They had also visited the ap Rowans and her man-of-business in Chester and made the decision to sell Fenwick Manor. She had decided to sever all ties with that place and its sad and frightening memories. Part of the money had been used to help towards the cost of building a larger ship and the rest was in trust to provide Tabitha with a dowry when the time came. Most important of all was that they were secure in each other's love.

'You look bewitching,' said Jack.

Anna smiled. 'You like my gown for the blessing ceremony?'

'Indeed, I do.' He took her hand and twirled her round.

The material was expensive cotton imported from the East to Italy and specially woven in Lombardy before being dyed a deep blue. The actual design was Anna's own. A couple of seamstresses in the town had done the bulk of the sewing, but she, herself, had embroidered the flowers and leaves that decorated the scooped neckline and the cuffs of the sleeves.

'But I love the woman inside it even more.' He kissed her and, releasing her, went over to the door.

'I almost forgot, I have another present for you.'

Her eyes widened. 'What sort of present? You've already been more than generous to me.'

'This kind of present,' he said, going outside and returning with a brand new lute.

She clapped her hands and gave a cry of delight. 'But you fixed my old one.'

'But it's never sounded the same. I thought you deserved a new one.'

She took it from him and plucked the strings, remembering the day when he had come to Rowan and handed her first lute to her. She had admired him then and did so even more now she knew him so much better.

She smiled into his eyes. This last year had been the happiest of her life. 'I love you, Jack. And that isn't only because there are a lot of advantages to being married to a merchant venturer,' she teased.

He took the lute from her and placed it on the chest and brought her close to him. 'And I love you. And, though not a witch, you have the power to enslave me in such a way that I never want to break the bonds that tie me to you.' And, bringing down his dark head he kissed her.

* * * * *